Coloring for Dark

Coloring for Dark

LINDA POWERS-DANIEL

COLORING FOR DARK

Certain characters in this work are historical figures, and certain events portrayed did take place. However, this is a work of fiction. All of the other characters, names, and events as well as all places, incidents, organizations, and dialogue in this novel are either the products of the author's imagination or are used fictitiously.

iUniverse books may be ordered through booksellers or by contacting:

iUniverse
1663 Liberty Drive
Bloomington, IN 47403
www.iuniverse.com
1-800-Authors (1-800-288-4677)

ISBN: 978-1-4917-4244-0 (sc)
ISBN: 978-1-4917-4245-7 (hc)
ISBN: 978-1-4917-4246-4 (e)

Library of Congress Control Number: 2014913966

Printed in the United States of America.

iUniverse rev. date: 10/14/2014

For my Celtic Appalachian Mountain heroines:

Victoria Singleton Turner
Juanita Turner Powers

Acknowledgments

First and foremost, I would like to thank my late husband, Edwin C. Daniel, former editorial writer for the *Kansas City Star*, for his encouragement and support in the undertaking of this book. His invaluable belief in me to delve into the dramatic and compelling history of a family and to write a story of historical fiction shows the confidence he had in me that materialized with the last words of this book.

It was important to me to render the historical story line with the dark, light, and shades in between of Southern Appalachia and a way of life. There are family members I wish to thank for their input and loving support, including my mother, Juanita Turner Powers; sisters, Myra Powers Breeding and Charlotte Powers-Sutherland; daughter, Mary Beth Collins; son, Byron Louis Collins; granddaughter, Phoebe Zadora Collins; and niece, Sadra Victoria Hayton.

During the first two years of this project, I lived in Apalachicola, Florida, on the Gulf of Mexico and had the ongoing support of my "Dream Sisters," who met every week at Trinity Episcopal Church. Each one had a unique talent that contributed to the underpinnings of this endeavor. Thank you with love to Rev. Kay Wheeler, Ellen Ashdown, Bella Ruda, Anne Eason, Lane Autrey, Elaine Kozlowsky, Paula Kroll, and Cass Allen.

A special thanks to Debe Beard, a confident and talented friend who spent many hours and a few glasses of wine giving me valuable feedback and encouragement.

Finally, thank you to the individuals whom I had an opportunity to speak with about their memories of the rugged settlers of the Sandy Basin and life from the Great Depression to the flood of 1977.

Prelude

Mother called on Good Friday, April 1977, with the news of the flood. "Laurel, you need to come home, or what's left of it. Water is up to the chimney, and God has moved us out." I looked at my two children trying on their new Easter clothes, and my heart sank as I wondered what else God would put on this family. We were like the Joad family in *Grapes of Wrath,* traveling and traveling with hardship after hardship.

My husband, Luther, followed me to the bedroom, arguing all the way. He closed the door behind us and cornered me in the room as he always did. "You need to stay home," he said. "They can take care of everything, and you need to stay with the children, where you belong. What will Beau do here with just me, Mother, and Laura Beth? You are always running back to Virginia over every little thing that happens. You've got that chip on your shoulder and expect me to feel sorry for your mother and sisters. Just because your daddy got himself murdered when you were six years old, you act like you all are joined at the hip—the Powers family against the world."

I looked him in the eye but didn't miss a beat as I continued to hurriedly pack my clothes. I wanted to get an early start, with it being a six-hour drive from Swedens Cove, just outside Chattanooga, to Haysi, Virginia.

I knelt down and picked up my beautiful blond, green-eyed, cherubic baby Beau, who was eighteen months. He knew something was wrong when his daddy kept talking and talking, and I began to get the hives. I set him down, got the shot out of my purse, and stuck it in my thigh. The welts began at my ears and moved down my body, quarter-sized, red, angry, and itchy. My throat began to close, and my stomach cramped. It was beginning to happen more frequently.

Laura Beth, who was ten years old with big, soft doe eyes and long, straight blonde hair, was used to seeing me this way. She picked up her brother and said, "Mother, we will be all right. I'll put together Beau's Easter basket and hide it for Easter morning."

Hugging her close, I said, "You are my brave girl, and I will be back home soon."

Luther followed me to the car just as his mother, Alma, drove in. "Why, Laurel, are you sure you want to leave the children here? Beau always cries for you, and we won't be able to do anything with him. You remember when Laura Beth had surgery, and we had to call you at midnight to come home because he wouldn't stop crying for you?" Alma spoke in her condescending tone and southern drawl, which sounded whiney coming from her.

I saw red about that time and said, "If two teachers with master's degrees can't take care of two children for a few days, then I wouldn't be telling anyone." I threw my bag in the car and waved to Laura Beth and Beau at the door. Rolling down the window, I said, "I love you. I'll call when I get there." With that, I blew a kiss and headed for Virginia and my childhood home, knowing it was already gone.

Once I got to Abingdon, just across the Tennessee line, I knew I would be there in two more hours. The hard part of the drive was ahead of me in the coal fields of Dickenson County, also known as Virginia's Baby. Driving through St. Paul, the mountains were a blanket of redbud and dogwood blooms making a canopy of beauty. I felt my heart tug at the mountain woman in my soul. The dogwoods represented

Jesus on the cross and the blood he shed for our sins and was Virginia's state flower. Driving up Dante Mountain and winding around the "get acquainted curves," named by my first boyfriend, Sheldon, when I was in the tenth grade, I smiled as I remembered mountain climbing with Sheldon just this time of year, kissing under the redbud and dogwood blooms, and running into the game warden. "What are you two doing up here?" he'd asked. I remember I was scared, and Sheldon smiled when the game warden asked, "Aren't you the quarterback of Haysi High?

As I topped Dante Mountain, the beauty was interrupted by the strip-mining eyesore scattered on the mountaintop, ravaged landscape that stretched for miles. For years, mountain people had sold their mineral rights to the strip miners, and the once beautiful mountaintops now showed the damage that represented the hard lives people had gleaned from these rugged mountains as the owners made their fortune and moved on. The coal miners came from a long line of coal miners and were at the mercy of ruthless coal operators. They had courage found in a few who would work miles underground with the constant danger of roof falls and explosions. This courage formed a level of pride coal miners shared to stay in the mountains and continue family traditions.

Winding down Dante Mountain to the valley below, I reached the mining camp at Trammel where the row houses all stood with their same weathered clapboard walls and tin roofs. I had left Dickenson County and loved coming home but only for a visit because it was both majestic and depressing. Struggle was written on the faces of the coal miners and their families.

I finally got to the new road at Clinchco and decided I would have to detour through Big Ridge because of the flood.

I thought it was funny it was still called "the new road" because it was now twelve years old. So again from the valley I traveled straight up Big Ridge Mountain's winding, narrow two-lane road. I stopped the car off the shoulder of the road above the railroad tracks overlooking the tunnel where I could see the Fork Bottom on the McClure River. From there, I could see our yellow house with the big porch, flooded to the chimney. All the houses on our street were flooded, and trailers, refrigerators, and cars had washed down the river, striking some of the houses, and were now floating around. I'd been told our house had been hit by a mobile home, which knocked the four large pillars on the front porch and caused a whiplash that took it off the foundation.

My mind became clouded with memories of moving there. It had been April then too. I was six years old, and my younger sister Gee, short for Georgiana, named from a book Mother read, turned four two weeks after the move. Her birthday was two days before Daddy was murdered. Our baby sister, Scarlet, was born the following fall, and Grandma Victoria (whom people called Tori) moved in to take care of us when Mother had to go to work. We grew into young women there but were sheltered and raised unaware of the cheating and lies in our Daddy's life that had led to his murder. I had asked Grandma many times to tell us about our daddy. All she would say was, "Ask me no questions, and I will tell you no lies."

Tears flowed down my face as I remembered our childhood years and thought about how, in a matter of hours, all the family pictures; yearbooks; white-boxed, faded long-stemmed roses; my satin and brocade prom dress; Little Joe's picture of our favorite TV show, *Bonanza*; Gee's Shirley Temple doll; and Scarlet's Barbie car were floating down the muddy, swollen McClure River. Where the McClure River met the Big Prater and Russell Fork Rivers, a backup of all the flood debris made it impossible to travel anywhere in Haysi, a town nestled on the banks of three rivers with mountains on both sides.

All the bridges had washed out, and the Chevrolet car dealership and Taylor's Hardware were completely ripped open in the back, allowing the river to sweep floating cars and supplies all around. No one could travel through town because the first bridge at the Big Dollar was gone. Some people who lived in town had taken supplies from the hardware and grocery stores, climbed up the mountain, and made temporary shelter.

We moved to town in the Fork Bottom on the river when I was six and ready for first grade. Daddy said I was too wild on the mountain, always slipping off, eating wild berries, falling out of the barn loft, and having broken my collar bone twice. I loved going to the chicken house and getting the eggs for my mud cakes. I wore boys' clothes with combat boots. They had belonged to my brother, Jimmy, who died in a fire when I was a year old.

I loved our new house in town more than the farm. We lived next door to our neighbors Edwin and Maureen and their daughter, Mary Katherine, who was my age. I thought she was a real princess with long blonde hair curled in hair rollers (unlike my unruly red curls), blue eyes, and a wardrobe of dresses. We became childhood friends and shared everything from first grade until graduation.

I looked across the street from our house to Old Goldie's house, and it was gone too—washed away. Realizing this made me think of all the trouble she had caused. She was nosey, watching everything we did and always commenting with sharp, mean-spirited talk. She was a tall woman with a bony frame who wore long skirts from days in the distant past, her gray hair was severely pulled back, and she was always pointing her finger when she talked. It was from her I learned the news about Daddy.

Gee and I had been playing on the porch that morning when a strange man came up and asked us, "Is your daddy home?"

"No, he's not home." I remember feeling scared and took Gee inside. It had started to rain anyway. Our babysitter, Katy, was listening to Elvis's "That's Alright Mama" on the radio. She loved Elvis, and I did too.

I pressed my nose on the windowpane, wanting to go out to play but unable to because of the rain. A car pulled up, and two people got out and opened the door to the backseat and helped Mother get out. She looked like she was crying, but she wasn't, and her face looked like she had gotten hurt and was in pain. Her long black hair shadowed her face. They held her up because she looked like she was going to fall. Her gray dress showed that she was wet under both arms, with large round circles. When they brought her in, she did not even see us.

I did not know what to do, so I took Gee by the hand and led her in the back of the room by the window in the bedroom where they put Mother to bed. She did not say a word. I hugged Gee to me, and we did not ask the questions that were on our mind. Old Goldie never came to our house, but there she was standing at the foot of Mother's bed with a few other neighbors gathering around.

Finally, the first one to speak was Old Goldie. "Poor little girls and one on the way."

I did not know what "one on the way" meant.

She continued in her high-pitched, quivering voice. "You know, their daddy was found dead, shot six times and all sprawled out in the passenger side of the car."

I took Gee by the shoulders and hugged her close. We did not cry, and I didn't know why. I did not ask Mother about Daddy, because it seemed unkind. No one saw us hugging there by the window at the end of Mother's bed.

Mother was beautiful. She was twenty-seven years old, slender with curves in all the right places. Everyone said her black hair was her crown and glory, according to the Bible. Her green eyes, like spring grass, were framed by brows within a small face with high cheekbones and a pointed, slightly turned-up nose. She looked graceful and fine and had a beautiful smile that we seldom saw.

She was very serious back then, and still is. I only remember her being playful once. I was five, and Gee was three. We were out in the yard at our house, built on our grandparents' land on Backbone Ridge. Mother liked to wash her hair in rainwater to make it soft. The water was caught in a rain barrel at the back of the house. We were playing around in the yard, and she was drying her hair in the sun. She was sitting on the love seat Daddy had built her at the edge of the woods. She bent her head down and let her long hair fall over her face, and we ran up to her. She let her face stay covered and said, "I'm going to get you." We loved this peekaboo game and stored it in our hearts, not realizing it would be the only memory of a playful day with her.

Even though we had lived in our new house for only two weeks, our next-door neighbors, Edwin and Maureen, showed loving support after the news of Daddy's murder. Gee and I did not know why we were picked up by Maureen and taken to the beauty shop to get our hair styled. We were all dressed up in Sunday dresses with black patent Mary Jane shoes, and after that, we went to Bea's Drug Store for a fountain cherry Coke; it was our first, and we had a wonderful time sitting on stools that turned all the way around.

Another surprise was the stores in the business community opened their hearts and contributed to the needs of our family in the aftermath of our tragedy. Department stores in town sent clothes for Gee and me. I had asked Mother for the red Indian moccasins at Sutherland Department Store the week before, and she'd said no. Well, those red moccasins showed up for me, and I never felt so wonderful. This memory would carry me into my adult shopping excursions that always brought me out of the blue funk.

I was lost in my thoughts when Gee and her husband, Matt, pulled in behind me. They had driven from Richlands to help salvage any belongings left from the flood. I put my arm around her and felt I was home.

"Mother is at Donna Denver's house with Benjamin," Gee said.

Benjamin was our little brother from Mother's second marriage to JR Colley, but that is another story. I realized Mother and Benjamin had no home, and she must begin again. It was a good thing that Mother believed the Lord moved her out. Later, she'd say to me over and over, "I am a winner in Christ, and idle hands are the devil's workshop, so we will begin again. God promised me he will put me on a hill this time."

When Benjamin was two years old, his father left after a drunken brawl. Mother had her third "walking nervous breakdown." I was called home from Tennessee, and when I arrived, she was sitting in a chair in the living room. I had brought Laura Beth with me, and she and Benjamin were playing on the floor with a rocking horse. Mother was unaware that they were there. Her eyes were glazed and empty. She finally asked me to call Reverend Johnson to come and anoint her with oil. I knew that it was in the Bible somewhere, so I made the call. He came over with a small golden pottery bottle of holy anointing oil of pure myrrh. He put the oil on her forehead centered above her eyes as he made the sign of the cross and prayed to God in his familiar soft, loving voice. "Our Heavenly Father, minister to Maggie in her time of trial and heartache."

She began going with Reverend Johnson's wife from First Presbyterian Church to Women's Aglow meetings held all over southwestern Virginia. It was there that she recovered from her breakdown. She became slain in the Spirit, falling back in the arms of those praying for her. When she came to, she was filled with the Holy Spirit and began speaking in tongues, as described in the second chapter of Acts. She said, "You have to have a broken heart so God will speak to it, because only the devil would speak to the head." After she'd been slain in the Spirit, the Presbyterian church could not feed her spiritual needs. She described the congregation as being lukewarm and not wanting the gifts of the spirit or to be a winner in Christ. She felt because the Presbyterians followed a program that prevented the expressive and ecstatic worship practices, which did not please the Lord to reveal himself so they could fall under his power. As a result, their walks with God would be hindered.

Mother got up every morning singing in the spirit with different unknown tongues, and during the day, she smiled and shouted, "Glory hallelujah and praise be to Jesus." This all happened when I was twenty-five years old. I have to admit that I did not understand it and knew once and for all she was gone from us, even though I had never seen her face so beautiful. She looked like an angel or a picture of the Madonna. I began to realize she had not been with us since Jimmy died; I just didn't know it until then.

Jimmy was three, and I was three months past my first birthday when he died. Aunt Belle, Mother's sister, said that he was the most beautiful little boy and was the apple of everyone's eye. He was perfectly formed with blond hair and brown eyes, mischievous and fun-loving and too smart for one so young.

She said on the morning he died, he awakened early and told Mother and Daddy that he dreamed he'd died in a fire. Mother and Daddy would later that day go to Haysi, leaving Jimmy with Aunt Belle and Grandma Tori (Maggie and Belle's Mother). He climbed in a chair and got the matches on the mantle and went to the corn crib, into the corner in the back, and struck the match. Flames went high and could be seen all over Backbone Ridge. It was said that Daddy drove so fast getting back to the mountain that day that no one thought they would live to get there.

My thoughts of the past were broken when my youngest sister, Scarlet, showed up at Donna's house to help out. She was having her own nervous breakdown, being a young wife unhappy in her marriage and the mother of her baby girl, Rachel Patricia, who was almost three years old.

She had been to the doctor and was prescribed Ativan, which was helping her cope, but she was only eating soup. Her long, thick, straight chestnut hair came almost to her waist. Her face was angular and slim, and her skin was golden suntanned. She was beautiful but sad. Mother had been trying to get her to be filled with the Holy Spirit and be delivered from the curses that had come down through the generations. This was making her worse. She would sit and cry with her head resting on her knees, and her hair covered her to the ankles.

She had married Bobby Joe Kiser at sixteen after deliberately getting pregnant so she could leave home a little over three years after JR married Mother and ten years after Daddy died. Mother could have prosecuted Bobby Joe, because he had just returned home from the army and was twenty-four. Scarlet was the baby and had been for fourteen years when Mother got pregnant with Benjamin, making her feel like it was a different family. Her life became a nightmare as she developed into a woman; Scarlet could not bear JR ogling and touching her.

Once we were all at Donna's, we began helping Mother with a few possessions that were salvaged. As we worked silently and in shock, I began thinking about Swedens Cove and Luther. I was as unhappy as it gets in my marriage to my college professor, whom I'd met while at Southwest Virginia Community College. He sure knew how to put the moves on me.

I was an easy target, as I was married to my high school sweetheart, Tommy Lee from Hoot Owl Holler, in Grundy, Virginia. Everyone knew Tommy Lee, with the roving eyes and irresponsible ways. He was confident and cocky and always saying he had hair like Glen Campbell and eyes like Jesus, as he tossed his head making his hair swoop and smiling with a blue-eyed crystal gaze that would draw anyone in.

In 1967, my senior year, just before graduation, we eloped to Boone, North Carolina, where you only had to be eighteen to get married. Mother and I had argued every week since I'd met Tommy Lee. She said to me on my first date with him,

"Go ahead and ruin your life." I had no clue what that meant. I would soon find out.

Gee met Matt after she and Luke, her boyfriend of two years, had broken up. This first heartbreak had been hell, and she had not showed interest in anyone until Matt. She met him at our college spring formal, and even though he was the date of her friend, she caught his eye and he called on her the next day.

He drove an impressive 1966 GTO, candy-apple red. He called it "The Judge." After a five-month courtship, Matt was ready to settle down. I remember Scarlet, Gee, and I were lying out in the sun at Gee's apartment at college, and he came swaggering across the yard with his tall physique, dark hair, blue eyes, and magnetic smile. I liked him, but Scarlet did not, afraid she would lose Gee too. Gee and Matt married in November of that same year.

This reservoir of memories ended with the realization that I would go back to Swedens Cove and get my children. My plan was to leave Luther, with all the lies, bounced checks, and that last episode of misappropriation of funds at East Point Elementary School when he was principal. And the straw that broke the camel's back was the betrayal of my husband with Marge, my only friend and president of the PTA. Who would have thought that while we were in the sauna rubbing baby oil on our legs, talking about our husbands' problems, she was sleeping with mine?

Was it looking at our yellow house under water with all our childhood memories, including the secrets leading to Daddy's murder, or was it the look of hopelessness in Mother's eyes that made me feel like I was looking into my own filled with despair?

Chapter 1
Laurel and the Tree of Knowledge

The tree of life was also in the midst of the garden and the tree of knowledge of good and evil.

—Genesis 2:9

I turned twenty-seven years old the December before the flood of April 1977 in Haysi, Virginia, which took the home we had lived in since my sixth birthday. I was facing leaving my second marriage to Luther and moving from Swedens Cove, just outside Chattanooga, back to Virginia.

Swedens Cove was beautiful, nestled on the bank of a winding creek between two mountains. The Collier family had owned three hundred acres in the Cove for more than one hundred years, and gradually, it had been parceled off to the brothers and sisters in the family. Upon the marriage of Alma and Louis, Luther's parents, Louis had inherited the land on the creek side. Over time, he built two houses, a dairy barn, a large livestock barn, a chicken coop with a pump house for the well water, and a car/equipment port out back adjacent to the house. The main house was built in 1940 with cinder blocks poured by Louis himself. He built the second house in 1960, hoping one day Luther would move back home. And he did.

The first time Luther took me to Chattanooga, it was dusk as we crossed Missionary Ridge, and the city lights twinkled as we made our way around Moccasin Bend toward Swedens Cove in Marion County, Tennessee. I fell in love with that view, and over the years, it never failed that at the moment I topped the ridge I'd feel wonderment remembering that first time.

Tommy Lee had just bounced a check for Laura Beth's child support, and Luther was there when the landlord stopped by to tell me the rent check didn't clear. Luther acted in his cool, nonchalant way, pulling the crisp cash out of his billfold and counting as he handed it to the landlord.

I had finally accepted the invitation to go with him to Swedens Cove to meet his mother. His father, Louis, had passed away, and she was all he had as family. I packed Laura Beth's and my bag, knowing Luther would take good care of us. After the past two years of coming through for me, it seemed natural to trust him and let him take charge of my life.

I liked that he thought I was beautiful and bought me stylish clothes, even choosing everything I wore down to my underwear. He would sit and wait for me to come out of the dressing room and give the sales lady a nod of what we would buy, never asking me what I thought. He loved taking Laura Beth and me out on the town. He was impressed with Laura Beth's manners and the compliments he received from total strangers on his beautiful family, even before we were his family. No man had ever doted on me like that, and when he included my baby girl, I was on cloud nine.

That was more than four years ago. This blue funk had been hanging over me since I had been six months pregnant with my second child, Beau. It was just as Grandma Tori said: "Out of the frying pan, into the fire." Feelings of shame and loss had worn me down, and I hid my tears and fears behind my long hair, finding it hard to look anyone in the eye. I put on the brave front I had been taught and "kept my powder dry," remembering advice from Mother when I got married the first time to Tommy Lee.

I kept the game face for Laura Beth, who was ten years old, and Beau, eighteen months, but it was getting harder and harder to keep it up. Knowing I must go back to Virginia meant dealing with the past, which was coming back to me over and over in my dreams of flashbacks, beginning with the murder of Daddy the April I was six years old. I was also painfully aware that I would be running into Tommy Lee, my first husband, who broke my heart with his wild and unfaithful ways.

Everyone in three counties knew how he brought me down from a high school queen to a wife who couldn't keep him home. We were married for three short years, strewn together with lies and deceit. I buried and suppressed each one and put it away like laying a baby down to sleep, a sleep that I didn't want disturbed. Again, Grandma Tori's words: "Let sleeping dogs lie."

When my marriage to Tommy Lee was falling apart, I was able to separate myself from my breaking heart being chipped away each time he was unfaithful. Each chip would fall to the floor, and I would glance as it fell and never stoop to pick it up, not claiming it was mine but always looking around to see if anyone was looking. It didn't happen if no one saw and remained a secret.

Just as I did as a child, I continued to weave a make-believe life, keeping all the details to myself. I did not confide in my family or his. Scarlet and Gee knew some of the heartbreak and disappointment, but they followed my lead. Each time he would draw me back in with his charm, and at the broken part, he would kiss away and smooth out the grief with promises that he couldn't keep—promises that would help me hold my secrets. No one was allowed to see my heart dying by degrees, and going home to Mother was not an option because of our stepfather, JR.

It was as if the devastation of the flood was recalling the past with waves of intense and powerful memories. I am the oldest of three girls; Gee, twenty five, and Scarlet twenty, left to find out why we had never been told the truth about our father's death and why it would evade us, helping keep us in a world of mystery for twenty years. A burning desire surfaced to go back to the past and put together the mysterious pieces of this puzzle. It was a puzzle that caused us pain and sorrow as we grew up in a household of all women, pushing the loss of our father deeper and deeper into our psyche.

Even our community helped to keep the secrets. Maybe it was for Mother, named Mary Magdalene and called Maggie, the young, twenty-seven-year-old, beautiful widow who'd been left four months pregnant with a six-year-old and a four-year-old at home. I could not fully understand how she held herself together in a very public way.

There were more than two thousand people at the funeral. The newspapers were full of accounts that almost put her under, but all she would say was, "If you want to know anything about my husband and his murder, you will have to ask anyone else but me." She allowed no newspapers in our home and no record of that fatal morning when she received the news. The headlines had screamed at her:

> Brady Powers Shot at Point-Blank Range in Premeditated Grudge Killing over Coca Raven Colley; Elkhorn City, Kentucky, Tavern Owner and Money
>
> Local Man, Brady Powers, Murdered over Love Triangle and Money
>
> Brady Powers of Haysi, Virginia, Found Murdered in Taxi; Shot Six Times by Harley

Wilson over Grudge Fight and Tavern Owner
Coca Raven Colley of Elkhorn City, Kentucky

Mother was full of contradictions, strong-willed, although vulnerable, and had a compulsively wild nature when pushed into a corner. I tried to wrap my mind around the traits of her secretive personality and her ambition to excel and control her situations. It was in part an Appalachian Mountain trait of the Scott Irish bloodline, being able to rebound from disappointment, discouragement, and misfortune that came to the mountain families. It was also part of her childhood, loving an alcoholic father, winning favor, using her beauty and affecting shyness and modesty on men who went against the grain. She proved this in her choice of men who lived on the edge of excitement and danger while maintaining confidence and control.

The early isolation and the mountain religious influence grounded her in a special way with the gift of prophetic dreams, directly from God. This gift made her serious and special. She always waited to see if her dream came true before announcing it: “From God, given in my dream.”

She seldom laughed and did not love listening to music or dancing or being fun-loving. Her emotional unavailability had haunted me all my life, giving me a feeling of not knowing her at all. Before we left Backbone Ridge and moved off the mountain, I don’t remember Mother being with us that often. She left me with Grandma Tori, and after Gee was born, we were left with babysitters.

I now believe that after Jimmy died in that horrible fire in 1950 when I was a little over a year old, she had a nervous breakdown that robbed me of knowing her. When Gee was born in 1951, she had already gone to that mysterious place in her mind, never to return. I sometimes think it was fear that kept her there, turning more inward to her religion, allowing her to escape to God's will to "keep her from going crazy" as described by her. She was four months pregnant with Scarlet when Daddy was murdered four years later, and God's will sealed all emotional demands on her forever.

Mother had a high school education and took a job as manager in a local business, going to work when Scarlet was three months old. Grandma Tori did the cleaning and cooking with her sweet but silent presence. Mother began taking night classes from the University of Virginia and eventually had almost two years of college. Grandma Tori gave her wrath about college, and we began to expect her to be home only on Sunday.

Haysi was located in Dickenson County, Virginia, tucked away in the beautiful Appalachian Mountains. The president at Cumberland Bank and Trust arranged for Mother to finance the house we had only lived in for two weeks before Daddy's murder. She was instantly raised from the wife of a dangerous player to a heroine with three little girls all beginning to look like her. She was revered as "salt of the earth," turning down marriage offers and any semblance of a social life. Women were jealous of her where their husbands were concerned. No one was more beautiful even after she cut off her long black hair. The non-emotional façade must have made her more desirable to the men, and she'd say, "I have never felt close to women anyway, and I don't care what they think."

We were always referred to in a crowd as "Brady's girls," not "Maggie's girls." We never knew the people who whispered in their little groups, but it was a realization that our innocence was being lost, a little more each time. That tragedy was a shadow of grief combined with shame hanging over our heads, marking us forever as "Brady's girls."

Our lives were just like our friends' lives except if the shadow surfaced. When it did, amid whispers and stares, it took a devastating toll on us. We did not know anything about how Daddy got himself killed and realized everyone else knew more than we did. We knew not to talk about it and not to ask questions, but it was always there and grew each year into an even bigger shadow. Grandma Tori always helped keep a lid on it when we would ask about Daddy. She'd say: "Your Mother doesn't want me to talk about it," or "Ask me no questions, and I will tell you no lies." So, we gradually quit asking. In our house, there were no pictures of him, nothing that belonged to him; it was as if he never existed except he was now part of our secret selves.

With Mother being absent and Grandma Tori taking care of our physical needs, Gee and I began to live a make-believe life as we went along. I read our neighbor Maureen's magazines and books from her library since our only book was the big Bible on the coffee table in our living room. I became a voracious reader and kept up to date on the latest so Scarlet, Gee, and I were in the know of how to dress, talk, and handle our situations. *Ladies' Home Journal, Redbook,* and *Glamour*, in addition to Mary Katherine's *Ingénue* for the teenager, became a monthly ritual of scouring over and drilling Gee and Scarlet to make them proper young ladies.

It was obvious Mother was a great fashion follower, and even though she was a penny pincher, she wore Jonathan Logan dresses and Mr. John hats; she just didn't talk to us about it. I remember her advising, "Wear the right underwear, or your clothes won't fit properly," meaning wear a Maidenform bra and panties. We began a practice of adopting everything we liked about certain families' décor, style, and traditions, and over the years, practice made perfect.

I held etiquette classes for Gee and Scarlet, cooked the meals, and required dressing up for dinner. I knew Mother was ruled by the concern of what people would say about her girls, so she was on board with most of my changes. This formed our personalities of becoming pleasers and achievers and "keeping our powder dry." Gee and I mothered Scarlet and spoiled her like she was our Christmas doll. She developed an attention-seeker personality and learned to use her beauty to get her way. Gee became feisty, strong willed, and controlling. She hid the lack of love and affection deep in her heart. Being petite, she learned to use her strong will to overcome anything that didn't suit her, and it worked. I was a bookworm and aspired to adopt traits from strong female characters like Jo March, Jane Eyre, and Hester Prynne. In eighth grade, I secretly read Frank Yerby's *The Vixens*, sneaking it from Maureen's shelf. The book was set in the South after the Civil War and starred the beautiful, golden Denise Lascals; it was my first lusty novel. This gave me a secret power about love, men, and lust, and I knew at the right moment I would rely on this book to help me in a future situation, just like all the other books I'd read.

I innately knew I was well liked, and my outgoing personality made me a leader. I could fool the adults, because I knew what they wanted to hear. But I would later know that my gullibility to the falsities of people would be a huge flaw, following me through the years. I was protective of my little sisters and quick to defend them against any odds. We all had traits of strength, vulnerability, intelligence, and beauty, but the loneliness felt by each one of us would prove to be a liability in our personal lives and an asset later in our professional lives. It just grew up with us and formed a life of its own.

When Gee and I became teenagers, we heard rumors about Daddy for the first time. No one directly spoke to us, but people would talk within earshot, saying "What a shame their daddy got himself killed over a woman and did not live to see them grow up." This would be from people we did not know well enough to be able to enter into conversation with them or ask questions. One was a cleaning lady for Maureen next door who did not like Mother. She talked all the time.

We would not ask Mother or Grandma Tori about what we heard because it was a closed subject, but we began to ask Mother how she and Daddy met and fell in love. Mother gladly picked up on this and began telling us how handsome he was, with the most perfect physique, and how he sang to her a beautiful love song, "Nobody's Baby but Mine." This made it easy for her to talk about him, and she would show a slight semblance of a smile as she remembered her love for him.

We had never seen Mother like this, so we kept it going just to see her in that moment. It was as if she was not our Mother but someone else, like a beautiful, tragic heroine. Gee and I both remember the love seat he built her in the edge of the woods on Backbone Ridge, where Poppy let them build a house on the land. She made him a total romantic and never mentioned anything that would take him out of this light. We put him on a pedestal, and he became our hero even though we knew something about him was "bad and dangerous."

One of the first big stories to hit us square between the eyes was that we had a half- brother who was four years older than I was, Jake Anderson. Aunt Belle brought it up one weekend when we were all visiting her on the farm. I was twenty years old at the time and remember we were outside having a picnic, and I turned to Mother and asked her if it was true. I was in shock and couldn't remember how old Jake was as I tried to add up if he was born before Mother and Daddy married but dared not ask her. Mother was angry with Belle and said, “It was told and that didn’t make it true.”

Thinking back to my high school years, he was on the basketball team the year we won state and was a football player when I was a first-year cheerleader in eighth grade. I remember when I came home after the first football banquet and told Mother that I had sat across the table from Jake Anderson and Bill Owens and that I was so excited I could not eat a bite. Jake did not pay me any attention at all but Bill teased me about his little brother. As I was talking, Mother turned white as a sheet. After that, she made sure I had a chaperone for every ball game. She then became so protective of me that I was not allowed to date until I was sixteen, and even then I had to beg her.

When I was nineteen, I heard for the first time about the woman Daddy was killed over. Edwin from next door was telling Tommy Lee: “They raised themselves after their mother was forced to go to work,” and “Their daddy got himself killed over a woman named Coca Raven, and she had owned a tavern in Elkhorn City, Kentucky.” He said something like, “She was a Melungeon of mixed ancestry and was looked down on.”

I did not dare ask any questions because he and Maureen were close with Mother and protective. But little by little, bits of the secrets were leaking out. I did not have anyone to go to for answers to my many questions in order to find out what was true or untrue. When I was twenty, Mother would not confirm this but said, “Since you are the oldest, there was a woman, but she did not appear at the trial.” She maintained that the story had already been told, and she would not help carry on the tale of the last day of Daddy’s life.

I was angry and resentful that at twenty years old I was just learning this about Daddy's past. All the years of asking and being told nothing seemed to be spilling over like water from a dam but never hitting the bottom. Not confirming the events leading up to his death became the first of many cryptic conversations with Mother. It seemed she had no qualms about letting cryptic remarks drop like a bomb with no concern for the fallout or damage.

Remembering the morning of April 9, 1955, Gee and I knew we'd seen the killer, Harley Wilson, when he came to our house looking for Daddy. We were on the front porch playing, and he walked into the yard. We didn't see a car. He asked, "Where is your Daddy?" And we said, "We don't know."

I remember feeling fear, and I quickly took Gee and went inside. I also remembered a lot of bits and pieces after the murder and funeral—things I heard, things I saw, and things I imagined. Growing up, I could not distinguish what was true and what was my child's imagination, and again, I did not ask.

Gee and I were taken to every trial and pranced around in our Sunday dresses, I imagine to add more sympathy. Gee would run up and down the corridors of the courthouse and loved the water fountain. She could not reach it, so I would lift her up again and again. Mother's lawyer, hired by Daddy's brothers, picked us up, took us to court, and bought us ice cream. I wished he would be our new Daddy.

Remembering Mother's lawyer struck a chord with me that Gee, Scarlet, and I must try to get the records from Mother's lawyer, who was now a famous judge in Clintwood, Virginia. I was sure he had all the facts, good and bad. We would be able to see what he used to convict the killer and what he didn't use that put Daddy in a less-than-honorable position, giving reasons that tipped the already violent nature of a man capable of premeditated murder. We had read that Harley lived up Hurricane Holler and that he had many relatives still living there. We hoped someone would talk with us.

One thing was for sure: I was convinced that Daddy's murder and the twenty years of mystery and silence had played a part in the formation of our personalities and the way we handled ourselves with others. It was also part of the underpinning foundation of our choices in men, the decisions we made, and the paths we took, and it was time to learn the truth. What would it take to purge our emotions of the years of living with these ghosts of the past?

The family was split about digging into the past. Scarlet was not interested, trying to be protective of Mother, so she sided with her. I knew it would be painful for Mother, especially after all the years and effort she'd made to erase the past. In her own words, she believed she was "not of this world." She was one with God, and it was becoming increasingly difficult to have a mother who was not of this world.

When I told her of our mission, she said, "Leave it in God's hands. You girls are better off than if your daddy had lived." This struck a chord with me, and it was the first time I realized the anger she had felt for being left alone to raise a family. She was the keeper of the secrets that had humiliated her and the questions we would later ask: "Mother, tell us what really happened to cause Daddy to be murdered, and why did you stay with him after all the things he did?"

After two years of trying to research the past and talking to a lot of relatives, Gee and I approached Mother, who was then eighty-two. Once again, we took a different angle, wanting to record Mother's story, which would include Daddy's story and, ultimately, our story.

We had read the courthouse records and saw a copy of Harley's confession to the murder, recounting the last day of Daddy's life. The confession backed up the story about Coca Raven, but we still had a long way to go.

Before I sat down with Mother, I asked her, "Will you allow me to tell your story? Your story as a young girl growing up during the Depression, living during World War II on Backbone Ridge, marrying Daddy at age seventeen, losing your firstborn son in a tragic fire, living through Daddy's murder, raising your fatherless children, beginning your new marriage to JR, giving birth to your son Benjamin, ending your marriage to JR, having another breakdown, and coming under the power of Jesus and then the flood?"

She stopped me to explain and make sure I understood. "Coming under the power of Jesus, that happens with the heart and not the head, which is Satan." I told her I understood, but actually, it was over my head. I thought we needed the heart and the head, but I was willing to delve into it because I wanted her story. She finally agreed and wanted her story told. She sat with me many hours and talked as I took notes. As she talked over the course of many visits, I realized she may have been unhappy with the story, because she even quoted the Bible: "The truth will stand and will set you free." I knew she did not practice this proverb, because she allowed her daughters to be raised up in this mystery so important to her that the damage did not matter. Even after agreeing to speak she announced, "There is more that will go with me to the grave." Like the old saying goes, finding out her secrets would be as scarce as hen's teeth.

Because everyone in three counties knew about the murder, we were always running into people, who, by chance, would bring up a related fact. Gee's sister-in-law's mother knew the aunt of the killer, and Gee asked her to arrange for a visit.

The aunt was Rebecca Deel, age eighty-five and living in an assisted living facility. She was very gracious to help us to learn of the fate of our daddy. Her mind was keen, and as she spoke of the past and her sister, Harley's mother, Delia, she related that no finer soul had ever lived.

Rebecca was an elegant woman and well-spoken as she told of the family home next to hers on Hurricane Holler. There were four brothers she recalled as she shook her head back and forth, saying, "They were all a bad lot, always fighting with knives and guns. The house was full of weapons. Poor Delia could not do anything with them after the death of their daddy. Grown men lived at home operating a moonshine still up the mountain. None of them were married, and when one went missing, no one reported it and everyone feared he was killed and buried by his own."

She said, "Harley and your daddy went way back as moonshine partners and drinking buddies."

As I researched and recorded the time line of Daddy's work history, it was evident that he worked the mines as a cutter between Logan, West Virginia, and Buchanan County, Virginia. He would quit the mines and run moonshine for Harley, showing a regular pattern.

This was backed up when Mother allowed me, for the first time, to go in her cedar chest at the end of her bed and look through any records there. Buried under Jimmy's beautiful clothes was a large brown paper bag. Someone had drawn a sketch of a car with notes.

Daddy had a 1940 Ford with a flathead V-8 that became customized with a Cadillac engine and was altered to conceal the weight of one hundred gallons of moonshine. The car had a one-brake wheel and special switches installed for headlights and taillights. As I read the car description to her, she said, "When the cops came after him, he would quit and go to Baltimore and work on the docks at the shipyard until things cooled off." Mother went on saying, "Your daddy had a reputation as the fastest driver in the county, and he did good deeds with his car too, carrying old people and children to Richlands Hospital, all the way singing his favorite driving song, 'Jack o' Diamonds, a.k.a. Rye Whiskey' by Tex Ritter. It went something like this:

Jack o' diamonds, Jack o' diamonds and I know you of old
You've robbed my poor pockets of silver and gold
It's a whiskey, you villain, you've been my downfall
You've kicked me, you've cuffed me, but I love you for all

It's a whiskey, rye whiskey, rye whiskey I cry
If I don't get rye whiskey, well, I think I will die

Beefsteak when I'm hungry red liquor when I'm dry
Greenbacks when I'm hard up and religion when I die
I'll go to yonder holler, and I'll build me a still
I'll give you a gallon for a five-dollar bill
If a tree don't fall on me I'll love till I die

If the ocean was whiskey and I was a duck
I'd dive to the bottom and never come up
But the ocean ain't whiskey and I ain't no duck
I'll play Jack o' diamonds and trust to my luck
Rye whiskey, rye whiskey I cry
If the whiskey don't kill me, I'll live till I die."

I remembered, as Mother continued talking, about the Christmas of 1953. I had just turned five, and Gee three when Daddy came home in a taxi. "Pack our bags because we are leaving on a train to Baltimore today," he'd said.

She said to me, "He was running from the law again."

I remembered he brought in all the toys from the backseat of the taxi and put them in the house. I told her, "No one brought our new dolls with us," and we cried in every train station seeing the Christmas dolls on display.

"Yes," she said. "Your memory is right; you both cried every time you saw a doll."

Chapter 2
Maggie and the Rose of Sharon

The wilderness and the solitary place shall be glad for them and the desert shall rejoice and blossom as the rose.
—Isaiah 36:1

I grew up listening to the grown-ups talk about life on Backbone Ridge. I was taught children should be seen and not heard, so I always stayed close to Grandma Tori when company came. In late spring when it was warm family members would meet at Sandlick on the Russell Fork River to camp out. Mother would never go because some of the family and friends would pass around the moonshine, but Grandma Tori didn't seem to mind and enjoyed the music and the stories. This was precious time because conversation was scarce except for funerals and church socials. By the camp fire, snuggling close to her, I heard things that frightened me, made me laugh, and were for grown up ears only. She never asked me to leave and over the years I heard some of the stories so many times I could repeat them word for word.

Mother was named Mary Magdalene Turner, called Maggie since her birth on September 8, 1927. She grew up during the Great Depression and was next to the youngest of ten children. Her parents were James (Poke) Emmett Turner and Victoria (Tori) Singleton Turner. They had married when she was a mere fourteen years old to his twenty-four. Grandma Tori would go on to have a child every two to five years until she was forty-four years old. She had twelve children, including stillborn twin girls.

Life had been hard, living on a carved-out existence on one hundred acres on Backbone Ridge, Virginia. James (called

Jim Poke, because he never got in a hurry) was called Poppy by his children and grandchildren and was one of five brothers who settled there in the late 1800s to early 1900s on approximately five hundred acres with their parents, Sparrow and Rachel Turner, who had traveled from Pennsylvania and settled in the Sandy Basin.

The dirt road wound its way to the top of the mountain, taking the shape of a backbone. It was a picture to look at, but there was not much flat land. Rolling hills sloped down deep through the valley to Laurel Creek, named for the mountain laurel that bloomed each spring in a shower of pink and white. Early on, all the laundry had to be carried down and washed against large rocks in the stream and then carried back to the house to hang out to dry. Grandma Tori's rule of thumb was "one set of clothes on your back, one on the clothesline, and one in the wash."

The house was made of clapboard and had two stories with three bedrooms upstairs and two bedrooms downstairs. Each bedroom had a fireplace that burned wood and coal, which was dug from the seam that ran on the sides of the hills and kept in supply in the coal buckets by the fireplaces. Except for Poppy and Grandma Tori's room, all the bedrooms had three beds lined up against a wall. Each had feather bed ticking made with duck feathers and were aired each spring or after an illness. There were many quilts, and in severe weather, cold bricks were warmed, wrapped, and put at the foot of each bed.

Out the back door of the kitchen was a small mud room with a bathtub in the middle of the floor. Once a week, water would be heated on the wood-burning stove, and over a two-day period, each family member would take a bath. Sometimes two children at a time would be put in the tub.

Grandma Tori sometimes allowed travelers to sleep in the hayloft in the barn and gave each one a quilt made of wool scraps collected over the years and tacked together with yarn. Just off the back porch, a mound of grass had been formed and a dirt root cellar built for potatoes and apples with shelves on the walls for canned food.

In back of the house was the smokehouse with long tables and jars of salt. Meat would hang from the ceiling and smelled of salt and blood. Around the road was a natural spring coming from the steep hillside where a cave-like formation with a poured cement floor was used to keep milk, cream, and butter cold. When you opened the door, it was cold, and the running water helped keep the churn of butter cold by sitting in the deepest carved-out part of the floor. The barn was the largest building on the property. It housed cows, horses, and chickens and had a large hayloft. The corn shed held the corn and husks that would feed the livestock in winter. Later, a cistern was built at the top of the hill, and water ran into the house for everything except drinking.

An outdoor toilet was beyond the smokehouse and had two seats, one large and one small. There were always corncobs of white and red. You used the red cob first and then the white cob to see if you needed another red cob. And there was a Sears, Roebuck, and Company catalog always lying on the floor.

Poppy was dearly loved and a playful buddy when he wasn't working at the mill or on the public works road program. He liked to take the little ones down to the stream in summer and let them swim and then to dry off their clothes they would travel the secret path to the moonshine stills. It was well-known that Poppy favored his moonshine. Mother was his best girl and took care of him. One of her jobs was to follow him around and remember where he hid his moonshine in case he overindulged and forgot. So she always knew and would never let him down because he always paid her. He would sometimes drink himself sleepy in the early evening and then wake up the entire household in the middle of the night to cook breakfast, thinking it was morning when he woke up. That meant going out to the root cellar to get berries to make berry gravy for his biscuits in the dead of the night. She would cry, and he would tell her to go back to bed and let the older girls make breakfast.

Poppy was a tall, angular man with high cheekbones, rugged and thin with a rather stern look. He always wore suspenders, a hat, and his gun holster and pistol. Once when traveling to see his youngest son, Bill, at Fort Bragg, he even took a shower with his gun and holster on. He wasn't as ambitious as Grandma Tori but was known to be mild mannered and did not like to use four-letter words.

Grandma Tori had long, thick, wavy gray hair that hung from her widow's peak down to her waist. She braided it and wore it pulled back in a severe bun. She also had Celtic heritage with striking high cheekbone features and was very slim from farm work and bearing children. She would not embellish her looks and was very serious, prim, and proper.

She was the worker in the family, making a crop twice a year, loading up her horse Whisper and riding down the mountain to barter for sugar, fabric, ribbon, and other wares. She was a woman of few words but would hold her own with Poppy. He adored her and would ask her where she was going, and she would say, "You could stand by the chimney all day, and it is for me to know and you to find out," and "What's good for the goose is good for the gander." Everyone said he loved her sparring with him and would smile as he waited for her to return.

She was religious in her practice but didn't talk about it and attended the once-a-month meeting with several traveling preachers that lasted all day. The meeting was followed by dinner on the ground outside the church. She did not try to persuade anyone or participate in the ritual worship of shouting, washing feet, and praying over top of others. She liked the line singing that was well known because only a few people or preachers could read. The preacher who could read would say the first line of the hymn in a special cadence, and then the congregation would repeat the line in song until the finish.

Sometimes the worship would get turbulent with shouting, jumping, and leaping and then some would fall under the spell of the Holy Spirit. Grandma Tori was quiet and never left her seat. She believed in angels, though. She told me that once when she was pregnant and working in the garden while no one was home, the labor pains had her bent over and almost unable to walk out of the garden. She barely managed to get herself up the hill, not knowing what she would do when a man on a horse road up. She cried for him to go get a midwife, and he turned and left. The midwife showed up and delivered her baby girl, Myrtle. Both Grandma Tori and the midwife said they had never seen the man before. Grandma Tori firmly believed he was an angel sent by God in her time of need. She never saw him again.

Mother was the apple of her parents' eye and had developed into a beauty. She was five two and about 110 pounds. Her eyes were a spring-grass green, and she had a slender face and high cheekbones that showed the angular, Celtic features of her father and mother. Her long black hair framed her face in a widow's peak, just like her mother, a sign of beauty everyone knew. She liked to curl it every night in the dark, after the lamps had been blown out. She became an expert with twirling it around her finger and pinning each curl with bobby pins. She had a small waist and boyish hips. By age fourteen, she had developed a full bust and had slender legs with a well-turned ankle and slender foot. With her lithe figure and dark hair, she made a striking presence everywhere she went.

Following the Great Depression, Mother benefited from the public works program brought into Appalachia by Pres. Franklin Roosevelt. Her mother allowed the programs to be held in her home so they could learn about preserving food, sewing, and using patterns, and she was about twelve, the perfect model for the new clothes. She saw another world during this training and developed an ambition for making good grades and wanting further education. She and her friend Meryl memorized 104 Bible verses to qualify to go to summer camp with the missionaries who had migrated to the mountains bringing Methodist and Presbyterian training. Camp was on the Pound River and was a two-hour drive from Backbone Ridge. It had been a barn and was turned into a makeshift camp. They studied with the missionaries and learned to swim; it was the first time she had been away from home.

Her first seven years of school were in a one-room school on Backbone Ridge, named Turner School after her grandfather, Sparrow Turner. She had decided she would go on to high school in the fall even though it meant she would have to walk off the mountain three miles down and three miles back. She dreaded the walk in the winter because of the weather and rutted-out road from the cars. Poppy still traveled by horse and did not own a car. Her parents did not encourage her to go to high school because they did not have the opportunity and believed a girl would just get married anyway.

Neither of Mother's parents could read or write. Her mother, Tori, had a way with numbers and could get the answer without following any particular format. It always puzzled her that her mother could do math in her head. She would be the only one of ten children to go to high school. The boys left for Detroit to work for Chrysler, and the girls were all married before they were sixteen, except Belle, who was smart and had a good job in Detroit. Some of her cousins were the same age or older.

It was 1940 and she was excited to attend high school located on the Russell Fork River in Haysi. She described wanting to look pretty on her first day, so she'd pin-curled her hair the night before. By morning light, the roosters were crowing, and her mother was putting coffee on the wood-burning stove in the kitchen. She came into the kitchen in a gray pleated skirt, short-sleeved black sweater, ankle socks, and new black-and-white saddle shoes she had bought with money she'd earned from babysitting her sister Ivy's four children. Her hair fell down her back in long curls and was tied with a red ribbon.

Her mother had a biscuit ready and fresh cow's milk. She looked at her and said, "You can go to school if you want, but you don't have to. You are just going to get married anyway."

She left the house on her first day and walked the path to the road where she was joined by other boys and girls to walk the trip together. A light rain began falling, and by the time they got to the school door, her curls had gone and her clothes were wet. She was embarrassed when the girls got off the bus and laughed at her appearance and wished the bus would come to Backbone Ridge, but she shrugged it off as best she could.

But the first day turned out to be wonderful. Her math teacher, Mr. Fletcher Owens, was twenty-five years old and very handsome. He asked each student to stand and give their name and to tell who their parents were. Because her last name was Turner, she was one of the last ones to stand, and he asked her to stay after school. She wondered what she had done wrong.

When everyone was gone, he told her, "I want to play a game called 'I'm going to catch you.'" He put his arms around her and added, "You are a beauty. Run again, and I will chase but try to get away." It was fun. He would catch her and pull her close to him as he ran his hands around her back and down to the waist while he held her close.

She said, "I have to go meet Poppy and take him the horse to bring home the cornmeal, but we can play another day." She liked the game, and it made her feel better because of those mean girls with their perfect hair and store-bought clothes.

She was sad when he went off to the war and was killed two months later. She missed him and the attention he gave her.

Early that spring, as she headed home, several boys taunted her all the way up the mountain dirt road. "Hey, little girl, I'm going to drink your blood." She couldn't see anyone and kept going, acting like she was not afraid even though she was terrified. She heard grapevines swinging in the air as she walked and heard footsteps keeping up with her, but she could not see into the woods enough to make anyone out. She was so happy to get past the big curve at Pride Perrigan's house where everything had been cleared for a pasture. She stepped it up, turned at Allifay Compton's house, and finally felt safe on their little dirt road as she passed the spring house. Once she got close to home, there were men in the yard who yelled at her to watch out for snakes in the road. Sure enough, there were two long snakes stretched across the road side by side.

"Copperheads and mates," they said.

When she got home, her sister Belle said, "Mommy has been taken to Cobern to Sister Mattie's house to see a specialist in female problems. Don't ask any questions." Belle then sent her to the spring house for fresh water in the water bucket and asked her to bring butter as well. When she returned, Belle was cooking supper and making pies. "Go to the smokehouse and get the ham closest to the door," she directed. She hated going in the smokehouse and looking at all the meat hanging from the ceiling; she quickly grabbed the ham and closed the door on the salty, bloody smell. The pies had been put in the window, and as she got close, she could see that they looked like custard with the meringue piled high, but she was scolded not to touch the pies.

All of her sisters treated her that way, keeping secrets and whispering things they said she was too young to hear. They even had a special hiding place for their "once-a-month curse" as they called it. They did not include her. When she turned fourteen, it was a good thing Cousin Patsy told her about the "curse" and showed her how to put together small, clean cloths to use during the days of bleeding "down there," named "God's special purpose."

Patsy had said, "The curse was brought on to all girls since the beginning of time by Eve sinning in the Garden of Eden from the Bible."

She hid her special cloths in her pillowcase after taking them down to the stream to wash and dry. Maggie never mentioned this to her mother or sisters, and they never mentioned it to her. This made her feel like an outsider, and she only shared her thoughts with Cousin Patsy and her friend Meryl.

Their mother got back from Cobern just in time for the once-a-month church meeting and dinner on the ground. Mother always went with her, so they dressed in their Sunday best and carried the custard pudding, walking all the way on the winding path to the Primitive Baptist Church. A table was out in front of the church building with several pitchers of water, and each one had a dipper. Anyone who was thirsty was allowed to go up and take a drink. No one ever did, but the preachers needed a lot of water before the day was over.

As usual, about five preachers were up front, and they referred to each other as "brother" and would preach over top of each other until one would sit down. The one left standing would begin to yell and walk back and forth with one hand over his ear while he shouted about hellfire and damnation. Everyone knew the one left standing was led by God, and no one questioned it. After he got tired and sat down, another preacher would lead the line singing in the familiar syncopated rhythm.

Sometimes the first two rows would practice foot washing at the end of the service, just as Jesus washed the disciples' feet, setting the example before he was to be betrayed by Judas. She and her mother did not ever sit down front because her mother was a very quiet and private Christian, but they watched in respect.

At the end of the long day and as everyone went out the door, one of the preachers would stand at the door and hold his hat upside down for the offering. The offering was the only way the preachers would get paid. Grandma Tori was very firm about contributing and did not believe preachers should go for education at the seminary or be paid a set salary. She always explained that she placed no faith in educated preachers because a preacher should be born with the gift of preaching, which could not be taught. One might as well not go to church rather than to attend one with an educated and paid preacher.

After church "let out," everyone went outside to a grassy, shady area cleared for dinner on the ground, which always proved to be a great affair. White tablecloths were placed on the ground, and the women brought their favorite dishes of fried chicken, mashed potatoes, green beans, corn pudding, slaw, corn bread, and pies and cakes of every flavor. But Mother's favorite time was the walk back in the evening with her mother, through the mountain laurel, wild berries, and the sweet smell of honeysuckle.

That week at school she was chosen to take a test, and because of her high score, she was allowed to move to the tenth grade. She heard some girls saying that the White Star Cafe was hiring high school girls on weekends and over the summer to serve food and get soldiers coming home to spend money in the jukebox.

She asked Mommy and Poppy if she could work to make money for shoes and things she needed, and they both agreed that it was up to her. She couldn't even think about a time when they told her no. So she stopped at the White Star and met Virgie Johnson, the owner. She took a long look at her and said, "With those green eyes and long black hair, those young soldiers will play the jukebox with you all night long." She was hired but not allowed to sell or serve alcohol. Virgie offered her the opportunity to stay in an apartment upstairs with two older girls on weekends, and she accepted. She was so happy that she skipped up the street and began the long walk up the mountain toward home. When she told her mother what Virgie had said about her being pretty, she reminded her that "pretty is as pretty does."

Fall came with the splendor of the turning of the leaves. This was the favorite time of the year for her, and she always chose the deep purple, red, green, and orange for fabric for new clothes. She never chose brown and always thought it dreary. At Thanksgiving, there would be a hog killing, and the men would hunt for wild turkey. She hid for the hog killing, avoiding hearing the shot and seeing it brought up on a rope to hang and let the blood drip in a big tub. Aunt America, called Merica, would come and get the blood and make blood pudding for the men, who considered it a must for holiday cooking.

Aunt Merica was no favorite. She had once told her that she looked like a Jezebel with her new bangs. Her mother had told her not to pay her aunt any mind before heading out to the backyard, picking up a chicken, slinging it to snap its neck, and throwing it into a cast-iron pot hanging on the fire pit and filled with boiling water. She would later pluck the feathers and then save them for pillows and feather beds to use on cold winter nights.

Thanksgiving Day was a feast. The table was filled with pork loin, fried chicken, wild turkey, mashed potatoes with butter in the middle, gravy, green beans, shucky beans, corn pudding, blood pudding, slaw, fried squash, okra, homemade biscuits, and chocolate gravy cake. The children could not come in to eat until they were called. The men ate first, then the women, and then the children. Poppy would sit by the fireplace and sip his moonshine, thinking no one was paying attention, but everyone was just leaving him alone.

Winter came with snow and ice that covered the mountains and trees. The cars rutted out the roads, making it hard to walk to school. It was also hard for Poppy to walk to all the moonshine stills, and if it wasn't too cold, the children would follow behind him. He let them swing on grapevines out over the bluffs and valley below. If the grapevine had broken or if one had let go, the fall would most likely have broken their neck. Grandma Tori put up canned food and dug holes in the ground of the root cellar for apples, sweet potatoes, and Irish potatoes. There was nothing better in the winter than when she took the biscuits out of the wood-burning stove, lathered with butter, and finished them off with sausage gravy and chocolate gravy. Mother knew from having so many brothers and sisters that the two gravies were a staple at every breakfast.

Poppy could not get much work in the winter, and he would get depressed. He was fond of saying, much to Grandma Tori's dismay, "The sun won't shine on one dog's ass all the time. Either the dog moves or the sun moves."

Poppy didn't cuss or act angry when drinking his moonshine. And it was known among the older children that if Grandma Tori had been gone on one of her long trips to barter by horseback that when she got back she would send all the children out to the garden or barn and she would take Poppy to bed.

It was Christmas, and school was out. Aunt Mattie's husband, Colin, asked Mother if she wanted to go with him to Richlands to get his new car and promised her that he'd take her to see a Christmas tree. It was a two-hour drive, and she had never seen anything so beautiful. Right in the middle of town was a huge cedar with different colored lights all the way to the top where a big twinkling star rested. There was never a Christmas tree at home, so she did not know what she had missed. They always had a wonderful meal, but there were no presents. Poppy would go to the cellar and dig up apples for everyone, and Grandma Tori would make a ten-layer spice cake made with molasses. Once Uncle Colin came and brought chocolate candy. Mother wanted to save hers, so she put two pieces above the elastic in her bloomers. It began to melt as she stood by the fire and ran down her legs. Everyone laughed, but she ran out of the room and hid.

Spring came at last with the redbuds, Bradford pear, crabapple, and finally dogwood trees during dogwood winter at Easter. The dogwood had the sign of the cross with a red spot in each bloom standing for the blood of Jesus. This time of the year, Mother enjoyed walking to school with all the moss, berries, and ferns lining the road. She couldn't wait to get to her new job at the White Star. The soldiers loved her and kept her busy serving them and playing the jukebox. She beamed from the attention and got invitations to go for walks. Each night she would count her money and hide it in a sock, as she was saving up for a new winter coat for the following year.

That same spring Billy Vanover came home on a furlough. She thought he was so handsome when he walked her home from the White Star. Belle sent them to the spring house for fresh, cold milk, hoping he would be bored and go home, but he stayed. She and Billy cupped their hands and drank the fresh, cold water as it came though the tube from the underground mountain spring. As they laughed, Billy bent over and kissed her wet mouth. This was her first kiss, and her stomach tingled. She swore to herself not to tell anyone.

She worked all summer at the White Star. She packed a bag and moved into the apartment above with Ella, twenty-five, and Mae, twenty-eight. Ella was in love with Clayton, the local sheriff. He was married and promised Ella he would leave his wife, Effie, and marry her. It had been going on for seven years. Mae was different from anyone she had ever met. She just liked to strip naked and stand on the landing of the stairway, teasing any man that would look her way. Maggie learned quickly about men, women, and life.

Ella thought she was pregnant and was scared to death. She had left Greenbrier Holler and moved to Haysi when she was fifteen years old. She was beautiful with dark hair and blue eyes. She only went to school through seventh grade but was smart. She had a way with men but held out for love, and then she met Clayton. Her mother had died when she was sixteen years old, and her father had remarried. Ella's stepmother was jealous and gradually wore Ella down so she would leave home. Ella had been taking a mail-order tincture to take during a certain time of the month to prevent pregnancy. It was called Womanette, was laced with an active ingredient of willow bark, and would help her to wait until she and Clayton were married to start a family. Ella said she had finally "come around" and that Womanette had helped her again for another month.

Mae didn't like men to touch her. She just wanted to tease them and make them want her. Mae had black hair and golden, cat-shaped eyes and was very sexy. She dressed to show off her breasts and legs. Men stared at her and whistled when she entered the room. She would swear, smoke, and drink bourbon. Once when she'd had too much bourbon, she told them that her father had "had his way with her" when she was thirteen years old.

She said, "Daddy would wake up the entire household and hold a gun on mother to make her sleep with him." Her mother had born eight children and hated him to come to her bed when he was drunk. He was a mean man and beat the children. They would hide under the house in a crawl space, and he would beat them with a fishing pole. The girls were all subject to his advances. Mae left home when she was fifteen years old after seeing her mother in the washhouse washing clothes and her father pulling up her dress and pushing her up against the washing machine. She turned and ran in the house, packed her bag, and began walking to Haysi and the White Star.

She liked Ella and Mae, even though they were so different, but she was saving herself for her true love. She didn't want babies at fifteen or sixteen like her sisters, and she liked having her independence and earning her own money. She turned fifteen that fall and started back to school. All her brothers and sisters had already left home, so there were just the three of them. She loved her newfound freedom and being the favorite of her parents. She excelled in all her classes and avoided the attention from boys.

Just before Thanksgiving all the neighbors were having a "stir off" to make molasses at Ernest Turner's house. Everyone would come and watch the sugar cane being put in the large vats, and then stirring began with long, large paddles. It would turn a black-golden brown, and some of it was called blackstrap and was used for illness in the winter. The molasses that was pure in golden color was used at breakfast with biscuits and butter and for spice cakes. Bonfires were lit, and all the children ran around sucking on sugar cane sticks. Some of her school friends were there, and boys were flirting with her and making themselves look daffy. She paid them no mind and was not interested. At the end of the night, all the neighbors would take home molasses because it was a community project.

She was coming up Backbone Ridge two days before Thanksgiving when she heard the rustle of the bushes in the woods on both sides of the road. It was a long stretch before she would be at anyone's house, and she walked the middle of the road. She heard that same taunt: "I'm going to drink your blood." She then heard more than one set of footsteps following her, but she could not make out anyone in the heavy wooded undergrowth and grapevines. She started running, making sure to stay in the middle of the road, and more footsteps began running. They all began making scary noises, taunting her, and she became terrified. All of a sudden, a car came up behind her and blew the horn because she did not hear it. She turned around with terror, tears, and gratitude because it was Old Doc Sutherland on his way to deliver a baby.

The noise in the woods had completely stopped, but he knew something was wrong with her. He hadn't delivered her, but he had made a house call when Poppy got shot and fell off his horse after a quarrel with one of those "no-good Rickys" who had moved in the gap. He told her to jump in and offered to take her to the road to her house. She was so thankful and told him what had happened. He explained that "Boys who don't go to school just like to get into meanness, including scaring girls." This time, she told her parents when she arrived home, and they told her to always walk with someone.

The next day it was all over town that a young girl was found in a barn on Backbone Ridge, barely alive. She had been beaten and raped over and over. She was identified as Dora Christine and was fourteen years old. Her family lived halfway up Backbone Ridge back in the edge of the woods. Her mother, Euta, was German and was a war bride coming home with her soldier, Delmer Wright. He was a mechanic at Powers Chevrolet and they had built a modest house and were well respected by everyone except a handful "who did not cotton to the Germans," according to town gossip.

After six weeks, Dora was able to identify two of the boys who had attacked her, and they identified the other three. They were high school dropouts and were all eighteen to twenty-one years old. The trial was held at Clintwood, the county seat, and they were sentenced to ten years in prison. Obviously, these were the same boys who had taunted

Mother. Her parents thought she was saved by the grace of God because they had named her Mary Magdalene.

Uncle Colin came for Christmas and took her to Richlands again. She marveled at the Christmas tree and shopped for her first new coat. It was red wool trimmed in black velvet and had shoulder pads and a matching hat. She was so proud to have worked and bought it herself. When they got home, Aunt Mattie was there, and they all had Christmas dinner together. Some of Belle's friends stopped by, and they, along with Mother, got into Poppy's moonshine and decided to dress up and go to town.

She had on her new coat and hat, and Belle, tall, slim, and willowy with dark wavy hair, was dressed up in the suit she'd worn working at the courthouse that day. They headed to Haysi walking, and the moonshine caught up with them about the time they reached the big curve at Pride Perrigan's house. They became tired and decided to sit down in the tall sage beside the road. When they awakened, Mother's shoulder pads had fallen down her sleeves, and her nylon hose had holes at the knees, as did the other girls' hose. When they arrived back home, Grandma Tori met them at the door, scolding them and leading them to the back bedroom. "Sleep off that devil water," she told them. The next morning, much to her dismay, Belle discovered she had lost the courthouse keys and was forced to retrace their steps. She finally found them in the sage brush where they had stopped.

At the end of the eleventh grade, she was looking forward to working the summer at the White Star. In September, she would be sixteen and a senior and would be the only one in her family to have graduated high school. A month before school was over, someone set a fire and the entire high school was burned to the ground. She was devastated. The students were told everyone would pass to the next grade, but it would be a year before the school could be rebuilt.

Belle was going to Michigan to work and had an offer to share an apartment with some other girls in Hazel Park. She asked Mother to come along. She was shocked at the invitation, because Belle did not usually include her, but she felt the time was right for her to go to a big city. Her parents did not try to dissuade her, so she packed all her clothes in her new suitcase, and off they went, riding the bus through Kentucky, Ohio, and finally Michigan.

Belle instructed her to say she was eighteen and she could do office work. The truth was she had no problem getting an office job and settled in with ease. She was excited to be in a city and be able to buy nylon hose, shoes, and good underwear. She learned that the underwear made a big difference in how she looked in her clothes and soon became just like any city girl, except her southern accent made her more charming. She was teased and asked to say "corn bread and butter" one more time. She did not take it personally and was more than happy to be the center of attention in a mixed crowd. The young men doted on her, but she was firmly holding out for the love of her life. Some of the girls drank and smoked, but she only experimented with smoking, and she liked it.

Holidays in the city were the most exciting thing she had ever experienced. Colored lights were everywhere, and trees were displayed in all the windows. It was a hustle and bustle and caroling of Christmas songs. She shopped for Mommy and Poppy. She bought handkerchiefs trimmed with lace and beautiful tortoiseshell combs for Mommy and nice socks and a red flannel shirt for Poppy. She also sent them candy, one of their favorites.

Mother and Belle went to all the parties, and she said, "It was the first time that I realized how much I loved Belle." Belle was a different person in the city. She lit up and loved dancing and music, laughing with a vibrancy she had never seen. They became close for the first time.

That spring, she went to the fair with her new friends and rode all the rides. She had the time of her life, having never experiencing anything like it before. She loved the Ferris wheel but ended up having to drink a seltzer after feeling like she had turned pea green.

It had been almost a year since they had moved when they received news that Poppy had suffered from a stroke. She and Belle packed up to go home. She was glad to be going home with new clothes and money in her new purse. By the time they got home, Poppy was out of the hospital, and it was clear he would not be working. She and Belle moved back in with their parents, and Belle began dating Harvey, a man from a local family. He was in the service and wanted to get married. Belle wanted to also, but she was hesitant after being on her own, earning her own money, and living independently. But one thing was for sure, she was crazy about him, so she said yes. Belle met him in Richmond, Virginia, and they were married by the justice of the peace.

After Belle's wedding, Mother went back to the White Star because the high school was not ready and moved back in with Ella and Mae. She had a way about her now. She knew the ropes and how to handle herself and situations. She walked with confidence and was the prettiest girl there—everyone said so. One night she was flirting and playing the jukebox with a few soldiers when in walked a tall, dark, handsome man. He was slender with broad shoulders and a narrow waist. He dressed different. He had on a suit jacket, white shirt, and tailored pants, and his clothes were well fitted. Everyone wanted to talk to him. He walked into the bar with an easy swagger and smile. He noticed her at the jukebox because he loved music and always played his favorites and sometimes danced on the bar. He thought she was the most beautiful woman he had ever seen. Her green eyes were dancing, and she flashed him a big smile that slayed him on the spot. That was a first.

When he walked over, the other men sat down. What she didn't know was he was hotheaded and loved a fight. He would not start one but would never back away. She couldn't put a finger on it, but he was something she had not encountered before. She was glad she had on her new store-bought white fitted skirt and her blouse with the daisies all over it. She thought it was her best outfit except her suit. She also had on nylon hose and open-toed white-and-black spectator pumps. Her hair curled and fell around her shoulders.

The man said, "I'm Brady, and who are you?" Without missing a beat, he put a dime in the jukebox and played "Nobody's Baby but Mine." She knew he was the one. Brady knew she was the one. But what she didn't know was Brady was a player and had a girl in every town from Bradshaw, West Virginia, to Elkhorn City, Kentucky, to Baltimore, Maryland, but he would have Maggie for Virginia.

It was a whirlwind romance. He gave her plenty of dimes for the jukebox, and they played "String of Pearls," "Always," "Always in My Heart," "As Time Goes By," and "Nobody's Baby but Mine" over and over. After she got off work, he asked her to go for a ride. She had never ridden with a man in a car before, and she was a little nervous but too excited to say no. He started singing "Put Your Arms around Me, Honey," and she thought he had the most beautiful voice she had ever heard.

Brady drove her to the Breaks Interstate Park on the Virginia-Kentucky state line. He told her it was the deepest gorge east of the Mississippi River and was called the Grand Canyon of the South. They parked at a bluff, kept the headlights on, and looked over the deepest canyon she had ever seen. She thought it was odd she had never been there, especially since it was only five miles from town.

The moon was full, and they were all alone. She felt Brady slip his hand around her waist as he leaned closer; she tilted her face toward his. She was drawn to him like a moth to a flame. He kissed her. This was unlike her first kiss with Billy. It was a soft kiss at first, but then it changed. She could feel the kiss in her breasts and all over her body. It scared her, but she couldn't stop. He was very gentle, but when he pulled her closer, she could feel his hardness. She stepped back. She felt a little wet down there, excited, and scared and told him, "I need to get back to my apartment." He kidded her to not be afraid of him and assured her that he was harmless and would always treat her like a lady.

When they got back, they parked in the parking lot at the White Star. They sat and talked. He had traveled a lot and had worked in the coal mines in West Virginia and Virginia as a cutter. He told her that it was the highest paying job and the most dangerous, and sometimes he would go to Baltimore and work at the shipyard in the harbor. He asked her if he could come back and see her after work the next night, and she said yes.

She noticed that when Brady walked in, all the men would step away, but she was so mesmerized she did not see any warning. She began spending every evening with him and had feelings surfacing that she had never had before. She had gone from picking four-leaf clovers and wishing for true love, having never experienced a lover, to bumps on her skin and butterflies when he entered the room. He wanted to meet her father and mother. She knew her father would not like Brady. She did not even know the reason or reasons. Her mother either.

She took him home one Sunday afternoon, and Brady tried all his charm on Poppy and Mommy. Poppy was a little taken in and liked his new car, but he said, "You know Maggie is almost seventeen, and you look a lot older than her."

Brady said he was twenty-six, although he was actually thirty-two. Mommy had that look that she could not be fooled. Poppy said, "Y'all would make pretty children." And Mommy was silent.

She invited Brady to a pie supper. It was a social event with music and dancing, and she made an apple pie. She had to make two actually. For the first one, her sisters had slipped in and put salt in her measuring cup. It was a good thing she stuck her finger in to test just before adding the braided crust sprinkled with sugar and cinnamon on the top.

It was custom that the boy bidding the highest would get the pie and sit with her during supper. When the bidding started, Brady bid on her pie and kept it going higher. Other boys wanted her and her pie, so the bid went higher than Brady could pay. It looked like there was going to be a fight, so she became afraid and left her pie and ran to the car with Brady running after her. She was so smitten that this warning sign also eluded her.

By the end of September, just after her seventeenth birthday, Poppy said yes to the marriage but asked Brady not to take her away from them. He offered land to build a house, thinking he would have Maggie close and that Brady and his car would come in handy.

She was so excited and went to Richlands to buy herself a new dress, coat, hat, gloves, shoes, and handbag. She chose a fitted lilac wool sheath dress with a black velvet collar and cuffs. The shape flattered her bustline and boyish hips. The coat was a deep purple wool swing coat with a matching sculpted asymmetric felt hat that crowned her head and above-the-wrist purple gloves with silk braided-closure pearl buttons up each side. Her shoes were black suede heels with an open toe and matching handbag with a tassel clasp. She said her wedding choice came from Proverbs 31 and its description of a virtuous woman who wore purple.

A date was set for October 5, 1944, and they traveled to Kentucky because she was too young to be married in Virginia, and Kentucky didn't require a blood test or waiting period. They went alone to Pikeville and were married by the justice of the peace.

Brady told her, "You are so beautiful," and she told him, "You look just like Gary Cooper in your new suit." They stayed three days at Beula Villa Hotel across Little Brown River from the Sulphur Well, an artesian well known to be good for one's health. People came from all over to take the cure.

Beula Villa was beautiful with rocking chairs out on a porch that wrapped around and twinkling lights everywhere—rustic but elegant. She thought it was a little out of the way. One evening Brady took a walk, and as she sat on the porch, she saw him talking to a man at the edge of the river. She never knew what they talked about, but it looked very businesslike. When she asked him who he'd been talking with, he said, "Just a man looking for someone about a job."

She thought her honeymoon was glorious. Her new husband was an experienced lover, making sure he took it slow with his virgin bride and leaving her with a physical love that would remain with her all her life. She was glad she had waited for true love.

After the honeymoon, Brady took her to his parents' home. They did not own a house, but Maggie did not know that at the time. They lived on Frying Pan in a big white house with a wide porch on the front and a small porch on the back where a large stream ran. His parents, Grandville and Mary Tennessee, fell in love with her, making her feel welcome instantly. She felt an undercurrent that they were worried about something.

Mary was a round little woman with dark brown eyes and a pretty face. She wore her gray hair braided and wound around her head from back to front in a circle, like a crown. She had a large bosom that met her waist, revealing that she wore no bra. Grandville was a slim, short man with curly hair and dark-brown eyes. He loved moonshine and women. He pretended he could not hear well but mostly when Mary was talking. She was very jealous of her husband and guarded him with her dark, piercing eyes. They had eight children, five boys and three girls, but everyone knew Brady was the favorite. She was soon to learn that they moved so many times people said, "The chickens would lay down to get their legs tied."

Grandville was known to drink away the money and would stay with relatives rather than come home and let Mary see for herself. He would sleep it off and ask that a swear-off-drinking letter be drawn up. He would then sign it along with a relative who would witness it so he could take it home to Mary.

She became the favorite daughter-in-law of Mary until she passed away. On her death bed, she sent for her. This seemed strange to the family, because Brady's parents never visited her and the children after his murder.

They ended up living in Bradshaw, West Virginia, after their marriage, telling Poppy they would build the house on his land after they saved some money. Brady was working at Red Jacket Coal Mines. Coal mining towns like Bradshaw owned the coal camps that were set up as row houses for the families of the coal miners.

They settled into a house in the coal camp that was bleak to say the least. She would scrub and clean, but the coal dust settled everywhere. The house was small, with only one bedroom, but at least it was on a top row where the better houses were.

She soon became aware that her husband's snake-charming personality would naturally have another side that could quickly turn hotheaded, and at the blink of an eye, he would make a decision to fight or walk off the job.

He said, "I can get another job running the cutter; there is no one better. What I don't like is our life to be owned by the coal company."

But unlike most coal miners, Brady would leave and go to Baltimore to work on the shipping docks, as he liked the city ways. He never believed the song "Green Rolling Hills of West Virginia," which called the state "the closest thing to heaven I will ever know." So Brady quit after a spirited argument with his foreman about coming to work "lit up on hooch."

After leaving Baltimore, they moved to Garden Creek in Buchanan County and rented a house, Brady taking a new job as cutter for Jewel Valley Coal. Maggie became pregnant, and after they were evicted from two houses, she asked Brady to take up her father's offer and build a house on the land close to her parents. Brady took her home to have the baby but did not build her the house. He went back to Garden Creek, and sometimes she would not see him for two months at a time. But when she did see him, he would charm her and act like he had never left. He would win her over again and again. She never thought to give him up; their physical attraction was too strong.

"He snared her and reeled her in like a magic spell," Poppy would say.

Jimmy Vencil Powers was born on September 9, 1946, at her parents' home, and it was a difficult birth. It took her mother, her sister Ivy, and a midwife during the long hours of labor to help Maggie, who needed to be in a hospital. Brady barely made it in time, but he arrived just in time to name the baby after Maggie's father, James, and his best friend, Vencil.

Because of the difficult birth, Brady hired his cousin Judy to take care of his wife and baby. Judy told her, "I had a dream, and you and Brady will only get to keep your Jimmy for one year before the Lord will call him home." Even though she was accustomed to hearing such dreams of the future, she felt a chill run over her entire body.

Brady would come and go from Garden Creek to Backbone Ridge to be with his family. Once he was gone for three months, but she always received love letters signed "Your Brady." This small gesture meant a lot to her and seemed to hold a special promise, like signing in blood. She knew he would stray but that he would always be hers.

When Jimmy was six months old, she wanted to surprise Brady, and they went to visit Garden Creek. Wilma Gilbert and Dean Sawyer were there. Dean was a married man, and she could not prove it, but she felt very strongly that Brady had also had a woman there after looking around at the bed cover and the state of the rooms. She took Jimmy and went back to her parents' home. Brady would come and go from Garden Creek and Backbone Ridge and was very good to her parents, providing transportation for trips to the hospital or doctor.

Brady once broke his leg when he got it caught between the cutter and the seam. He came back to Backbone Ridge after receiving a large sum of money for the accident. She loved having him home, and he and Jimmy became very close. She took control of the money while Brady was recovering. She made sure she and Jimmy had a new wardrobe and then put the rest inside a canning jar, dug a hole in the yard, and hid it from her husband. After Brady was well, he told her, "I'm going to stay off work until the money runs out."

Jimmy was a spirited, intelligent child and beautiful, with blond hair and brown eyes. He loved jokes and laughing. Belle always said he was too intelligent for his own good. Because Brady had been with him so much, he was attached and wanted to take Jimmy on a trip with him. She was upset and put her hand on the car and prayed for it not to start, and it didn't. She felt God had stopped Brady from taking her baby boy on a trip that he didn't need to go on. Another time he was leaving with Jimmy, She prayed for the car not to start, but it did. When God let her down, she picked up a large rock and broke the windshield to keep Brady from leaving. Finally, Brady succeeded and took Jimmy with him for three days, and she was sick not knowing where they were or how Jimmy was being looked after.

When they got home, Brady wanted to make up. He gave her money for the household bills and money for her to visit the dentist. What he didn't know was she had a plan to leave and take Jimmy. She would not stand by and allow Brady to take Jimmy on road trips to every honky-tonk in West Virginia and Virginia. She had thought about this for many hours and would tell no one, not even her mother. Two days before she was to leave Backbone Ridge she dug up the jar in the yard, and with the dentist money, she went to the Arrington Drug Store in Haysi and bought a bus ticket to Christiansburg, Virginia. She knew the tickets could be used on any day, so on the day she left with Jimmy and a small bag, she walked off the mountain three miles and then rather than board at the drug store, she walked another two miles carrying Jimmy and the bag. She waved the bus down on the road in front of Doc Sutherland's house and boarded, assuring that she would not be traced. Her plan included gong to Aunt Jane's house in Christiansburg, and even though she was Poppy's sister, she had never met her. After the four-hour ride, she and Jimmy arrived and took a taxi to Aunt Jane's house.

The house was a huge, plantation-style with a big, wraparound porch and a well-kept, luscious green yard with beautiful flowers and trees that went down behind the house and on to forever it seemed. As she approached the house, she became a little timid for the first time, realizing that Aunt Jane may not welcome her and the baby. A tall woman who looked just like Poppy answered the door. She introduced herself and Jimmy and asked if they could stay until she could get a job and support herself and her baby. Aunt Jane was more than happy to help her niece and even volunteered to babysit Jimmy to help her pass the time, as she had just buried her husband the previous year. She and Jimmy were taken to their own room, and they even had an inside bathroom. She was ecstatic that her plan worked out even better than she had anticipated, but she had a fleeting heaviness in her heart about not telling Mommy and Poppy of her plan.

Before long, she was able to land a job at the VA Overall Factory making overalls. Aunt Jane wouldn't let her pay anything for board and keeping Jimmy. Instead, she told her to save her money so they would have a better start. Soon, however, Aunt Jane became worried about Jimmy, who seemed unhappy and cried a lot. After six months, she realized that she must take Jimmy and go home. It simply wasn't fair for him to be so unhappy, and she knew Aunt Jane was frustrated.

She didn't want to admit it, but she had settled down and was thinking straight. She knew she couldn't run away from her problems. Before she left Aunt Jane's, she went shopping and bought herself and Jimmy a new wardrobe. For their trip home, Jimmy wore camel wool pants and a matching jacket trimmed in brown velvet that came to his knees with a hat. She chose a red coat and hat for herself, and they both sported new shoes. They boarded the same bus after a tearful good-bye with Aunt Jane and were bound for the drug store in Haysi. The first person she saw after stepping off the bus was Brady. He helped her down and took Jimmy in his arms, giving him a big kiss.

"You have your nose stuck up so high in the air, you'll fall and break your damn neck," he said to her. Laughing all the while, he led them to the car. He acted like they had never left as he took them home to Backbone Ridge. That night, Brady held her close and whispered to her, "I will always love you, and there will never be anyone like you, my little spirited beauty."

On December 13, 1948, I was born in Richlands Hospital and named Laurel Victoria Powers. Again, it was a difficult birth, and Mother was severely damaged due to her small pelvis. Dr. Bower said if she had any more children she could die, as well as the child. I had a lot of coal-black hair, long enough to make a big curl on top, and golden-brown eyes. The nurses carried me all over to show me off to the staff.

I was laid in my new white satin bassinet when my big brother, Jimmy, picked up a handful of coal from the coal bucket by the fireplace and threw it in the bassinet. "I don't want her," he said. "Take her back where you got her."

I had turned a year old in December. It was early March, and Poppy was preparing to burn off the garden patch to get ready for spring planting. Three-year-old Jimmy was fascinated by the fire and worked side by side with Poppy all day. That night, everyone was tired after the hard day of work and went to bed just after dark.

Early the next morning, Daddy and Mother got ready to go to town for plants and seed for the new garden. Just before they left, Jimmy awakened, and he, Daddy, and I began playing on the floor. As we played, Jimmy told Daddy he'd had a dream. "I was burned in a fire." When Mother heard him, she got a chill remembering what Judy had said: "You and Brady will only get to keep your Jimmy for one year before the Lord will call him home." She shrugged it off, because he was now three years old. She began to laugh watching us play as Jimmy walked on Daddy's back and sang, "I'm Walking the Floor over You." They left Jimmy and me with Belle and Grandma Tori, saying, "We will be back directly."

News reached them in town that a fire started in the corncrib and that their baby Jimmy had been trapped in the back of the crib. The drive to Backbone Ridge was like living in a nightmare and not waking up. Folks would later say they did not know how Daddy and Mother got home alive because he'd driven so fast and slid around the dirt road curves. They could see the smoke for miles, and upon reaching the home, they saw that neighbors had gathered around.

Mother jumped out of the car and ran to the burning corncrib. She had to be held back by her uncle, Professor John, who lived on the adjoining property. She sank to the ground and Daddy with her, lying together in their haunting cries and moans of death. He held her in his arms, and her arms reached to the sky as she cried from her soul. "Lord, why have you taken our precious Jimmy?"

Their lives were transformed that day. The talk was that Mother's eyes took on an out-of-this-world look, and Daddy moaned "noooooooo." They both had to be lifted from the ground and carried into the house. There must have been at least twenty neighbors and family members gathered around the young couple who followed them into the house.

Professor John said, "This is nothing but an act of negligence."

Belle and Grandma Tori recounted, "He put a chair in front of the fireplace, got the matches from the mantle, and took them to the back of the corncrib full of dry corn for feeding the livestock where he set the fire." The chair was still there.

Jimmy was buried on Backbone Ridge on the highest hill in the Turner Family Cemetery. He was the first to be buried there. Mother chose the plot at the entrance where the view of the mountains and valleys were majestic, almost like standing in the clouds looking as far as the eye could see.

It was a cold day that March when they laid their baby boy to rest. They walked behind the small casket up the hill. Mother swayed and had to be supported by Daddy and his brother, Leonard. Her feet did not touch the ground. She couldn't speak, and her face was stoic and dry of tears. Her mouth trembled, but she didn't say a word until they lowered his casket into the ground after the final prayer. It was then that she let out a scream so primal it sounded like a wounded animal filling the sky on and on until she split in two. She shattered and would be forever left in this world agonizing about that fatal day when they left Jimmy singing and laughing. She was carried off the hill and put into bed where she stayed for days and days. She did not want to eat, bathe, or talk to anyone. Doc Sutherland was called, and he said the only medicine was time.

Belle said Mother did not get out of her bed for any length of time until it was time to place the marble grave marker at Jimmy's grave site. It had his picture embedded in an oval frame, taken at the Powers family reunion. He had been wearing a white jumper suit and was holding his white wooden baby chair. Mother began getting out of bed and walking up to the cemetery. She planted flowers and grieved for her baby. I stayed with Grandma Tori.

Everyone waited for Mother to come back from wherever her mind kept her, but she never did. She became angry at God and angry at her mother and Belle because they had not seen him climb up to the mantle. She was angry at her husband. He was never there to console her, drinking and carrying tear-stained pictures of Jimmy in the front seat of the car while he stayed away for weeks at a time. She noticed the pictures in the front seat were so soaked in tears that his beautiful image had faded away.

Daddy continued to stay away for weeks at a time, and Mother spent her time at the cemetery. She planted white crepe myrtles to the south of the rolling hill behind Jimmy's grave. Around the other three sides she planted shrub roses of yellow and peach, adding lilacs and wisteria by the fence just across from the tall rhododendron that had been there for years. She went early every morning and came home late in the afternoon. I stayed with Grandma Tori during this time of grief. Grandma Tori never was one to talk much, but her guilt over Jimmy's death was overwhelming because it seemed every time his name came up she would busy herself with sewing and other household duties. Mother never discussed Jimmy with her sister or mother, so it seemed the three women bore their feelings in silence.

Mother was inconsolable, and Daddy just wanted his wife back. She had lost weight and still had trouble eating and sleeping. He needed to feel connected to her again. No other woman could console him like her. She told him she was numb and angry that he was thinking of sex at such a time. Toward the end of that summer he took her to Chattanooga to see his sister Pearl, leaving Laurel with Grandma Tori. They enjoyed the rolling hills of Tennessee and stopped in Knoxville for the night as they traveled back home. It was in Knoxville where they came together in their feelings of isolation and suffering, and Mother found out six weeks later that she was pregnant.

The next spring in early March, she began to bleed. She knew she and her child were in jeopardy. Old Doc Sutherland was sent for, and he told her she must go on bed rest and carry the baby as long as she could. The baby was due in May, so everyone was preparing for the worst.

On April 9, Mother knew she must get to a hospital, but there was no one home that day except her, Poppy, and baby Laurel, who was two years and four months. She packed a small bag and told Poppy to watch the baby and then left, walking to her sister Ivy's house about two miles up the winding, steep Backbone Ridge road around to the gap. Ivy's son Johnny took her to Richlands Hospital, as she was going into premature labor. Mother did not know where Daddy was, and once again, she was embarrassed, because the family always talked about him never being there when she needed him.

Just after Mother left, Poppy went to sleep, and I must have decided to follow Mother. They said I had on a pink snowsuit, and one of my lace-up shoes had come off. I tried to put it on, but it was too difficult for me. I left Poppy sleeping and began the long walk around the ridge to Ivy's house with one shoe on and carrying the other. According to all accounts I was almost to the curve of the dirt road leading to Ivy's house when Poppy's brother, Larkin, who lived in the gap, saw me with one shoe on and went down to the road and picked me up. I told him I was going to find my mother, and he figured she must be at Ivy's. Ivy could not believe I had gotten that far and took me back to Poppy; by that time, Grandma Tori was there. They were amazed that I could walk by myself almost two miles following my mother.

Once Mother reached the hospital, Dr. Bower was called and performed an emergency cesarean section. Georgiana Paige was born on April 11, 1951, weighing four pounds. She was called Gee because she was so small. She was named after a famous duchess Mother had read about in school. Gee was a month premature, she had no hair or fingernails, and her arms and her legs stayed in fetal position as she was placed in an incubator.

Mother waited for her husband to come. When Sunday came, he was still a no-show, and she began crying uncontrollable sobs. The nurse called Dr. Bower, and he prescribed her a sedative. Belle reported back home to everyone that Mother had the baby blues. She felt hopelessness creep into her soul, and Belle took her and the baby back to Backbone Ridge to her family, also feeling her hopelessness that Daddy was nowhere to be found.

When Gee was three months old, she traveled with her children to Clinchco to her sister Sophia's house, hoping for a change from the feeling that had taken over her life. She wanted to rid herself of the irritable and exhausted day-to-day existence and knew that no one there would ask her about her husband and why he had not been home once to see the baby. Sophia was hard on her, though. She always thought Daddy was a rounder and not good enough for her sister. At the same time, she was oblivious to her own husband's past with the rumors of dark stories and hoped her sister never heard anything about it.

It was about midnight and everyone was asleep when the entire household was awakened to shots begin fired up into the air. Mother was sleeping with us and looked out the window from upstairs. There was Daddy, standing down in the yard yelling for her. "Maggie, I want to see my little groundhoggie."

Mother became livid and gathered her children and went into the yard. Daddy was smiling and took Gee out of Maggie's arms and began dancing all around the yard singing "On Top of Old Smokey." I joined in the singing and was ecstatic to see Daddy. He picked me up, and along with Gee, we danced around the yard as he sang "Tennessee Waltz."

Sophia came running out of the house screaming. "You are blind and need to take a look at yourself and pray that God Almighty helps to change your ways." Then she added, "Leave before you wake up the neighbors."

Daddy danced to the car and turned around and said, "You always thought you were the berries, but I am here to tell you Maggie is."

Mother got in the front seat, picking up a moonshine jar and putting it under her skirt between her legs. Daddy drove fast back to Backbone Ridge as usual, something she never got used to.

Within a week of Daddy coming back home, Mother had a dream as vivid as if she were awake. She dreamed she was trying to leave Daddy. She was packing her clothes as well as her children's clothes and searching for the car keys, trying to get everything ready so she could make a clean break. She packed the car and came back into the house, not turning on the lights, hoping to leave before dawn. She slipped and fell between the chair and sofa, trying not to awaken anyone. She was unable to get up, and a voice said to her, "Until death do us part." A chill ran down her entire body, and she bolted upright in her bed in a sweat.

Sensing something different about Mother, Daddy finally decided to build the house on the land Poppy had given them. It had two bedrooms, a living room, and a kitchen with an outhouse out back. Running water came from the cistern at the top of the hill above the house. Daddy placed rain barrels behind the house for hair washing because Mother said the rainwater made hair soft as silk. The entire family carried water from the springhouse in lard buckets. Gee's was the smallest, and by the time she had walked up the hill, the water had splashed out of her bucket. Grandma Tori made curtains and slipcovers for the sofa and chair out of a fabric covered with large cabbage flowers of blue and white.

Gee did not have any hair until she was almost three years old. Mother thought it was because she was premature. The beautician in town told her to rub freshly made butter on Gee's head, and it would begin to grow. So every day Gee had a bald, shiny head covered in butter. Sure enough, Gee's hair began to grow in a soft black sheen. By this time, Gee loved to dance when visitors came over. She had a natural ability and practiced with the babysitter and the radio. When visitors came, she would go behind the cabbage curtain, and I would announce her and she would come out from behind her "curti" and dance to the Carter Family's "Wildwood Flower" playing on the radio. She danced in hoedown style and her own variations, and everyone thought of her as a gifted dancer.

Once the family settled into the new house, Gee and I had babysitters taking care of us. We didn't know where our mother was. First, we were dropped off at Pliney Turner's house for his wife, Dora, to look after us. There was a playhouse out back, and Gee went straight for it. It had windows and curtains and everything just like a real house except it was for little girls. Gee and I thought it was magical, but we were warned that it belonged to their now grown-up daughter, Azzelea, and that we were not allowed to play in there.

Gee kept trying to open the door, and Dora scolded her again and again. Once when Dora went to the henhouse, I took Gee, and hand in hand, we left and began walking toward home. It was about a mile, and we passed Fairy's house and saw her working in her flower garden. She walked over, but we kept walking as she called out to us.

"Does your mother know where you are going?"

"Uh-huh," I responded, although I knew no one was home.

Gee and I continued on and went by the springhouse, picked up our clean lard buckets from inside the door, and dipped them into the cool mountain spring water. Then we walked up the hill to the house, and by the time we got there, Gee had sloshed her bucket empty. We went in, and Daddy was asleep after working the hoot owl shift. I quietly opened the refrigerator door and took out a Mable Black Label beer. I couldn't open it, so I got a hammer and a nail and drove a hole in it. Gee and I then shared the beer. As we drank, I noticed that Gee's shoes had become untied during our walk, but I couldn't tie them back up no matter how hard I tried. I decided to take Gee to Ivy's house, thinking maybe Mother was there. We went to the main road and started walking the two miles, but once we got there, we discovered she wasn't there. Ivy took us back home where I received my first whipping from Daddy.

I continued to get in trouble. In the winter, I once put Gee on an upside-down ironing board for a makeshift sled and sent her down the hillside to Grandma Tori's house during the first big snow. She held on tight to the ironing board legs, but by the time she got to the bottom, she had wet her snowsuit and was crying. I ran down to get her and found her freezing and shaking. Daddy was right behind me and spanked me again. He said he was going to hire a babysitter to stay at our house from now on.

In the meantime, Mother came home, and lucky for me, Gee was already dry. She had gone over to a large crock in the corner of the kitchen and took the cloth off the top and had her nose in, sipping the top. Mother ran over and grabbed her and covered the crock back up. I was still crying from my spanking and asked Mother what was in the crock.

She said, "Every awful old thing your daddy could find he threw in there."

Little did I know that Daddy was making "his old family recipe" in the five-gallon crock. After three days, he would put it in fruit jars until it was "just right." Daddy told me that opening the jars too soon would make them explode. So Gee and I made sure we did not touch the jars.

Daddy began dressing me in Jimmy's clothes, which they had kept in the cedar chest. I looked just like a boy except for my long reddish-blonde hair curling down my back. There were certain clothes I didn't wear that were kept in the cedar chest, like his hats and coats with matching jodhpurs and shoes. After they took out the combat boots and sturdy country clothes, Mother closed the cedar chest, and we were not allowed in there. I fell in love with the boots that laced and buckled up to the knee. I began wishing I was a boy.

My parents also began dressing me in denim jeans because I had developed an allergic reaction to everything outside that touched my skin. With Jimmy's boots, my outside adventures grew and grew, and I was getting braver each time. I slipped out in the barn and took the chicken eggs and broke them into my mud pies to make them moist so they would stick together.

I climbed into the barn loft and fell through the hay hatch, breaking my collarbone. The doctor taped my chest, and as soon as it healed, I jumped over Laurel Creek and broke it again. Back to the doctor we went where he taped it again.

I wandered over the hills, valleys, and streams of the farm, looking at cows, horses, and a hornets' nest. The nest was up in the tree that looked like the old boogieman that came and got little children who didn't behave and mind their parents. It sat high up in the tree on the roughed-out road going past the barn. It was a wrinkled gray face with big eyes set deep into his head looking at me. I always ran away, but when the cousins came for a visit, we threw rocks at it, and it broke, sending swarming hornets everywhere. We ran back home with red stings on our bodies, and mine were huge red hives from an allergic reaction. Grandma Tori made an onion poultice wrapped in muslin cloth and tied it around the stings.

My favorite adventure was wandering all over the farm and eating all kinds of berries: blueberries, blackberries, raspberries, strawberries, and mulberries all hanging lush for the picking. I found a berry that did not have a name. It grew in a bush of greens and was dark red-purple. I ate them and became very ill. I was rushed to the hospital and admitted in serious condition. One bad memory of that stay in the hospital was first being put in a large iron baby bed. I had never seen a bed like that. Then a nurse came in to take my temperature and said, "In your bottom." I knew instantly I was not going to let her do that to me. As soon as she got close, I grabbed the thermometer from her and threw it on the floor, breaking it into tiny pieces. After that, she put it under my tongue.

It was Christmas, and Gee and I were listening to the radio. "Christmas time's a coming … snowflakes a falling … holly in the window … and I know I'm coming home." We sat side by side on the blue-white cabbage flower sofa, rocking back and forth and singing with the music. All of a sudden, Daddy came in and said to Mother, "I have a taxi waiting outside full of toys." The load included new dolls for both Gee and me. To our surprise, he brought in all the toys and at the same time told Mother, "Pack our bags. We are leaving on a train for Baltimore."

She was upset with him but packed the bags, and they loaded us into the taxi. Neither of them remembered to bring our new dolls. We were taken to the train station in Coburn and boarded for Washington, DC, where we would change trains for Baltimore. We were met at the train station by Aunt Delta Lee and Uncle Grant and would stay with them while Daddy looked for a job. Gee and I were still crying after seeing all the storefronts with toys and dolls in the DC station. Aunt Delta Lee told us Santa had left presents for us at her house, and we quickly dried the tears.

Daddy said, "You girls are spoiled rotten and rurint with everyone doting on you."

Mother told Daddy that we were not staying at Delta Lee's for longer than four weeks or until he got his first paycheck and found us an apartment. She was quiet and proper. We knew not to say anything. She later told Delta Lee that Daddy had been hiding from the law again, "something about moonshine."

Daddy got a job at the shipyard but made no move to find an apartment. Mother decided after his second paycheck to take the money and buy us tickets back home. We left Daddy at the train station, and as we boarded, a young soldier said, "Ma'am, let me help you." He took Gee from her arms and carried her to our seats. He stayed with us until we reached Cobern, our last stop. Mother thanked him, and he said, "This little one was light as a feather."

Mother got a taxi and directed the driver to her sister Mattie's house. When we arrived, Mattie had just gotten home, and she was all dressed up and had on a wide-brimmed blue hat with feathers. I asked her if she'd worn the hat all day.

She said, "Yes, why?"

I replied, "Because it makes you look tacky." This began my love of hats.

Mattie lived in a beautiful house with a big yard in the valley outside Cobern. Mattie was a recent widow. Her deceased husband, Preacher, called that because he was a preacher, had asked Mattie to allow him to see Mother undress. He wanted her to open the curtains as Mother undressed, and when she refused, he withheld money for groceries. He finally got sick and Mattie began inviting a young man to sit on the front porch for sweet tea and Preacher was unable to walk out of the bedroom, but he could see her. She said all she did was "play around," but she laughed as she told this to Mother and Aunt Belle, who also laughed when talking about this. Preacher got his just rewards, dying after six months.

Mattie had chickens and a rooster out back between the yard and the garden. I ran in the middle of the chickens as they ran around my feet, when, all at once, the rooster came out of nowhere and began flogging me. My shirt was ripped off, and there were big, angry scratches bleeding down my chest. I became terrified and screamed as Mother witnessed the attack from the kitchen window, ran outside, and pulled me on the back porch. Once I was inside the kitchen, they rubbed balsam of myrrh ointment on me, saying it was a miracle cure. It came from Grandma Tori's Singleton family rolling store. They traveled all over southwest Virginia selling hard-to-get important goods from the backs of their trucks.

Mother sent word to her nephew Randy who finally came and took us back to Backbone Ridge. On April 11, Gee's third birthday, Mother put Gee in the high chair and sat her birthday cake with candles in the middle of the tray. We were singing "Happy Birthday" when Daddy walked in with presents, singing and grinning like he had been there all along.

That evening, Mother and Daddy went to the love seat, and he put his arm around her. I was playing behind the love seat in the green, thick moss. Mother told Daddy, as she looked straight ahead, "I am going back to school to finish my senior year."

He said, "This is the worst time to go with Laurel being five and Gee three."

She said to him, "I have not been any benefit to anyone since Jimmy's death, and I am afraid I am losing my mind."

My parents didn't know I was there listening. Daddy pulled Mother close, but she didn't turn her face to look at him. He said, "You can begin in the fall. I will find a babysitter for the girls."

Grandma Tori was getting ready for church when Poppy fell to the floor. She couldn't get him up, and he was talking like he had been in the moonshine again. She called for me, and I ran in as she directed me. "Go get your daddy, quick."

I ran up the hill and was so out of breath I could hardly speak. I said, "Daddy, come quick and bring the car. Grandma Tori said to tell you Poppy is very sick."

Everyone wanted Daddy when they needed to go somewhere, because everyone knew he drove faster than anyone in the county.

Daddy had just worked the hoot owl shift at the Splashdam mines but jumped in the car and carried Poppy to the hospital where we learned he'd had a stroke. The doctor did not give much hope. Mother was heartbroken; she was his favorite little girl. Daddy knew she was in bad shape and sent her home with her brother, French, saying he would stay with Poppy. Daddy was good that way and stayed until Poppy's soul was taken to heaven.

Grandma Tori did not cry and kept a straight face. I did not cry and spent the night with her, and Gee went home with Mother and Daddy. That night she threw two potatoes in the fireplace, and after a while, she took them out and peeled the black skin off them and we ate them on a plate with butter and salt in front of the fireplace and she didn't say a word. Then we went to bed, and I slept with her.

Poppy's funeral was at the Turner Family Old Regular Baptist Church. At least four preachers preached about Brother Turner and for salvation on his soul. Grandma Tori and her ten children sat in the front row, but she allowed me to sit with her. After the funeral, Poppy was taken to the Turner Cemetery and buried across from Jimmy. Mother fainted and had to be carried down the hill by Daddy. I held tight to Grandma Tori's hand and felt her white handkerchief trimmed in lace. I loved her handkerchiefs. Some had flowers in the corner and some had lace, but they all were white, stacked in the top drawer of her chifforobe. Belle carried Gee, who did not know what was going on, and we all went back to Grandma Tori's house where the church women had prepared a large dinner.

After Poppy's funeral, Mother was still going to the cemetery all the time. She tended the flowers around Jimmy's grave and began to plant flowers around Poppy's grave. She began losing track of date and time and would sing, "I'll Fly Away."

> Some bright morning when this life is over,
> I'll fly away
> To that home on God's celestial shore
> I'll fly away
> Just a few more weary days and then
> I'll fly away
> To a land where joys will never end
> I'll fly away.

Daddy kept his word to Mother and hired a babysitter named Katy Mullins. She began coming early that summer and would stay until she fixed supper. Daddy was home more, and Grandma Tori decided she wanted to go to Michigan to visit with her youngest son, Bill. I was heartbroken and began crying, unable to stop. They didn't know what to do with me, and finally, Daddy took off his belt and threatened me with a whipping. I ran outside Grandma Tori's house around the big oak tree in the front yard, and every time I came around, Daddy gave me another lick with his belt. He picked me up and took me screaming, "I don't want her to go," and put me in the car.

Grandma Tori finally came home after a month, talking up a storm about the city, Bill's apartment, and Johnny Cash. Uncle Bill had a new stereo and records, and he even had the new album *Cry Cry Cry*. It was odd hearing her talk about Johnny Cash, because she never talked that much. It was also the first time I heard the grown-ups talking in a hushed voice, "Tori has broke-up housekeeping." I did not know what that meant, but I did not like it.

One morning, early in the summer, I didn't want to get out of bed. Mother felt my forehead and said, "Laurel is burning up with fever." They took me to town to Doc Sutherland, and he diagnosed roundworms. He sent us home with a bottle of medicine.

I had a terrible pain in my tummy and could not stand up straight. I did not get any better taking the medicine, only worse. Mother wanted Daddy to take me to Richlands Hospital, but he said," "We need to trust Doc Sutherland because he is always right." Daddy called an old buddy who was a medic in the army to come see me. He told my parents they needed to give me a tablespoon of lard, but when Daddy tried to get me to swallow it, I began crying and wouldn't do it. He finally offered to pay me a dollar if I did it, and I agreed. Mother later told me that I began being unresponsive, and she pled with Daddy to take me to the hospital. He said that he wouldn't because the medicine needed time to work.

Mother sent to town for a taxi and took me to Richlands Hospital. When we got there, she carried me in and said, "Her eyes have already rolled back in her head."

The doctor took one look at me and said, "Prepare her for surgery."

As they wheeled me away, the doctor told her that he had no idea what was wrong with me but that I was in the hands of God. The exploratory surgery of my abdomen revealed a ruptured appendix. I was in ICU for eleven days hanging on to life. Mother told me that she'd carried me to the chapel with the tubes attached and prayed for God not to take her second child. At the time, she weighed 110 pounds, and I weighed 48 pounds. When Daddy showed up and saw all the tubes and IVs, Mother said he went outside and vomited. Then he went to town and bought me a new doll and a big dollhouse.

Mother said, "I did not leave your side even though he was there, and I could not face him, because if I had listened to him you would have died. There was a silence between us for many weeks."

My roommate in the hospital was a little girl named Anna Mae who had been there two weeks with third-degree burns. Her mother gave my mother an extra set of clothes. She would take them home at night and wash them, and Mother would watch her little girl along with me. I could only see Anna Mae's face. She could not move and was wrapped in white bandages. After four weeks in the hospital, I was allowed to go home. Before leaving, I gave my dollhouse to Anna Mae, who had to stay. My last wish was to go to the floor where people came to pick out their babies, and Mother took me to the pediatric floor. I was surprised that you could choose a baby of any size but accepted her story about where babies came from.

After being released, I was taken home to Grandma Tori's. I remember it hurt to walk and that I had a big scarred-over hole on my right side. I wore long white cotton gowns and loved being with Grandma Tori. I would lay my head in her lap, and she would stroke my hair. I spent the rest of the summer there, but she told me, "Once you are better, Laurel, I am going back to Michigan to your uncle Bill's."

I was so sad she was leaving me again. There wasn't anything I could do, and I did not want another whipping. I decided not to cry.

After Grandma Tori went to Michigan, I went back home. Mother told me that one night Daddy got into his home brew and dropped a picture out of his wallet, and he didn't see her put her foot on the picture. When he turned, she picked it up. It was a picture of Daddy with his arm around a beautiful woman. Mother described her as being dark skinned with long midnight curly hair with eyes turned up at the corners. Her lips were full in a perfect heart-shaped face. Her dress was cut low, showing ample breasts, and she was smiling a sly smile. Mother went on to say, "I had suspected women all along, but to see this picture of the beautiful woman with your Daddy looking at her with his smile that could charm a snake just made me sick, and it was pukey."

Mother said that she hid the picture in wax paper in the flour bin behind the sifter. She would take it out from time to time and get angry all over again. She knew there was something about this woman that Daddy thought was special. She kept her sorrow to herself and did not mention it to anyone. She would bury this one in the bottom of her heart with the rest and "keep her powder dry," so to speak. Her dry powder was second nature because crying was a sign of weakness; everyone knew that. She told me that she often thought to herself, "The woman in the picture was the kind of woman who would show her ass up to the red," just like Poppy used to say.

I turned six on the thirteenth of December, and it was an exciting time because the Sears Christmas catalog came. Gee and I sat on the sofa for hours looking at all the toys on every page with our eyes big and wide. Daddy brought in a spruce pine, Mother's favorite, and we decorated with strings of popcorn and peppermint sticks. We bundled up and went outside for Daddy to shoot the mistletoe out of the tree. Mother put a red ribbon on it and hung it in the doorway. We saw Daddy kissing Mother under the mistletoe, and she would later tell us that one day a boy would do this to us.

That was the first year Gee and I saw Santa Claus. We went to Richlands, where Mother had gone as a child, and saw the same tree in the middle of town. We were in awe, because our tree at home had no lights or star on top. Then we went to Johnson's Five and Dime, and there was Santa waving for everyone to come in. Gee and I fell instantly in love with the mysterious Santa and Christmas.

After Christmas, Mother began to get sick every morning before she went to school. I heard Aunt Belle say, "Maggie is PG again." I asked what "PG" meant, and she said, "Why, honey, she has a bun in the oven."

Mother was so upset and sick, so Gee and I left her alone. The truth was she had a blinding, red-hot rage just thinking about the woman in the picture and Daddy having his way with her in a night of weakness. She could not resist him, and now this was her cross to bear and the thorn in her side and many a woman's fate.

Daddy went around singing "Hey Good Lookin'" and "If I Knew You Were Coming I'd've Baked a Cake." Mother sang too, but her song wasn't happy. It went something like:

> Gonna lay my burden down
> Lay my body in the ground
>
> When I get to the other side,
> I'll put your picture way up high.

It was April 1, 1955, when we moved from Backbone Ridge to our house in the Fork Bottom in Haysi. Daddy had broken his tibia in the mines but could walk with a cast on the lower part of his left leg. He was excited about our house, which was located close to where the three rivers, McClure, Big Prater and Russell Fork, met and formed a peaceful settlement of families. Most of the fathers were coal miners, but we lived next door to the principal of the high school, Edwin and his wife, Maureen, and their daughter, Mary Katherine, who was my age and would become my best friend.

Our house was one of the best-looking houses on the street. It had a long front porch with four large round columns and sat on a corner lot. It had three bedrooms and an indoor bathroom. We moved in, and our babysitter, Katy, came with us. It had a long front porch with a swing on one end and a glider on the other. I loved the apple tree out back and climbed it our first day there.

It was different from living on the farm, with streets in front of the houses, which were lined up in rows close together. Daddy got me by the arm and squeezed it hard saying,

"Laurel, you better stay out of the street and keep Gee out too. I don't want you hit by a car."

He scared me, and I said, "Yes, Daddy, and I will take good care of Gee."

During the day, Mother went to school, and Katy played the radio, singing along with Elvis's "That's Alright Mama" and dancing in the kitchen with us.

Since Daddy could not work in the mines because of his broken leg, he worked as a taxi driver for his buddy, Clyde Vanover, who owned Riverside Café. Daddy had pointed at Riverside Café as we were driving by. "Look, Laurel, that's my old stomping ground." It was nestled back in the tall pines just outside of town across the river. As he was talking, Mother was silent like it didn't seem important.

We went on to my grandparents' house and sat on the front porch visiting. Mother was dressed up and had on pearls; her long dark hair framed her face. She was holding Gee, who was dressed in a little yellow dress with smocking around the front. Her legs were tan, and she wore no shoes. I leaned into Daddy with his arm around me. I had on a green-and-white basket weave pattern dress and was also barefoot. Daddy had on dress slacks and a short-sleeved button-up shirt of a lightweight beige fabric. He wore sandals and no socks. Later we saw the picture that has been taken that day, and it was the last one of us before Daddy was killed.

Things were to change forever. Gee turned four on April 11, and Daddy missed that birthday too. In fact, he did not come home for two days and nights. Mother was used to his absence, so she continued to go to school, and of course, we had Katy. That first morning was just like any other morning, except it was raining, and Gee and I had to play on the front porch. The porch was high at one end and low on the other, built with the lay of the land. Gee and I loved to swing and sing “Sixteen Tons” by Tennessee Ernie Ford.

A man walked into the yard. I had seen him before. I once heard Mother say he was a lowlife, and she did not want him around us. She said, “He’s a buddy of your daddy, and they spend a lot of time together.” One time Daddy showed up at midnight with him and demanded Mother fix him something to eat. They were loud and drunk, and Mother sent me back to keep Gee in the bed. She was afraid, so she made him fried eggs. I was sure this was the man she talked about.

“Is your Daddy home?” the man asked as he approached.

I grabbed Gee and pulled her to me, backing up toward the door. He did not come any closer. I said, “No, he is not here.” I was scared and pulled Gee inside the door before he walked off. I always wondered if I helped him find and kill Daddy.

On the second day, I pressed my nose against the windowpane, knowing I could not go out to play because of the rain. A strange car pulled up, and I watched as a man and a woman opened the door to the backseat. I saw Mother. She seemed unable to help herself out of the car. Each of the people with her let her lean on them, and they brought her in. She looked like she was hurt, but she wasn’t crying. Her hair was down over her face, and she looked like she was going to fall. When they put her arms around their shoulders to keep her from falling, I saw big wet spots under both of her arms on her gray dress. They took her to the first bedroom, the room I shared with Gee, and placed her on the bed. She was shaking, and they put the cover over her. She didn’t see us standing there. I didn’t know what to do. I pulled Gee toward the foot of the bed where we stood silently. I wanted to take Gee and get in bed with Mother, but I knew we couldn’t. I remember wondering what was wrong and why the neighbors were coming to our house. Gee looked at me with her big dark eyes, and I pulled her close and hugged her. Somehow she knew not to talk. I don't know why I couldn't ask the questions in my mind, but I remained silent, thinking I was supposed to and somehow thinking it would be unkind to Mother.

Old Goldie from across the street had come into the room. She was intruding, I was sure of it, because she never had a kind word to say. I couldn't figure out why she would be there. I was afraid of her, beginning with her tall, boney frame and piercing black eyes. She said, "Their Daddy has been found dead, shot six times and left beside the road just in Buchanan County at Council. Poor little girls and one on the way."

I stood there and thought, *Daddy is dead. He won't be singing my favorite lullaby, "Bye Ole Baby Bunting."*

> Bye ole baby bunting
> Daddy's gone a hunting
> To fetch a little rabbit skin
> To wrap the baby bunting in

We didn't cry, but I wanted Mother to say something. We were in a room full of grown-ups, and no one noticed us at the end of the bed. It was a dark room of silence. Since there was no one crying, we did not cry either and became stuck in a threatened frozen state with no grown-ups to help us.

By the time we got back to our house, after getting new haircuts with Maureen, it was full of people. The living room was being prepared for bringing Daddy home, they said. Relatives were coming in from as far away as California, Maryland, and Michigan. Neighbors brought food, and I heard some talking about "sitting up with the corpse." I later found out that once Daddy was brought home, he would have people stay awake and not leave him alone through the night until his soul was taken to heaven at burial.

Grandma Tori arrived with Uncle Bill from Michigan. She took us to the bedroom off the kitchen and closed the door, and we slept with her. I remember wishing that Mother would come in and sleep with us. The next morning was noisy, and more food was being brought in. Gee and I followed Grandma Tori around as she checked the clocks to see if they were set at the time Daddy died to prevent bad luck to the living. She said, "When you don't know for sure the time of death, God will honor the time the family was notified." She covered the mirrors with black cloth she'd brought with her. She told us the first one to look in the mirror when a corpse is in the house will be the next to die. Since we were six and four, we took it all as gospel.

A long black car pulled in front of the house, and they brought in a foldout wire table with gray velvet covering the front and placed it against the wall in the living room. Flowers hung on the velvet, and the room began to smell sweet, very sweet. Furniture was moved out, and folding chairs were put in place. Then they brought in a stand-up piece of heavy metal and placed a long gray shiny box on it. They sent for Mother, and she was brought in supported by Aunt Delta from Baltimore, who was much bigger than Mother. Mother was not crying, but she looked like she was hurting, whimpering low and broken.

She was saying, "No, I don't want to go in there. Please don't take me in there."

When they got to the shiny gray box, they raised the lid. There was Daddy, but he did not awake. I began shivering and wanted to cry, but I didn't. His face was puffy, and I saw blood on his white shirt right in the middle and turned away.

Delta was holding Gee and she said, "Where are my daddy's legs?"

Mother took Gee from Aunt Delta, and I grabbed hold of Mother's leg. It was the first time we had touched since they brought her home. Just as Aunt Delta took our picture, Grandma Tori stepped in, saying something about people taking pictures of the dead. She took all three of us out of the living room. I wanted to run far away and wondered if it was really blood on Daddy's shirt. I couldn't ask anyone.

The next day, Daddy was picked up by the same long black car. Everything was loaded up, and the living room became empty. We were dressed up for church and taken to the funeral at Mt. Olive Church. They had Daddy up front with the lid open again. They put Mother in the front pew, and she was holding Gee.

The preacher finished, "Brother Brady has met his maker. Are you ready to meet yours? Now let us pray."

I didn't understand why I wasn't sitting with Mother, and my cousin Silvie was asking me, "Do you want to see your daddy one more time?"

I answered, yes, thinking but not understanding he would be gone forever. Then she took me outside through the side door to the end of the line, and we went through again and again. I remember wanting someone to take me out of the line, please, but no one saw me. We kept going until the last line had paid their respects by viewing Daddy and speaking to the family.

They brought Daddy to the Turner Cemetery right beside where Jimmy was buried. It was a long walk up the steep hill. We followed Daddy in his box carried up the hill by our uncles. Once we were there, they let us see Daddy for the last time. Then they lowered him in a deep hole. After the prayer, a woman sang "Amazing Grace" in her haunting, mountain, bluegrass style, as Mother was brought up close. They wanted her to pick up a handful of dirt and throw it in on top of Daddy, but she did not respond. She began swaying in her black dress, pulling off her hat and veil as she turned away from Daddy. Uncle Leonard caught her, and Gee and I followed them, leaving Daddy, walking down the hill as we held hands. We just left Daddy there, and I knew we would not see him again, but no one told me that. I wanted to sing, "Bye, baby Bunting, Daddy's gone a-hunting," because Daddy would surely go hunting in heaven.

Grandma Tori decided to stay with us. Mother was out of her own mind for many days, weeks, and then months. Mother recounted, "There were two thousand people at the funeral, and the newspaper articles were unmerciful." She became silent and a protective blanket over us except asking, "I want all talk to cease of my husband and their daddy in this house." Grandma Tori kept her silence, and the community did as well.

Chapter 3
Daddy's Atonement

And he is the propitiation for our sins; and not for ours only but also the sins of the whole world.
—1 John 2:2

It had been over fifty years since Daddy's murder. Mother said she had another dream of Daddy. He had spoken to her through her dream. Over the years, she had nightmares of his murder, and I was surprised it was a good one. Even though she was eighty-five years old, she looked much younger, and her mind was very keen. As she reclined on the sofa with the sun coming in the window, her face took on that beatific look that I had come to enjoy over the years.

As she spoke of the dream, it came to mind, a phrase she had used many times: "I am one with God." "I named the dream Brady's Atonement," she said. I was taken aback, because I always believed Mother felt guilty because she was glad he was gone. In moments of anger, she had said to me, "If your daddy had lived, you would not have had it near so good." This mysterious reference made me angry and sad when I was younger, but I had come to believe his death gave her instant martyrdom, crown and all. I was determined to use her cryptic announcements collected over the years to glean information of the untold story of Daddy, his life, and his murder.

So I began to catch her in moments of repose when she was both in this world and in God's world to gently lead her in her memories. It was such a time when Mother and I were relaxing at my home on the Gulf of Mexico, and she was in a wistful mood and talked about Daddy. I used a tape recorder to capture her words and her intonation.

The sun was setting on the Apalachicola bay like a giant fireball of orange and red, splashing with threads of hot pink and purple with a hint of silver. Just as it began to touch the bay, she said, "It's coloring for dark." I asked her what she meant, and she said, "The sun is setting, and this is my favorite time of day."

It suddenly struck me that this old saying describing dusk, "coloring for dark," described her life and our life with the light, dark, and shadows of our story.

In her dream, Daddy was standing with his arms toward heaven. He was in an open, luscious green field below the corncrib where Jimmy died and was wearing a white shirt that was glistening, except for a crimson spot just at the heart. As she walked up to him, the spot faded and was gone. He opened his arms to her, and she ran to him with tears of happiness streaming down her face. As he folded her into his arms, the tears were dried away, leaving a trace of salt like lace on her skin. She said, "The salt lace residue was like a beautiful pattern, kin to snowflakes."

I was speechless as she began to cry. I had never seen her cry. We don't cry; mountain women don't cry. I cried too.

She related to me that this was, "A word of wisdom," given to her that she would see her Brady in heaven. She continued on in a pensive voice filled with happiness and joy. "Your Daddy saw Harley there pointing the gun. He was sitting on a gun, as all taxis had a gun under a cushion in case of robbery. In that instant split second, your Daddy begged God for forgiveness for his sins and the hurt he had caused the people he loved, the ones who loved him, and those loved by others. The first of six bullets pierced the middle of his outstretched open hand; the other five entered his heart, and reconciliation with his maker began. Heaven opened up in a blinding path of gold, his blood flowed away from his body, and the cessation of life as he knew it transformed him into his heavenly body. He was one with the Lord God Almighty, and just as Jesus died on the cross, it was finished." This was her Word of Knowledge, a miracle from God, to be able to tell us that Daddy was in heaven and forgiven.

It was as if she did not want to contain the information within her being any longer. She drifted in her thoughts. "It was cold that weekend your Daddy did not come home." She remembered that she had been preparing to build a fire in the fireplace, and a bird flew down the chimney. She screamed, and Gee and I went running to her. She said, "This is a sign of a death," and later she said, "My Brady was killed that same morning and was already dead." She cautioned to be quiet and listen to God and trust that he would speak when he was ready. He would choose the way, whether it would be in a sign, a dream, or his voice. The catch was you wouldn't know for sure until time passed and it came into fruition.

She looked grateful as she spoke about her dream of Daddy's salvation. She went on to say, "I have never told you girls about the calling on your daddy's life. I couldn't because he ran from it, and the life he led took him far away from the voice he'd heard as a boy of twelve. As you girls were growing up, I kept you in church and tried every possible way to keep your daddy's sinful deeds secret. I didn't want you all to be influenced by his example. I don't think I could have gone on with my life, with all that already happened, if even one of you took his path.

"He broke down and cried after Jimmy died and told me how God had spoken to him. He said the revival preachers formed camp meetings following the Scots and Irish immigrants' settlement along the spine of the Appalachian Mountains. They would come around in warm weather, and everyone would be getting ready. The young men would go into the woods and cut brush that was lush and round to form a brush arbor cover for weeklong services. It would lean to a rolling hillside on the back, and on the front the branches would be attached to two lean poles. Musicians would gather from all over the county and set up to play old-time religious songs."

She went on to say that this is how Daddy had told her the story:

It was the first evening of the worship. Brady had gone with other boys out of curiosity after listening to them talk about looking up the dresses of women falling on the floor while coming under the spell of Jesus. He had been to church with his mother, a God-fearing woman, and had seen her shout and wash feet in the manner described in the Bible. But this felt different. The first preacher up in the front was young and good-looking with curly blond hair. He called himself Brother Allen. Brady had never seen a preacher that young, so it caught his attention.

The preacher led off by saying, "Devil, get behind us. This is sacred ground of believers doing God's work."

Then Brother Allen took his hand and made the sign of the cross. Brady was fascinated as the people drew closer, wanting to be touched by this man who was demanding demons come out of the possessed. He was charging back and forth, and the excitement was building with his power to deliver miracles. Then came the healing service as he performed the laying on of hands to a man in the front row. He was in a wheelchair and said he had a bad heart due to rheumatic fever. Brother Allen touched the man and cried out, "By the power of Jesus, be healed," and the man jumped out of his wheelchair and danced around the crowd. "Praise be to Jesus," was chanted until the crowd was in a frenzy.

All of a sudden, Brady got goose bumps running up and down his body and felt his hair stand up on his head. A commanding voice interrupted his thoughts, and it was as if no one was there except him. God said to him, "Brady, I am putting a call on your life; before you were born, I chose you for a special work."

Brady shouted with joy, and Brother Allen grabbed him and said, "Brother, are you ready to be saved and born again by being baptized by the Holy Spirit?" Brother Allen then led him into the glassy still river behind the camp.

As Mother wrapped up the story, she added, "Your daddy said many times that he would do anything to have that feeling again. Your daddy walked in his special walk with God until he was sixteen and began working in the coal mines. On his first day, miners were gathered around waiting to go on shift. They ranged in age from sixteen to sixty or maybe a little older. Most were family, made up of fathers, sons, nephews, and grandsons.

"Everyone knew that an explosion due to methane gas being released from a coal seam could happen at any time and that no one would come out alive. The deeper the seam, the more likely it would happen. Most young men saw their fathers take a drink or two of hooch to calm their nerves before going down to the work area deep in the mines. Nerves were running high as word trickled from coal mine to coal mine of the explosion in Mather, Pennsylvania, in May 1928. That explosion killed 195 men who had just gone on the night shift.

"Your Daddy faced danger, disaster, and death every time he went down. He began to count on the hot, burning feeling of the hooch going down, warming his body and numbing his mind.
He moved to Keystone, West Virginia, named for Keystone Coal and Coke Company of Pennsylvania. There he worked as a cutter when he was seventeen years old. He began going with the men who were ten to twenty years older than him to madam coal camp brothels spread out along the railroad tracks. His favorite was Crystal's in the Cinder Bottom Red Light District, one of the famous ones, which was labeled the Sodom and Gomorrah of the coalfields. Once he chose the path of sin, he took on a shell of secrecy to protect the mysterious hold on him of the glitzy parlor with the young ladies made up in fancy robes who lounged around waiting for the door to open."

Mother took a deep breath before continuing her story. "Her name was Gloria, and she was of a certain age, meaning older than your daddy. He told me once that she was a blonde-haired beauty, experienced but still looking young and alluring. He dared to say that she was pleased and not at all shy about getting the attention of many men as she walked across the room. Her face appeared perfect in the low lights of the parlor. I know she sauntered across to your Daddy, who was young and wet behind the ears. Unknown to him, she was not after his money because she knew he was not like her well-to-do, older clients. Her goal was more sinister than that. This lady of the night wanted his immortal soul by seducing his mortal body."

I had never heard Mother talk in such a knowing way about ladies of the night. She continued her story. "She kept him from a pure and holy relationship with God and robbed him of the true Lover of his soul."

It dawned on me that Mother had referred to Revelations in the Bible to understand Daddy's past, and she stood firm that until the moment of atonement in her dream that Daddy was lost to the woman referred to in Jeremiah 51.7: "Babylon hath been a golden cup in the Lord's hand, that made all the earth drunken; the nations have drunken of her wine, therefore the nations are mad."

I did not know how to respond. I hoped she would continue, but she was meditative as we sat in silence holding hands. That was the first time Mother had seemed real to me.

Mother would then slip back into her old memory and the description of "her Brady," instilling in me the strong physical hold he had over her. Again, she would tell me like I had never heard it before. "Your daddy looked better in coveralls that most men in suits; he was tall and slender with broad shoulders, a narrow waist, and muscular arms. His face was well chiseled with high cheekbones and a cleft in his chin resting below that easy smile. His wavy dark hair was combed back, and his eyes were a velvet dark brown. His presence caused notice with his well-dressed swagger and mysterious gaze. He loved clothes, and some said he looked like Gary Cooper. He was always the life of the party, singing and dancing on the bar and charming women and men alike."

As always, I acted like this was the first time I had heard her description of Daddy, but I could repeat it by heart.

Through our growing-up years, I thought I was a coal miner's daughter. As I got older and more curious about why Daddy had gotten himself murdered, I began to see his pictures didn't have the hard, weary look of a coal miner. I realized that the quilt Mother made me, for my first marriage, was from his suits—rich fabric of pin stripes, tweed, and good wool. Coal miners did not own that many suits. The more

I delved into it, the more I learned he had gained some city slicker ways. This was apparent in his arrogant attitude for authority. He was a rolling stone from West Virginia, Kentucky, and Virginia to Maryland. He was streetwise and a player, running from creditors, law enforcement, and old grudges. Mother had not been willing to own up to any of this, but with her latest revelations and the information his cousins were more than happy to disclose to "Brady's girls," the pieces began to fit in the puzzle.

The cousins said, "He fancied fast women, cars, music, dancing, guns, and moonshine."

Everyone knew Grandma Tori said he looked like a wolf in sheep's clothing when he came calling, smitten with the seventeen-year-old Maggie. She said, "He hid in the attic of our house when the local police came looking for him."

Grandma Tori was not as impressed as Poppy with the cavalier and maverick attitude. She did agree with Poppy that they would make pretty children. However, she and Mother had always drowned in silence when we would veer off the path and ask questions relating to Daddy's darker side. It began to dawn on me that Mother was intrigued with the ruggedness and in-control aspects of his "dandy personality" and even possibly felt a sense of power. Being impressionable and young, she had passed the point of no return.

Daddy was the eldest of eight children and only had a sixth-grade education, but he was smart and streetwise. I am sure he gained some of his bravado, at age sixteen, while working in the coal mines, having a big drink of moonshine, singing the words:

> Where it is dark as a dungeon and damp as the dew
> Where danger is double and pleasures are few

> Where the rain never falls and the sun never
> shines
> It's dark as a dungeon way down in the mines.

He hated being paid with credit scrip and tokens to use at the Company Store. This indebted the coal miners and robbed them of hope. By keeping this anger on the surface, he would end up being a hothead, get in a fight, and lose his job.

There was more to this lovable rogue's wild disposition. He was adventurous and a risk taker who lived by his own code of honor. His good deeds were know by many a downtrodden coal miner's family, and he could be relied on and was seen as a light at the end of a tunnel, having walked in their shoes, and easily justified his actions. Daddy worked for the coal mines when he was not running moonshine or escaping to Maryland just ahead of the law. His cover for running moonshine or skirting the law turned out to be one of the big secrets Mother kept from us. Keeping the secrets both helped and hurt us.

She said, "Daddy and Harley's relationship went back a long way. They met at Riverside Cafe, Daddy's stomping ground. Harley had come home from the army with a self-inflicted gunshot wound to his right foot. This gave him a dishonorable discharge, and he bragged about being insane and pulling one over on the army. Harley knew he didn't have normal looks; in fact, he was ugly, and women were never sexually attracted to him. Your daddy was the opposite, and Harley considered him to be masculine in every way."

Based on what Mother was saying, I concluded the pairing of Daddy and Harley put them on a collision course of no return.

Good fortune landed in our lap about Harley's family. Gee found Harley's aunt by happenstance. One day she'd stopped to visit her sister-in-law's mother, Vada, who had been ill. Vada lived in what used to be a mining row house in Keen Mountain Camp, Virginia. They were talking about Harley Wilson and Daddy's murder.

During the course of their conversation, Vada said, "My maiden name was Wilson, and my family lived up Hurricane Holler with all the Wilsons." She continued, "You won't believe this, but his aunt was named Rebecca Hart, and she moved to an assisted living facility at Claypool Hill just a few miles from you."

Gee knew we had made another breakthrough on the past and stopped at the assisted living facility on her way home and asked permission to see her.

Gee knocked on Rebecca Hart's door, and a small-framed, well-dressed woman smiled and thanked her for coming to see her. Gee quickly explained why she was there. "You don't know me, but I am the daughter of Brady Powers, who was murdered by your nephew, Harley. I don't know if you want to talk to me. I just want to know more about my daddy since I was only four years old when he died."

The woman smiled and said, "Child, if I was four years old when my daddy died, I would want someone to talk to me too. I will be more than happy to tell you anything you want to know."

So Gee set a time for the two of us to go back and talk with her about her memories of the past to help us put together more missing pieces of this puzzle.

When we interviewed Rebecca, she said, "My sister, Delia, was a saint if there ever was one. She couldn't do anything with her five boys after their daddy died. Harley was about forty years old when he planned and carried out the murder of your daddy, Brady. He was known as a lowlife, even if he was my nephew. He was about five six and 190 pounds. His hair was blond but thinning. Eyes were a steely gray, giving the appearance of icy calm and showing no soul. Everyone said so."

After a brief pause she continued. "It was a common occurrence for Harley and his four brothers to fight at the moonshine still while brandishing guns and knives. One day, their little brother Samuel disappeared, and no one reported him missing. Don't know for sure but suspected a brother or brothers accidently killed him during a drinking brawl and argument."

As she talked, I felt a cold shadow still dark from that time when Harley came into our yard the day he killed Daddy. She ended by telling us how to go up Hurricane Holler and see the house, which was empty but still there.

Gee and I set out early one Saturday morning and drove up Hurricane Holler and took a winding, narrow paved road to the mouth of the holler, just as Rebecca had described. The house was set back on a grassy knoll, across a car bridge, and over a winding stream called Hurricane Creek. It was partially falling down with missing steps. We decided we did not want to get out of the car; it was too eerie, like ghosts were haunting the house and grounds. Vines were growing up the chimney in a spiraling choke, and the front door was open. A feeling of evil came over me.

I imagined we parked in the same spot as Daddy did the day he waited for Harley with no thought of his last minutes of life. We looked at each other, and tears came down our cheeks. We were almost to the end of our search for answers to Daddy's past.

Our last step in that quest would be to visit Mother's lawyer who had handled the murder trial. Daddy's brothers Radford and Leonard hired a criminal attorney because they thought one of the brothers might take justice in their own hands and they wanted Mother to have the support throughout the trial that she wouldn't receive from the prosecutor. Gee and I made the trip to Clintwood to visit Ransome Phillips, who by then was a judge in Dickenson County. The meeting was surreal, especially for me because I remembered him, but as a little girl under the age of ten. He was still handsome and gave us both a hug. I remembered I had wanted him to be our new daddy.

He showed us to the library and had the file on a table, bulging with paper, held together by large rubber bands. He said, "When your daddy's brothers hired me to travel to Grundy, in Buchanan County, to represent the family against Harley, I took the highly sensational case, because as a young lawyer, this would help set my career on the path to becoming a judge." He continued," "I realized I would work as long as it took for this beautiful young widow and her girls in order to convict the killer."

Mr. Phillips explained that he hired an investigator to go to Elkhorn City and Hurricane Holler to get the background story on the woman who owned the tavern and on Harley so he could put together the evidence ensuring all the elements for premeditated murder.

We found out that Harley liked to run around with Daddy and touted him to be the best moonshine runner in Virginia. He told stories about Daddy, how he could outrun any officer with his hot rod, one-brake wheel, making many a 180-degree turn. Daddy knew every curve on his run and outfitted his Ford with the ability to turn off the taillights or blind the officer with his souped-up headlights. All the while he was likely singing "Rye Whiskey" and "Sixteen Tons." In every bar, Daddy had people hanging around him, his charisma drew people in. Harley was there too, but no one noticed him. This was particularly apparent when he and Daddy went to Coca's Place just across the state line in Elkhorn City, Kentucky. In fact, they had frequented houses with prostitutes, and word got around that Harley always laid a weapon down when he paid his money.

After discussing some of the file, Mr. Phillips left us in the library and told us to take as long as we liked. Gee and I were glued to the file. Finally, the "Woman, Coca" had come to life as we read, and it was as if Daddy had come back to life in a way we never imagined. We looked at each other, and our hands shook as we took the center file from the brackets. We were as ready as we would ever be to put the facts with the rumors.

As we began to read, Coca's history was revealed to us.

Coca Raven Colley was beautiful. She had grown up in what amounted to squalor. Coca's father was a Melungeon, meaning he was of mixed race, usually black, white, and Indian or other ancestry. Coca's grandfather, Hollis, was named for the plantation owner where he had been a slave until he was ten years old. He fled into the Virginia Mountains, far away from dusty cotton fields when the Thirteenth Amendment to the US Constitution freed him in 1865.

He met and fell in love with Gabby, a beautiful Irish girl with red hair and green eyes. They were not allowed to marry but had one son, Sampson. Sampson was a handsome, strong boy. He had dark auburn hair, green eyes, and golden-tan skin.

Sampson followed his Daddy's footsteps and worked in the mines in Harlen, Kentucky, until after the boom and fall of World War II when railroads could not depend on coal for fuel to drive locomotives. He hitched a ride to Pikeville, Kentucky, and worked for Fats Warner, a minister and local businessman who died of a heart attack in the "midst of passion" with his mistress. Lucky for Sampson he could pass as white and was headed to Clinchfield Coal Company in Clinchco, Virginia, when he met and fell in love with Willa Pearl, whose father was also a coal miner.

They had only one child, a girl named Coca Raven. Sampson was injured in a coal mining accident and died of his injuries soon after Coca was nine years old. Willa Pearl was forced to go to work. She had never worked outside the home but needed enough money to support herself and Coca. Having no education or experience, she found work in Elkhorn City working for Mamie at Mamie's Place.

Mamie's Place was a local tavern where a man could buy a woman's company for the same price as his shot of whiskey. They had been there three years when Coca's mother became sick. Within a year, she knew she was dying; she was hiding her bloody handkerchief from Coca. Mamie was just and fair, and also seeing the sensual beauty budding in Coca, she promised Willa Pearl that she would take care of the girl. Willa Pearl was desperate to know her girl would have a roof over her head and food to eat.

Mamie was right. Coca grew into a sensual beauty. She was petite and voluptuous. Her Melungeon heritage had blessed her with long, wavy midnight hair, silvery green eyes that turned up at the corners, and a heart-shaped face. Her lips were naturally full. Men old and young stared at her, and the women turned their backs to her and gossiped as she went past.

Coca was smart as well as beautiful, and being the shrewd businesswoman that Mamie was, she quickly realized Coca was an asset. She was right from the day she made her promise to Willa Pearl. Mamie came to love Coca like the daughter she never had, but business was business and at age fourteen, Coca made her first business transaction with a man. Coca also took on more responsibility in keeping the books and ordering liquor and moonshine for the bar. When Coca was twenty-five, Mamie died and left it all to Coca. She was proud when she hung the new sign: COCA RAVEN'S.

It had been three years, and Coca was more beautiful than ever. She was tough; she had to be in the line of work she was in. She was dead-on with a shotgun or a pistol and kept both behind the bar. She was flirty and coy, and even though she did not have male customers anymore, none of the men minded. They were just pleased as punch that she had smiled her beautiful smile their way.

One hot night, the moon was full, and the tavern was hopping. The men had just been paid, and their spirits were high. Drinks were flowing, and her girls were busy as could be. In walked a man unfamiliar to Coca. He was the most beautiful man she had ever seen. Moreover, she had seen men from all walks of life from politicians to businessmen to preachers. But this one was different. He looked at ease and walked with grace. His clothes fit him like a glove, showing his perfect physique. She thought he looked like a Philadelphia lawyer, and he was looking at her. Their eyes met and held. He walked up to her, took her hand, and kissed it, never losing eye contact. "Good evening, ma'am. I'm Brady. I would like to buy you a drink."

Coca appeared not to notice Harley with the beady eyes and walked away with Brady. Later, Coca took Brady to her room, and he didn't have to pay. Brady was clearly as taken in by Coca as she was by him.

Harley was tired of not being noticed. He knew he was short and squat with thinning hair. He also was not a gentleman and didn't think Brady was either. Brady would put on a show, a real ladies' man, pulling out all the manners and charm. Harley knew Brady used vulgar humor sparingly. It was like he wore two hats. If he had on an old Greek fisherman-style hat, open leather sandals, and a shirt with a beach scene that wasn't tucked in, he would use the colorful expression "I like my coffee strong as stud-hoss piss with the foam farted off it." If he had on his wide-brimmed fedora, he was likely to have on a three-button suit, a white shirt, and a short, wide silk tie with a clip. He would be glib and pulled out all the stops: "Do I have a pistol in my pocket, or are you just glad to see me?" Brady always trumped, Harley believed.

Aunt Belle had given a statement and we read her words: "My sister's husband, Brady, seemed to separate his feelings for Coca and Maggie. Maggie still took Brady's breath away. Everyone knew he was a visceral man and lived in the moment, not thinking about tomorrow. Maggie seemed to take it in stride. She was high-spirited, especially when angry, and would do anything to make her point. She would take to praying when he was leaving. She'd pray the car wouldn't start, and if God didn't answer her prayer on the spot, she would pick up a rock that seemed so heavy she would not be able to lift except with the strength from God and would throw it into the windshield. And she would use Brady's belief on hell with him. 'There is a hell and a hot one, and you will go there if you don't change your ways,' she'd say."

Aunt Belle's statement went on to say that Mother had known something was up. Daddy and Harley had been going to

Elkhorn for eight months. He was in good humor before he'd left, she said, and had tucked us in, singing: "Bye ole baby Bunting, Daddy's gone a-hunting to seek a little rabbit skin to wrap the baby Bunting in."

At the end of the file was the confession hand-printed on binder paper Harley had made of premeditated murder. It was the same one Gee and I had read at the courthouse.

> I went lookin' for Brady that mornin', and his two little girls were playin' on the porch singing, "If You've Got the Money Honey, I've Got the Time." I scared 'em real good. I went back to town and caught a ride to Riverside Café where I found Brady waitin' for his next fare. Brady thought he had beatn' the hell out of me with that fistfight over his car and Coca. He was used to me kowtowin' to him but I had been plannin' on gettin' him back for a good while. He had tore up the house on Hurricane Holler and the shed at the still for money he said I owed him for the last load of moonshine before he quit runnin' it for me. I had tried to reason with him that he was overpaid, and that as far as I was concerned we were even. He became so mad and began shootin' holes in the still and set fire to the shed. If there had been moonshine in the still it would have blown to kingdom come.
>
> Now Coca, he was real sweet on her, and she was the first woman I truly loved other than my Ma. Brady had beat me with his fist after I rolled him out of his car, sleepin' off a drunk, went to Elkhorn and picked up Coca, and brought her back to Hurricane Holler. She

thought I was bringin' her to him but she was dead wrong. I wanted her for me. She began yellin' at me to take her home when she saw Brady was not there for her as I had promised. She was getting hard to handle when a car pulled up with Brady and a buddy.

Brady slammed the car door and came at me like a chargin' bull. His eyes were full of hate and I raised my hands up over my face tryin' for protection. He came at me like a buzz saw, and there was no turnin' back. His face was white and he began cussin' me with every word I had ever heard. About the same time he grunted and threw a punch at me as I tried to dodge him. That first punch hit me dead on in the stomach and then a quick one to my throat ending with a kick to my manhood landin' me on the ground. He said get up, and I couldn't, and he kicked me until I blacked out. He had it comin': the time had come. I hired him to take me to Coca's Place in Elkhorn City, Kentucky. I was right reckonin' that he would think he was gettin' paid to go see her. Once we got there she took him to her private quarters. We stayed all day. I tried to pace myself so I could carry out my plan. We left late in the evenin' and I had him to stop three times to buy beer. The last stop he said he better go in for me, that if the law was in there I would get taken in. When we got to the holler I told him I had to go in and get the fare. I went in and got the thirty-eight special, which was already loaded. I came down to the car and when he turned I fired six bullets into him, watching his shocked look as blood spattered everywhere.

> He never saw it comin'. When you dance you have to pay the fiddler.

Mother said the news of Daddy's murder was broken to her just one month shy of graduating her senior year by the assistant principal Mr. Stacy Ratliff. He had announced for her to come to the office over the intercom. Mrs. Ellen Donovan, the librarian, was also there. Mother said she knew instantly it had to do with Daddy, and her heart sank.

She said that Mrs. Donovan was holding the new high school yearbook and had a marker at her school picture. The caption under her picture read, "She keeps her worries in the bottom of her heart and sits on the lid and smiles." Mother figured Mrs. Donovan knew of Brady's reputation when she put the caption under her picture. She gave the book to Mother as Mr. Ratliff began slowly telling her that Daddy had been found murdered beside a road in Council, Virginia. He'd been shot six times, Mr. Ratliff explained. He said the car had been moved because Daddy was on the passenger side. The taxi he had been driving for Riverside Café was soaked in blood with the owner's gun still under the driver's seat. She recalled that he related in a sympathetic tone, "Your husband was taken by surprise and didn't stand a chance."

Mother said that she simply couldn't take in what Mr. Ratliff was saying. It was like she could see him talking, but she couldn't hear his words. Her body began to tremble and numbness covered her from head to toe. She felt ringing in her ears every time her heart beat. Her head felt like a band was being tightened around it and pulled tighter and tighter until the room became dark.

When Mother awakened, she recalled, she was in the teachers' lounge on the sofa. Mrs. Donovan had smelling salts. Mother said she then informed her that she was four months pregnant and became faint again. Mrs. Donovan told her that she herself had been unable to tell anyone that she was six weeks pregnant and shared the suffering of being married to an unfaithful husband. This was the reason she dedicated the caption under Mother's picture, suffering in silence. Mother said once she was able, Mr. Ratliff and Mrs. Donovan helped her to the car. She said she was terrified to go home to us, her little girls.

Chapter 4
Brady's Girls Stomping the Grapes

Take us the foxes, the little foxes, that spoil the vines; for our vines have tender grapes.
—Song of Solomon 2:15

Gee and I did not know we were getting a baby sister. Scarlet Jewel just showed up one day on our bed with lots of dark hair and dressed in white lace. She arrived just five months after Daddy was murdered. Our cousin, Kathy, told us she was too small for us to hold, so we would lie on the bed beside her. Gee took a baby blanket, held it close to the fire to warm it, and then brought it back to bed and covered her tiny kicking legs. We loved her instantly. However, she was only on our bed for a while. Scarlet had a cradle in Grandma Tori's room with a beautiful pink-and-white satin coverlet with a little satin pillow laced with pink ribbon. Gee and I thought we had a princess living in that room. She was the first happiness in the house since we moved there before Daddy died. Mother and Grandma Tori were smiling, and we all huddled around her and watched her every move.

We would awaken to Mother screaming in the middle of the night. Gee would move over in our bed, and I would hold her close. This happened all our growing up years. I overheard Mother talking about a dream she had before they found Harley and charged him with the murder. She dreamed it was Harley, and he had taken off his bloody clothes and tried to wash the blood out to no avail. In her dream, he climbed into the mountains behind his house and had pushed the clothes as far as he could into a hollow log. When the sheriff came to tell her that the search dogs went straight behind Harley's house high in the mountains and found the bloody wet clothes, she told him that God had given her the dream and then related it to him. He was taken aback as he listened to her, looking into the dark green eyes on her grief-stricken face as he confirmed to her that she was right. The tracking dogs had gone straight to the hollow log high in the mountain behind Harley's house. The clothes were still wet and bloody. The sheriff was no churchgoing man, but he knew this young widow had something special between her and God.

Mother became very busy, meeting with her lawyer and the sheriff and finally going to the first trial in Buchanan County where the charge against Harley was premeditated murder. She said it was unbearable to be in court day after day, listening to them say those terrible things about Daddy. The way she described it, I always thought they were a bunch of lies. She gave the impression that the law didn't do their job and had used flimsy hearsay evidence describing a fistfight when Daddy beat Harley up over taking a woman in Daddy's car up a dirt road holler and burying it up to the axle without Daddy's knowledge. There was a longtime grudge over moonshine money from their past of making and running moonshine.

The Grundy County Courthouse was full of people wanting to see the murderer and the beautiful young widow and her girls. Being the oldest, I remember people staring and pointing at us. Gee would run up and down the corridors to the water fountain. I would lift her up time and again. When they brought the killer into the courtroom, a nice police officer would take us into an office. We were important being on parade, and everyone smiled at us all dressed up in our organdy dresses, crinolines, and black patent Mary Jane shoes, all gifts from Sutherland's department store.

We went to several trials, and then they just suddenly stopped. Mother said, "His silk-stocking lawyers pled that he was temporarily insane at the time of the murder and that he had tested at a below-average IQ. He had a history of showing less impulse control, especially when under the influence during bouts of drinking alcohol." She indicated his lawyer sounded like he had read it in a book.

Also, Harley's dishonorable discharge from the army was introduced as evidence, stating he had shot himself in the foot to make himself unable to meet fitness for duty. They argued this all contributed to a crime of passion while temporarily insane rather than cold, premeditated murder. The history of Daddy and Harley as recounted by several witnesses had the perfect setting. Harley and Daddy had many arguments over the moonshine money. Daddy insisted on being paid a large sum of money for running the moonshine from Harley's family still. He had the car, driving skills, and streetwise intelligence, delivering the moonshine on time and collecting the money. Harley was no match for Daddy in any way, and Harley knew it.

Harley wanted people to think he was running in Daddy's league. He had a reputation for bragging in local pubs about Coca Raven from Elkhorn, Kentucky, that she was sweet on him but was careful to never speak of it when in the company of Daddy. He was a ne'er-do-well outsider, and in every honky-tonk women surrounded Daddy, with his swagger and charming, easy smile; they were drawn to his dark good looks and flamboyance. He was the life of the party, and Harley hated him for it. He went unnoticed but liked to be in the action with Daddy, a dangerous pairing of Harley's short, stocky, balding, unattractive looks as a social misfit versus Daddy's handsome, confident, charismatic personality.

Witnesses testified that they didn't believe Harley's bragging, and everyone knew Daddy had beat him with his fist after he rolled Daddy out of his own car as he slept. Then Harley took the car to Elkhorn and tricked Coca into coming with him to Virginia on the pretense that Daddy had sent him to get her. He took her up the holler to his house on Hurricane Creek. Daddy, along with a couple of friends, caught up with Harley just in time to see his new car buried up to the axle in the muddy, rutted road and Coca Raven in fear of her life. Harley had put the moves on her, and she had resisted. She slapped him, and he backhanded her.

The court record shows that Daddy gave Harley a beating with his fist and left him lying in the mud and took Coca back to Elkhorn City. He would never have brought her to Virginia where his family lived. Coca was special but not as special as Mother. During the trial, Coca could not be reached and went into hiding until things settled down. Harley's lawyer did a good job of convincing the judge of the insanity plea, and he ruled that Harley would be sent to Southwestern State Hospital for the criminally insane until he was considered sane enough to stand trial.

Mother went deeper into herself as her life and the lives of her three girls were held in limbo. Over the next five years, she had to wait for the reports on Harley and thought he would never be released to stand trial. She continued to have nightmares and was emotionally numb to everything around her. She was going through the motions. Gee had the same recurring nightmare of a man with his head covered with a beekeeper hat running and running after her. She began wetting the bed and suffered severe anxiety when Mother was away. I would act out the funeral process of saying long good-byes and memorizing and singing songs of tragic death. My nightmare was also reoccurring. I dreamt that Harley would come back and kill us. If he wanted to kill Daddy, then he wanted to kill us too; it just made sense. Scarlet had the love from Grandma Tori and us, but with Mother away at work and so out of it, Mother was unable to bond with her baby girl, who never saw her daddy. For Scarlet, something would always be missing. We all waited and waited.

Finally, after five years, Harley was released to stand trial. Mother had to sit through another trial and relive every detail step-by-step. I was twelve years old, Gee was ten, and Scarlet was five when we were all taken to the trial. They showed the grown-ups the pictures taken in the taxi after Daddy's body was found that morning parked beside the main road in Council, Virginia.

Everything had changed. Life had gone on except for us. The high sheriff had changed to someone who had not investigated the case. Mother had agreed to let the judge sentence Harley and not go for a long, drawn-out jury trial. She thought Harley would have gotten more time from the judge, but he only sentenced him to twelve years to include the five already spent in the criminal insane hospital, stating that the conditions in the hospital were the same or worse than in prison.

In all, Harley served twelve years. He was released under the condition that he was never to return to Virginia. We later found out he killed a man in prison in self-defense. Once he was out, he moved to Greenville, Tennessee, married, died, and was buried there.

Life settled in our house with all women. Looking back, I liked it with Grandma Tori, Mother, Gee, and Scarlet and our routine with no men. Grandma Tori became the manager of the house, and Mother became breadwinner and father. I was the mother, because Mother held me responsible even though Grandma Tori was there. I took my role seriously. She left a list of household chores each Saturday for Gee and me that would keep us busy and out of trouble.

If we went outside, I was responsible for keeping up with Scarlet and making sure Gee did not get in any fights in the neighborhood. Gee would sometimes say four-letter words, and I made it my job to wash her mouth out with Ivory Soap. Bubbles would come out of her mouth for a long time. She was small, but so was a stick of dynamite. She was always blowing up, and I would have to jump in and defend her. Mother ruled by the telephone. When she called, I had to answer and give her a report of what was happening and where we were with our list. I learned to turn the big silver knob on the bottom of the big black phone up as high as it would go, so I could hear the ring outside. When it rang, I learned to run in and answer without seeming out of breath.

Early in spring on the anniversary of Daddy's murder, Mother wanted to be baptized in the McClure River, just up the street below the swinging bridge. I was seven years old and hanging back in the crowd. All of a sudden, the men called preachers were leading Mother out in the river. She had on a white dress, and her long black hair was hanging down in waves. Two preachers took her out into the deep. They put one hand in the middle of her back and one on the back of her head, and they took her under the water as the people on the side sang "Poor Wayfaring Stranger" and "Crossing over Jordan." This terrified me, and as I looked around, Grandma Tori was holding Scarlet, and Gee was holding on the hem of Grandma's dress, hiding her face. I did not know what they were doing to Mother. She came up crying, the outline of her slim body showing through the wet dress, and they walked her out of the water. I knew I never wanted to cross over Jordan with a poor stranger. All I knew was I did not like anything to do with preachers.

"When you hear nothing, say nothing," Grandma Tori said after learning the Old Regular Baptist Church had excommunicated Mother for cutting her hair. I heard

Grandma Tori say that Mother was thirty-three, the same age as Jesus when they nailed him on the cross. I thought it unfair. Who else could memorize 104 Bible verses? Besides, long hair had to be curled, and I heard Mother tell Maureen next door that she didn't have time for her hair after beginning to work six days a week.

Grandma Tori would only say the same words: "When you hear nothing, say nothing."

Mother said not to talk about it, and she never let her hair grow out again. Time began to erase Daddy with help from Mother and Grandma Tori. There were no pictures of him, and all his personal belongings had disappeared. Again, when we would ask, Grandma Tori would say, "Ask no questions, and I'll tell you no lies."

Mother began taking us to the First Presbyterian Church where God already knew who was going to be saved and gave us free will for our choices. I asked Mother what that meant, and she said, "Always take the right path, the one blessed by God." That sounded easy.

We loved Sundays. We dressed up in our Sunday dresses with crinolines, hats, white gloves, and black patent Mary Jane shoes. We had to wash our gloves the night before, and on Sunday morning, Grandma Tori would shine our shoes with leftover buttered biscuits. In church, sometimes Mother would pull the rubber band of our hat tucked under our hair and let it pinch the back of our necks if we were not paying attention. After church, we would stop by the drug store for cherry Cokes. I was allowed to buy a movie magazine, and that became my fashion guide and my romance with the stars. I became an expert on all the stars and their lives. After we went home, Mother would cook fried chicken, creamed potatoes, green beans, and slaw or roast beef with all the trimmings. She always looked beautiful wearing her Sunday clothes, high heels, and a crisp white apron.

It was the summer before seventh grade during a revival at the Sandlick Presbyterian Church that the minister was talking about being saved and going to heaven. I was there with all my friends, and I wanted so much to go to heaven and did not know if I was one of the chosen ones like the Presbyterians believed. I looked at the minister with his outstretched hands. He instructed the organist to play "Just as I Am" and then invited everyone to come forward and be saved. I wanted to go and kept waiting for the Lord to tell me to come. And I waited. All of a sudden, a light surrounded the minister head to toe, and I knew I must go forward. Just as they were beginning the song for the third time, I went forward and was saved. Thank God I would be one of the precious jewels for his crown like in the song "When He Cometh."

Later that summer we had some visitors at our house, and they asked us if we had accepted Jesus Christ as our savior, and I proudly said yes. Gee said no, and they told her she was not saved. She said she didn't give a damn. Grandma Tori said, "The devil is in that child, and children should be seen and not heard."

I thought they were rude to make Gee feel bad, and Mother called Gee down, saying, "God knows everything we do and even the number of hairs on our heads."

The Presbyterians said it was supposed to be a personal relationship between us and God. Mother explained that Gee had the chance to make her own peace with God in her own timing. Two years later, when Gee was also twelve years old, she accepted Jesus as her savior at Presbyterian Summer Camp during Vespers. Scarlet attended Sunday school for a perfect attendance pin with bars for each year that attached, and she proudly wore it every Sunday for eight years.

Our elementary school years were fun and filled with activities. We went to church camp, 4-H camp, and summer band camp and made many friends. Gee learned to ski and sew, took dance, and played ball at Presbyterian camp. She became a majorette in ninth grade and developed a curvy figure, although she was petite. I attended 4-H camp, participated in summer band, took majorette lessons, and learned to swim. Scarlet followed the camp routine, played trumpet in the summer band, and was afraid to learn to swim.

It was my fault she was afraid to swim. Each summer on Fourth of July our family, along with Maureen, Edwin, and Mary Katherine from next door, went to Caney Creek Swimming Pool for an all-day picnic and swimming. There was a long slide coming down to the pool. I encouraged Scarlet to slide down and promised I would catch her. I had no way of knowing that when she got to me, I would be unable to catch her and she would hang around my neck in a panic. We both went under, and I was not strong enough to get her out alone, so that fear stuck with her.

The three of us hated the first day of school each year when it came up. Each child had to stand up by alphabetical order and state their parents' names. We hated this, because we had to say both Daddy's and Mother's names, and his name was never mentioned in our house, so it felt like we were betraying them. It was like a really bad admission, especially to be repeated out loud, and sounded shameful. I was glad *P* was near the end of the alphabet, but that just made the waiting harder.

Our innocence was lost in the aftermath of Daddy's murder, gossip, newspaper stories, and standing every year saying, "I am the daughter of Maggie and Brady Powers." The play yard talk would be buzzing all around us until the teacher would ring the bell. Gee has said her only solace of those times was her friend, Mia Anne Peterson, whose father had also died, and their names were together. Gee and Mia shared the same humiliation.

As we grew older and were in crowds, the pointing started. "There's Brady's girls!" We began to feel "marked" by this tragedy, and it would hang over our heads every time we were thrust in the shadow of grief of that time and place. So at weddings, funerals, and other social gatherings, "the girls" naturally banded together. They noticed the pointing but kept talking and refused to look their way, which gave an air of haughtiness. As Grandma Tori said, we would "pay it no mind." Just an unspoken silence between us and what would begin to appear as "an air of haughtiness," which became our armor. The attention affected us each in a different way. There was no way of verbalizing the feelings that went with being "marked," known by everyone but not knowing them. It has never gone away. With the exception of Scarlet, who said she always felt special and famous and liked being pointed at. Gee and I had an arm of protection for her all the same.

It was during this time I began playing funeral. We gathered large flowers of yellow, orange, pink, and purple and laid them on top of Gee who would lie face up on the cedar chest. Then Mary Katherine would bring Scarlet in and tell her Gee was dead and that she would never see her again. Scarlet would cry, and we would all take turns being dead. Grandma Tori put an end to that game, and I almost got a spanking for being the ringleader. She did let us have funerals under the willow tree for all animals. We had full-service funerals with flowers, singing, and preaching. My favorite songs performed under the willow were “Pretty Polly” and “Knoxville Girl,” both about love and murder. I began an obsession with songs of love and death. I continued to add songs of death: “Teen Angel,” “Patches,” “Running Bear,” “Moody River,” and “Last Kiss.” I taught Gee and Scarlet all the words, and we sang them all the time. I was keeping that last day of seeing Daddy fresh in my mind.

“Brady’s girls” or “the girls” (as Mother called us) were keen observers and invented who we wanted to be, along with the traits already inherited and learned. I was a tomboy and avid reader who would shed my Sunday dress, bra, and shoes in seventh grade and become the Indian in the tree. Gee was small but could outrun everyone and would have if she’d been included in the games. She also liked to be the boss or the mother in any playhouse game. Scarlet was happy with her stick horse and her big, flat rock by the railroad track that jutted out into water. It was her safe haven getaway place where she loved to talk out loud about her issues, read, and write her thoughts. She also walked the railroad track when no one knew where she was. She had been warned it was dangerous, and she liked it. Once on Thanksgiving she hiked to the top of the mountain above the island. We were calling her, but she didn’t answer. She could see us but did not want us to see her. Finally, she would show up. She began to show traits of aloofness or, as Mother called it, “Scarlet is being vague and way out there.”

I read *Little Women* and wanted to be Jo so badly that I embodied her persona. I would have sold my hair if need be. I escaped the sadness that permeated our house and hid in the apple tree behind the house to read my favorite books where no one could find me. I would stay for hours reading and eating the tart green apples. When I heard them calling for me, sometimes I did not answer.

Gee like to wear her mink-tipped high heels and always did her housework all dressed up. She said when she grew up she would always wear high heels and makeup to do her housework. She was a neat little thing, always cleaning and bossing everyone around like she was the mother.

Scarlet would run out of the house naked when just out of the bath, and our neighbor Edwin would wrap her in a towel and bring her home. She began to call him Daddy, and he didn't mind, even if the people at church gossiped about it.

On Saturday evenings, Mother would bring home brown-and-serve rolls, a break from homemade biscuits and cornbread, and we would lather them with butter and eat in front of the television while watching *Bonanza*. Since *Bonanza* had four men, we would pick who our boyfriend was, and Gee always chose Little Joe. No one cared except we all knew she was in love with Little Joe, so we went along.

Our holidays were the best. Mother was going through the motions and always went to bed early, but she planned all year for the holidays. She bought our gifts throughout the year, and they were a sight to behold. On Christmas Eve, she would come home in a taxi, hiding them on the front and back porch until we were asleep. On Christmas morning, the tree towered over our wished-for gifts, and oranges, tangerines, and nuts filled the big wooden bowl on the coffee table to the brim. Gee and I decorated the house following the design we liked best in the neighborhood, and Grandma Tori baked for days. The three of us sat in amazement staring at our Christmas tree lights in the darkened room every night, making Christmas our favorite holiday.

Being the tomboy I was, I challenged the rule for Friday's softball games because it was boys only. Classes were always dismissed so the entire school could watch the game, and

I was the first girl to show that I could play as well as the boys. This was the same year Scarlet got the measles and pneumonia. Mother had her lying behind the little stove in the kitchen on a pallet on two chairs. She had a high fever and was talking about playing hopscotch on the stove pipes. The next day Gee and I stepped off the school bus in town, and it was snowing hard. Mother's boss told us she had gone to the hospital two hours away to take Scarlet who was, according to him, "bad-off sick." Gee thought Mother would never be coming home, and she cried and cried. I could not console her. She did not believe anyone until Mother arrived with Scarlet after a week. This event would further impact Gee feeling separation and loneliness from Mother, and this feeling became a part of her personality.

Scarlet loved the hospital. She was doted on and given ice cream anytime she wanted. The nurses asked her what her favorite TV program was, and even though she was five, she answered *Maverick*. Once she was home, she missed the attention of being in the hospital and began saying she couldn't walk. Mother took her back, and the doctor realized she was pretending she couldn't walk to be doted on like when she was there. Attention was fast becoming her friend.

The boys in sixth grade began to notice my breasts and teased me. In seventh grade, I wore a 34B. This caused a problem with posture because I was embarrassed. Mother told me if I didn't stand up straight, she was going to send me to charm school. I begin walking with books on my head every evening after reading that young girls learned good posture and modeling practices by walking with books on their heads.

Gee was so petite; she would be a late developer, I overheard Maureen saying to Mother, but she was becoming a dark-skinned, black-eyed beauty. Scarlet was like me and would develop early. This would be trouble for her, because she did not have the maturity to handle the attention. The same year, I got "the curse" for the first time while on a band trip to Norton. I called home crying, and luckily, Mary Katherine was with me and we took care of things. One good thing about the curse is you were not allowed to do any pickling during canning season. I learned that during the first summer canning season. The mix pickles won't pickle if you have the curse, so I was always claimed the curse during any pickling and canning every summer.

Gee had to be defended time and again because she was the runt. If she didn't get her way in a neighborhood ballgame, she would often throw the ball in the river, and we would have to chase it down the winding stream to save her from being beat up by older and bigger children. I was always coming to her defense in the neighborhood squabbles. Grandma Tori kept saying, "The devil is in that child." Once Mother was called out by a tall, large-boned neighbor woman, and I was so scared, because I thought she was going to hurt Mother. As it turned out, her little girl lied about Gee cutting the straps off her best shoes, and it was settled when it was apparent the little girl lied.

Many summer days we, along with our friends, would go over to the island and form clans to compete against each other in many different games. I was the only girl leader of a clan, and we were very protective of each other. The island was magical and was located just across the street behind the last house in the curve, on the shallow water side. It had lush green moss, blueberry bushes, and mulberry trees. We would pick and eat the berries after wading through the water and lie under a canopy of trees. The canopy made it shady and cool on hot summer days. From the land side, near the swinging bridge, we would walk barefoot on the large, flat river rocks to meet the clan test everyone had to pass for the island rules. Our bare feet became seasoned tough by the hot river rocks, and newcomers would cry and turn back. After leaving the rocks, the sand was white and deep in the middle of the island. A small hill was on the far side and sloped down to the river where the current ran swift. The hill was covered in moss and shrubs with tall pine trees for playing hide-and-seek.

Long, idyllic days were spent playing hopscotch and marbles, catching lightning bugs, and swinging from the grapevines out over the river. Gee had a special rock for hopscotch, and I had a special steely for marbles. We would pack our lunches and stay until dark when we would hear parents calling. The three of us would be the last to leave. I would pick Scarlet up and carry her home with Gee walking in her short stride beside me. If Mother was angry, then she would not switch me because I had the baby. Sometimes she got Gee, saying, "If I got the wrong one, you probably needed it anyway."

I was amazed to be so popular and happy that the boys thought I was pretty. This opened a surprising new world to me. But Mary Katherine, with her blonde hair, blue eyes, and cute figure, was the beauty I would aspire to look like. It could never be, with my brown eyes, curly auburn hair, and, worst of all, my bosom. I wished for straight hair and an eighteen-inch waist like Scarlet O'Hara, but I had a twenty-four-inch waist and my bust was a 34C. Mary Katherine had a twenty-two-inch waist and was a 32AA. We measured all the time. We would spend hours looking at *Photoplay Magazine* and modeled our look after Sandra Dee and Natalie Wood.

When the school paper came out, I was voted "prettiest legs," and the next time I got "best figure," which didn't faze me because pretty was never mentioned in our house, except Grandma Tori saying, "Pretty is as pretty does." Although, I heard Mary Katherine's Aunt Lois tell Maureen, referring to me, "She will be a heartbreaker," as she smiled, and I knew that was good. I had never known anyone "in love," but I loved reading Emilie Loring books and was always the first one on the book mobile that parked in front of Sutherland's Department Store. I had another of her books, *To Love and to Honor*, in my hand when my French teacher, Ms. Agatha Flowers, took it from my hand. Instead, she handed me *Jane Eyre* by Charlotte Bronte and *Rebecca* by Daphne du Maurier, saying, "Young lady, you are reading below your reading level."

Escaping the sadness by reading did not totally erase the shadow spirits of Daddy and baby brother Jimmy, which hung heavy in a veil of silence with Grandma Tori and Mother moving about, like a dance around the invisible shadows without anyone touching. We behaved like young ladies, making sure the neighbors would notice and say, "Their mother is doing a good job." We did this because Mother was always saying, "What will the neighbors say about my girls?"

I learned to be a people pleaser and knew what grown-ups wanted to see and hear. I excelled as an athlete and student and was willing to morph into the person who worked the best for the situation. I had a strong will and became an achiever with an aloofness toward my two little sisters, unless someone was treating them unfairly, and then I jumped in with both feet to defend them to the finish. At the same time, we all three had an innocence of not experiencing the world properly.

Being raised sheltered and unaware of life's many games and ulterior motives, we always accepted things at face value. We were taught not to live in the gray of life but in the black-and-white, to respect elders, and to never tell a lie. We were unaware if Mother had a problem with finances or of any other sort. We just knew that when she came home from work, she needed her space, and that did not include us. Scarlet could not lie at her breast. It seemed Mother's breast held a great hurt, and we were to never lie in her arms. Occasionally, Grandma Tori would let us lay our head in her lap, and she would rub our hair. She usually did this when she was sitting on the front porch glider. Other than that, there was no physical affection in our house except between us girls hugging each other. There was a bond of affection in the family that was ever present but not expressed.

When I was fifteen years old I decided to quit the band and head majorette. I had loved being in the marching band and playing concerts and vying for the position of first chair flutist, and it had been my dream since fourth grade. Now my friends wanted to try out for cheerleading. You had to have a B average and keep it, or you could not stay on the squad. I was chosen after tryouts and quit the band without a second thought.

This decision began my interaction with boys like Jake Anderson. Jake was a basketball and football star. He was tall, dark, and handsome. He also attended Young Peoples at the First Presbyterian Church. I could not look at him he was so handsome. I got butterflies. Once I sat across the table from him at the football banquet and could not touch my food. I could not wait to tell Mother, but she turned white and said, "Boys ruin your life."

Looking back now, it is apparent that Jake was our half-brother. Mother still maintained: "I was told that, but that doesn't make it true. It was all I could do to keep body and soul together after your daddy was killed and all the rumors that came up." She also reminded me that Daddy had never mentioned it. Every time I talked about it she got "mad as a wet hen."

While searching for the truth about Daddy and his murder, Gee and I found Jake and spoke with him. He was told all his life by his grandmother who raised him that Brady, our daddy, was his father. He seemed hurt and had a look that he was in a faraway place as he talked to us. I added the years together. Jake was three years older than I was and two years older than Jimmy. So Jake was born during the time Mother and Daddy were married but had not had any children. That explained the evening at the football banquet when I was overwhelmed with how handsome he was and Mother's terrifying response to me that I never understood.

I understood the implication and fear Mother felt with me in the same high school as Jake and people talking. When I tried to talk to her about it, she called people telling tales names like "blowhard" and "windbag." She maintained that there was no proof Jake was Daddy's son. I imagine when we were pointed out as Brady's girls, Jake was one of the many reasons everyone was interested. A life cut short for the choices he made, never once thinking about the ones he would leave behind. This included Jake.

Even though I was not allowed to date until I was sixteen, two football players would end up giving me their class rings. Accepting the class ring would mean we were going steady. To me, going steady was dating one boy. Some considered it a token that would guarantee going all the way. The first was Dallas Deel. He was three years older than I was and a running back for the Haysi Tigers. He was a gentleman and a sweet boy. He gave me my first French kiss on the hardware bridge at the beginning of football season. I felt like that kiss made me a woman, and I had a delicious secret. I had read about the French kiss in *The Vixens*, which I slipped in and read at Mary Katherine's house. Reading about it I could not imagine it being so wonderful, so I kept reading. When I got mine, I turned into a woman with a secret.

On November 22, 1963, I was on the stairs between classes when Dallas came to me and got me by the arm and walked me outside. With tears in his eyes, he told me President Kennedy had been shot. I did not cry, but I had a flashback to the day I heard Daddy was shot nine years before. Everything went from being fine and wonderful to a bleakness that set in all over me. I felt like I was in a daze. The principal announced over the intercom that school would be closing early.

I remember Mother had not been in favor of a Catholic being president, and at the time, I did not understand why that was so terrible. I heard Mother talking with a neighbor about what a state the world would be in if we got a Catholic president. She'd said that the Southern churches were deeply suspicious about the changes that would be made and felt the rituals were anti-Christ, not to mention having to have an intermediary priest act as intercessor for God's children. She believed praying "in the Spirit" was a gift to all who asked and that it was the most powerful prayer possible, especially "Where two were gathered together, or a mother's prayer."

We sat in front of our television and watched with the world as First Lady Jackie Kennedy held herself, her children, and the nation up through the days of the funeral events. I noticed something strange. She led her children by the hand and encouraged them to write a note to go with their father to heaven. I felt a strange feeling in my heart that no one had acknowledged Gee and me when Daddy died.

That spring, I was allowed to go to the prom with Dallas with a chaperone. Mother arranged for me to wear my cousin Janey's dress, and I hated it. It was yellow and had tulle puffs all along the bodice and straps. I pulled it all off down to the brocade on the shoulders and back bodice and cut off the long dress of tulle to the top of the knee with Grandma Tori's help.

She was a genius at changing the look of clothes, saying, "This was like making a silk purse out of a sow's ear."

There were only two freshmen girls at the prom, and I was one of them. I felt like I was on cloud nine and had a wonderful time. When we got home, Mother had the house and front porch lit up like a circus. I was sure everyone would see us. Dallas walked me to the door and gave me a French kiss, and I was embarrassed to tell him he was not allowed to come in. I was having a slumber party, and all the girls were waiting and peeking out the window.

Dallas was invited to go with us to Caney Creek Pool for the first summer picnic on the Fourth of July that year. We laid on beach towels in the green grass, and he leaned over and kissed me. Uncle Clyde saw the kiss and advised Mother to send me to Michigan with his family, hoping to break up the romance. It did. I mailed the ring back to Dallas on my first day back at the end of the summer. Then I went to the drug store and played "World without Love" by Peter and Gordon on the jukebox, and in walked Dallas. He said he was leaving for Norfolk and had another girlfriend. I didn't know what to do, so I walked up to the jukebox and played "Sealed with a Kiss." I wanted him to think I left a boyfriend in Michigan. And I didn't turn around.

That fall was full of excitement. Sheldon Sutherland was the quarterback, and on the team bus while riding back from the game with our rival, Clintwood, he slipped in behind me and whispered in my ear. "If you won't be mad, I want you to know your breasts look great in that sweater." I did not get what was so great about my breasts, but I was glad he was behind me and that it was dark and that he didn't know butterflies swarmed in my stomach. Sheldon was six three and very intelligent. He was a senior the year I was a sophomore, and I knew he would be "hot to handle" as I listened to the older girls talking, but that didn't stop me from being taken in by him. He was known to go out with girls who "came across," but I still wanted to try. He was the catch. Mother said I could not go out on a date. She had managed so far to allow me to meet boys at school functions until Sheldon asked me to go to Clintwood to see the movie *What's New Pussycat?*

I stopped after school at Johnson's Five and Dime where Mother worked as the manager, and she said, "No, you cannot go on a date, in a car, with Sheldon."

Finally, I went down to Sutherland's Department Store and asked Mrs. Sutherland to ask Sheldon to ask Mother in person. Well, it worked when Sheldon stopped by the store and used his best manners to ask her in person.

He picked me up in his Corvair, and we went to Clintwood. I was nervous, and his British Sterling cologne was making my nose run, which was one of my common curses due to allergies. I was so embarrassed, but I don't think he knew. He held my hand and put his arm around me.

On the way back, he passed the road to my house and went toward the high school. He said he knew a really good parking place out back by Smokers' Glory. He backed the car into the two-lane area and turned off the lights. I was getting nervous. He moved over close to me and kissed me for a really long time. He ran his hand above my knee, and I pulled back about the same time the town sheriff pulled in shinning a big flashlight in our direction.

Sheldon didn't seem nervous and said, "Good evening, sir." I, on the other hand, was dying by degrees because everyone knew the sheriff had a crush on Mother. I knew he would tell her, and that would be the end of my going on dates.

The sheriff said, “Maybe you kids don’t know, but you cannot park on school property.”

Sheldon took me home and walked me to the door. He kissed me good night, saying he would meet me during lunch on Monday. I went straight to Mother’s bedroom and got in bed with her, which I never did. She was startled, and I told her about going up to the school and the sheriff. I wanted to tell on myself. This, I learned, was a very good decision, and it always worked in the future.

On Saturday, I always did my chores, and the last one on my list was mopping the floors. On one particular Saturday, no one was there except Scarlet and me. Sheldon surprised me by stopping by and wanted me to go with him for a drive. I told him I couldn’t go, so he mopped the floors for me. I told him if I went, we had to take Scarlet. He was not too happy but agreed.

I asked if I could drive his car up the street, and he said yes. It was his mother’s long gray Buick, and I pulled in the last driveway on the street. All of a sudden, I hit a post with a clothesline attached and a mop hanging on it. The line broke, and the mop flew over the house. I backed out suddenly, and Sheldon said to stop. He checked the car for damage and got in the driver’s seat. I was mortified by the whole thing, and then Scarlet asked if we could stop at the drive-in for French fries. I later got in real trouble for going with him and taking Scarlet, but I was not sorry. Nothing could ever go wrong when babysitting a baby sister.

The following Monday, Sheldon met me at lunch, and we walked outside. Everyone looked at us, and I felt so proud. He was the star of the football and basketball teams, and it was the first time I felt the presence of sheer happiness in a grown-up way. As he walked me back to class, he slipped me a note. I waited until I was inside before I opened and began discreetly reading. The note read: "Hi, pretty girl. I am sorry I am so oversexed!" I thought, *Oh my God! What is wrong with him?* I could not share this information with anyone, not even Mary Katherine. Later, when we met just before practice, he leaned over and kissed me. I did not ask him about the note.

After the bonfire rally on Friday evening, Sheldon slid a gold chain around my neck with his class ring. "Will you go steady and be mine?" he asked.

"Yes," I said as I looked up at his dazzling smile, although I was still worrying about the "oversexed" problem.

On Saturday, he asked me to go hiking. It was a beautiful sunny day, and off we went up the mountain from where he lived. We were kissing, and he ran his hands down my back and around to the front of my sweater. I was afraid when he slipped his hand up the front. Just in time, a game warden came from out of nowhere and started asking questions. Of course, when he found out I was with the quarterback of HHS, he engaged in a friendly conversation. On our way back to the car, Sheldon said he was too oversexed for me. I was confused and embarrassed as I tried to figure out what he meant. He took me home, and at the steps of my house, he lifted me up and gave me a kiss.

After school on Monday, I stopped at Johnson's and told Mother that Sheldon was too much for me to handle. She made no effort to help me or ask questions and left me to handle it alone. I was so unhappy that I put the chain and ring in a nice box and dropped it off to his mother at Sutherland's Department Store, because I wasn't able to face him. The last thing that happened between me and Sheldon was that he dedicated a song called "Ivory Tower" to me in the school newspaper for everyone to see. I was humiliated by him insinuating that I was living in a cold ivory tower and did not want love. I could have run all the way home. Instead, I got a pass from Mr. Hilton to go to the library where I could hide in a book. The principal smiled and said "Okay, Jill." (He was always telling me I looked like Jill St. John.) After that, I felt better.

Mother said, "No more going steady. You have to play the field." She did not act thoughtful or explain it. She seemed to be mad because she was having to deal with it. I knew playing the field meant going out with different boys, so I was friendly to everyone who I thought was good-looking, an athlete, and older than I was. I never dated a boy in my class. So to my surprise, on Friday evening I was getting ready for a date with Will Mitchem, a good-looking athlete who also worked at Ratliff ESSO on Saturdays, Mother came in and asked me, "What do you think you are doing?"

I was startled.

She said, "There are four boys asking for you, and I am leaving you to handle this mess. I am going next door to Maureen's."

Grandma Tori said, "Your mother is mad as a wet hen."

I was still perplexed. I was friendly with the boys—that was all! Gee was laughing and said, "I will go out with one of them if Mother would let me."

I was afraid to come out of my room, but I finally walked out. Will was in the living room, and the others were on the porch. I just shrugged my shoulders and then turned to Will and said, "I'm ready." I simply ignored the boys on the porch.

Will and I went to the drive-in movie at Vansant, and I don't even remember the movie. All I remember is when we left, Will forgot to unhook the sound system from the window and when he started up the truck he pulled the post out of the ground. He had to stop and take it out to put it back. We never had another date. I was not good at "playing the field" and did not know why.

By spring, The Pink Room was open to teenagers on Wednesday and Saturday nights. It was part of a motel called the Hilltop Inn and was tucked in a curve on the top of Big Ridge Mountain. The Pink Room was pink and big and was furnished very modern with a bar that went clear across the room with bar stools. Beer was served if you were eighteen, but the girls always drank cherry Coke. The dance floor took up the middle of the room, and there were tables and chairs in a *U* shape. The bandstand was raised and could set up for a six- to ten-piece band. Mother was dead-set against Gee and me going. I was sixteen, and Gee fourteen. She said if Mary Katherine's parents let her go, then she would allow us. Of course, she thought her parents would say no, but to the surprise of everyone, Mary Katherine's parents said yes. So this would begin our favorite weekly outings, dancing at the Pink Room to a different live band every Wednesday and Saturday night.

One day as I walked home from the drug store, Bobby Puckett, who was three years older than I and had a black Chevy, asked me to get in so he could take me home. My pat answer was, "My mother doesn't allow me to ride in cars with certain boys." Two days later, he showed up with a bike, and I rode on the handlebars from the drug store across the low-water bridge to the front of our house. Before he left, he asked, "Are you going roller skating Friday night?"

Mother was furious. Attention was coming my way from boys as much as four years older than I was, and it was driving her crazy.

Mother and I were not close to begin with, and we were not getting along about anything. I had songs dedicated to me on the radio and phone calls asking for dates. I had never felt so happy in my life. After years of receiving no attention, Gee and I were the belles, and little Scarlet was turning into quite the beauty, following in our footsteps. She had been chosen to play Pocahontas by the high school drama club because she was so beautiful with her golden-tan body and long dark hair that fell to her waist. We were becoming a force to reckon with, a momentum of its own.

Word got out about the Pink Room, and we received pamphlets from Sharon's mother, Aleta, to educate us. They explained that dancing originated in the wine gardens where males and females stomped the grapes to make wine, which led to sin in the wine garden. I looked it up in the library, and our literature did not mention Dionysus, the ancient Greek god of the grape harvest, being involved with wine making with ritual madness and ecstasy. That would have at least referred to Greek mythology and made the allegation of sin more profound. So I couldn't find any backup about dancing being a sin. Anyway, in the three years we danced there, I never saw any wine.

The boys would go up Lick Creek to Old Man Creighton's house and pay for a pint of alcohol. Old Man Creighton kept it in his well out back, which was made of mountain stone and had a little roof over it. He would lower a bucket into the water using an attached handle and draw up the water bucket full of pint bottles, and the boys would pay for one each. The girls never asked for one and never took a drink. The businessmen in town belonged to the Moose Club downstairs from the Pink Room. They bought and kept their own bottles of special drink there with their names on them. You had to be twenty-one to go in the Moose Club and had to be accompanied by a member.

It was the summer before my junior year. Mary Katherine, Gee, and I were at the Pink Room. The three of us had golden tans. We had spent days lying out in the sun using a baby oil and iodine tanning recipe. I had on a fitted pink-and-green candy stripe sheath dress. It was two inches above my knees, and I looked grown up in my new gold T-strap sandals. My hair was reddish light auburn and in the style of Sandra Dee in *A Summer Place*, my favorite movie. I had curled my already naturally curly hair with the big drain-pipe hair rollers using a stale beer for setting lotion. I will never forget as I looked across the room and spotted about six older boys, maybe even college boys. They were not from our school.

The one in front had light-blonde hair and was dressed in a madras shirt, navy-blue blazer, and khaki pants. He looked straight at us, said something to the boys, and then pointed at me. He walked straight toward me with a huge smile, blue eyes with curled eyelashes giving him a playboy style saying.

"Hi, I'm Tommy Lee, and you are mine."

I liked it! The group was from Grundy, about a thirty-minute drive in neighboring Buchanan County. He said he was from Hoot Owl Holler, like he was proud of it.

They had just graduated high school and were headed to University of Virginia that fall. The band playing that night was called the King Bees, and Tommy pulled me onto the dance floor. He could dance. I mean, he must have had lessons. He knew how to hold the dance pose and move around the floor, and most of all, he was graceful. At the end of a dance, he would give me a deep dip like on *American Bandstand.* Sometimes we cleared the floor, especially when "Last Date" played by Floyd Cramer. That became our dance song, and everyone took notice.

He asked me out for Wednesday night to come back for teenage night. I said he would have to bring a date for Mary Katherine, and he said that was no problem. I had somehow forgotten Mother would not allow me to date. So Mary Katherine and I asked her dad first, and he said yes. Mother respected his opinion, and so we were allowed to double-date. On Wednesday evening, Tommy Lee called from the Dixie, and I asked him to bring me a package of peppermint gum, my favorite, just to see if he would. He pulled up in a burgundy Dodge and had a guy name JJ with him.

We kept them waiting a fashionable fifteen minutes (like we read in *Ingénue*). Gee came running in our bedroom saying, "Tommy Lee kissed so good." She loved pulling pranks like that. I really don't know if she kissed him or not; she had become such the little flirt.

Once we got to the middle of our porch steps, Tommy Lee turned me around and put his hands on my shoulders. "Are you the daughter of Brady Powers who was murdered?" he asked. He explained his mother had inquired of a neighbor who used to live in Haysi and knew my family. My heart sank, as I felt the sting of being always "marked" even though ten years had passed. Would it ever get easier to hear the name "Brady's daughter"?

Tommy Lee saw I was upset, put his arm around me, and gave me a big smile. "We will talk about it later," he said. "There were so many pretty girls in this town that there must be something in the water." I liked the way he handled the situation.

The band that played that night was the Reasons Why from Pikeville, Kentucky, and they had two girl singers. We danced the night away. JJ said he always lost five pounds dancing, and he was already skinny. So our summer was filled with the Pink Room and Tommy Lee, who always brought a date for Mary Katherine.

She was never asked for a second date, so we went through a lot of boys. I don't know why that was the case, with her cool blonde beauty and deep navy eyes. We played by all the rules we read about in *Ingénue* and had all the moves of the most popular dances. One thing I think hurt her chances with boys was trying not to act Southern and standing before the mirror for hours working with the vowels, A-E-I-O-U, hoping to accomplish a Midwestern accent. I thought she just wanted to sound proper, but her mother, Maureen, called it correct English. I did not like it, but I loved her. I liked it when people asked me to say corn bread and butter one more time. I was told I had a nice reading voice by our English teacher, so I didn't change one bit.

Mary Katherine was different, because she had her heart set on being the Key Club Sweetheart and valedictorian of our graduating class. She had straight As, but she wouldn't pick up a library book unless it was required reading. I read everything in sight and wrote book reports for three students. Many a night when we polished our fingernails and toenails she tutored me in Algebra II, and I passed with a B. She was a genius.

Our teacher had no patience for me. His name was Mr. Leon Powers (not related to us), and he said, "All the Powers have a head for math except you." He had a scar that ran down the entire side of his face; it was very fine and didn't hurt his good looks. He once said he knew my daddy, and they'd had some great times together he called "rounders." This always embarrassed me, alluding to "their rounders," because everyone knew they were of an unpleasant nature and were probably drunk. I made myself go to his class. He was an atheist and often said, "A prayer is the same as a telephone call when no one answers." And worst of all, he told Mother I was boy crazy, and she believed him.

Mother finally came to her senses over the summer about me and Tommy Lee and car dates. Tommy Lee took me to the drive-in at Vansant to see *Your Cheating Heart.* He was so excited and over the top and loved the song "I'm So Lonesome I Could Cry." When it got to the part "Hear that lonesome whip-poor-will / lost his will to live," tears formed in his blue eyes, and he put his arm around me. He pulled me close, but I was careful not to encourage him. I had heard all about the drive-in movie, and there being one thing on a boy's mind. I told him I liked walk-in movies best, but I thought it was so sweet that he loved that movie so much.

He asked me if we could go see it again, and I said yes. I wished I hadn't worn a skirt. I was careful to keep it down to my knees. His kiss was powerful, and he pulled back and said, "Don't worry. You can trust me."

I wanted to relax but was remembering everything about "nice girls" and "bad girls." The nice girls got the date, and when she was taken home and kissed at the door, the boy went out with the bad girl who would do whatever he wanted. I felt sorry for a few of the girls at school because they were the second date, but I didn't think of them as bad girls. More importantly, I was going to remain a good girl.

I was in love, really in love for the first time. Tommy Lee was leaving for college the following weekend. He asked to take my framed picture from the living room, so I quietly gave it to him. In the picture I had on my white brocade prom dress with golden thread. It was formfitting and from the same year I was voted "best figure." I wore long white gloves that came above the elbow and carried a small beaded clutch. Mother would have been upset if she knew I gave him that picture. I slid it out of the frame and wrote "Love Forever."

We went parking at the John Flanagan Dam, and after making out, he asked me to go steady and gave me his class ring. The song "Baby I'm Yours" came on, and he said that would be our song. Later, he bought me the record. I was thrilled. I played it over and over.

He came home every weekend and worked at Johnny's Flower Shop driving the delivery truck. When Mother saw the ring, she flipped out. She was so mad, and we argued every morning before school. I don't know why, but it would start before I would be dressed and she would switch me with her "keen switch" that she kept on top of the cabinet in the kitchen. I would have the stripes to show it, because I was only wearing a bra and panties.

"Spare the rod and spoil the child," she would say as I was trying to reason with her. "Raise a child up the way they should go, and they will not depart from it. This is straight from the Bible."

She called it talking back, and I called it making a valid point by deductive reasoning, like the scientific way. Grandma Tori would come in and scold me after telling me, "Once your Mother gets started, she doesn't know when to stop." I could not help but provoke her, as she called it.

I wrote Tommy Lee every night in the dark, because Mother wouldn't allow me to write him. One Friday when I got off the bus, he was waiting for me. I was excited but shocked. He had been to see Mother and convinced her to let us go steady.

All she would ever say to me was, "He talked in circles, and if you make your own bed, you have to lie in it."

My junior year was a whirlwind of spending time with Tommy Lee, cheerleading, staying on the honor roll, and participating in school clubs and activities. Tommy Lee wanted me to wear his ring on a chain around my neck for all to see. He liked to use the phrase, "You'll play hell if you flirt with her." I liked that he loved me so much he would say that. He always had his gang of friends to call on. They were all of the preppy types, with socks to match the pastel plaid in their shirts and cordovan penny loafers polished and shined. Sometimes he didn't wear any socks. He was cool and had style.

He and his friends were from good families with high aspirations for their education and future. But he alluded that his friends would come to his rescue and that they could get rough and "take care of things." For some odd reason, I liked being taken care of like that.

Mary Katherine's mother saw a bruise on Mary Katherine's neck. Mary Katherine had been out with Henry Fuller from Grundy, and she said he pinned her against the car door while kissing so hard but said not to tell anyone. She put a spoon in the freezer and held it on her neck to help it go away, but her skin was so fair it didn't work.

Maureen said, "You girls need a lecture on necking and petting. That bruise is called a hickey, and good girls should never have one."

Mary Katherine acted like she did not have one, but it showed against her blonde hair. I though the word *hickey* sounded disgusting and did not want one. We listened to her mother talk about the topics of making out, affectionate play, petting with or without contact with genital organs, and staying a virgin at all cost. I vowed to stay a virgin at all cost, as it seemed to be the prize called "God's special purpose to take to your marriage." This would be the only talk we would have about sex, except in biology we learned there were only a few days a month a girl could get pregnant. I didn't look up when I heard many sighs of relief.

With Tommy Lee, I was close to having the vapours, as I understood them to be. It was beginning to get crazy with him. I was trying to remember the *Ingénue* article on how to keep your boyfriend and stay a virgin. He told me that I acted like I had gone to the movies and never came back, and life was not like a movie. Everything I learned about love and sex was from a movie or a book, so I thought I was in the know by reading everything I could get my hands on. He was always bringing it up when we were parking and kissing. He used baseball language, which made me crazy. He put a lot of pressure on me by telling me if I loved him, I would at least go to second base. He even asked me to drop my dress to the waist just so he could see my breasts. I said no.

Then the stories came out about blue balls, a condition that boys would get that put them in the hospital when a girl would not allow third base. I really hated this part of our parking, because Tommy would always tell me which friend had been in the hospital with a bad case. I felt so bad about his friends and did not want him to get it. I asked him if he wanted me to sing "I'll Never Walk Alone," and he said yes. After that, we would leave the parking place, and he would be all happy, telling me how much he loved me. I had never been in love and was drowning in it, in an all confusing, consuming, and committed way. I was his, and he was mine; we were destined to be together.

Sometimes I would fake being sick on Sunday and skip Sunday school and church. Tommy Lee and his friends would stop on their way back to school. They would wait for him in the car, and I would be in bed in my Sandra Dee shorty lilac pajamas, just like she wore in *A Summer Place.* My long, tan legs, pretty as a picture, were perfectly posed in the filmy fabric, all lace and bows. Even though I had the cover pulled up, he would kiss me and run his hand up and down my leg. It was heaven. When he left, my special purpose was wet, and I was beginning to understand my body and feelings. I was a woman, soon to be seventeen. I could already put change down my bra, and it wouldn't fall through. Grandma Tori said when the change didn't hit the floor, it was a sure sign of a woman.

Tommy Lee gave me two records he said were our songs: "Baby I'm Yours" by Barbara Lewis and "The Twelfth of Never" by Johnny Mathis. I played them over and over each week until he came home on the weekends. He always signed his letters "Forever and A Day." I lived for stopping by the post office to pick up my letters and waiting for him to come home for the weekends.

Gee started going to the Pink Room with Mary Katherine and me. She was modern and liked to smoke in the bathroom. She knew all about sex even though she, like us, was a virgin. She and Mary Katherine came out of the bathroom after smoking and laughing. They called me over, and Gee told us how boys got a hard-on, and if you would watch, you could see it. She laughed even more because we were two years older and had never thought of getting a boy worked up just so we could notice.

Gee thought we were stupid bookworms and laughed at us. She was fully developed and even though petite at five two, she had a voluptuous figure boasting measurements of

34-21-34. The boys were crazy about her, but with her happy-go-lucky, sexy attitude, she didn't suffer the anxiety that I did about sex. She was all brag and tease.

Parker lived up the street and was cute with his Beatle haircut. He had a crush on Gee, so Tommy Lee asked them to go to Lover's Gap parking with us at the private airport on top of Lover's Gap Mountain. We had just arrived, and the radio was playing "Rhythm of the Rain" when all of a sudden Parker jumped out of the car. As we turned around, he was jumping up and down. His pocket had caught fire. Gee laughed and laughed and said, "Jeans too tight, and matches ignite." Their romance would fade due to his being drafted to the army and stationed in Germany.

During my junior year, Tommy Lee and I planned to go to the Junior-Senior Prom. I wore a blush-pink chiffon, strapless dress fitted at the waist with matching satin heels. Tommy Lee had on a rented tux, and we danced the night away. All the boys in my class hated the out-of-towner who came to our prom. The only thing that made it sad was that Gee was a freshman and had been asked by Sean Owens, a junior. Mother was going as the date of Mr. Allister, a school teacher, but would not allow Gee to go. It was heartbreaking because she had allowed me to go as a freshman. Gee would suffer disparity like this, and I never knew the reason. Maybe Mother wanted her to stay with Scarlet, or maybe she could not afford so many dresses for the prom and she knew Gee had two more years.

Gee began dating Luke Patterson from Clinchco. They looked like twins, and he had a TR7. She loved being taken to meet his family. It was a real family with a mother, father, and sister. And just like us, his grandmother lived with them. They all fell in love with Gee and she them. They had festive celebrations and would dress formally for dinner. Luke's parents were in love. It showed; when he came home from work each evening, they would have a cocktail on the back porch, laughing and kissing. Then he would grill steaks, and she would do the rest. Gee experienced the real family atmosphere, something Scarlet and I did not.

Soon you would not see one without the other. They fell head over heels in love. Our family loved him, and Mother did not give Gee the grief she gave me about dating. Gee felt true love for the first time, and it filled her loneliness that had been there since Daddy died. Luke was soft-spoken, kind, smart, handsome, and talented. He taught Gee to drive his four-speed TR7 on the way to Caney Creek swimming pool. He took her to get her driver's license, but she failed the driving test, never leaving first gear. She began to cry, and he bought her a doll that looked just like her. The second time she took the test, she passed, and they drove all over the county with the top down. They had the time of their lives playing pool, listening to music on the jukebox, and eating ice cream dipped in chocolate. Finally, she had a real family and the love she had always wanted. But little did Gee know, trouble was looming. Luke's parents wanted him to go to college and not get married young like they did.

It was Christmas of my junior year, and Tommy Lee was back from school for the holidays. Mother let him stay over on Saturday night with the order that he had to sleep on the sofa and go to Sunday school the next morning. We all went to Sunday school at the First Presbyterian Church. Ms. Mitchell was our teacher, a beautiful eighty-something woman with silver hair. She always wore sheer pastel blouses with a fancy slip underneath. She was very feminine except she was always fishing out her bra strap. For the room of teenagers, it was always a hoot.

Later that day, Tommy Lee, Gee, Scarlet, and I went back to Backbone Ridge where my grandparents had lived to get a live Christmas tree. I accidentally got us on the adjoining property, and we cut the most beautiful tree we had ever seen. Mother had to speak with the owner, who was mad as hell, and she did not have her pay even though he said "I would not have taken one hundred dollars for that tree." We all decorated it together.

Gee and I decorated the house with holly, painted snowflake designs on the windows, and hung mistletoe that had been shot out of a tree by Edwin next door. Tommy Lee bought me a heather sweater in teal and a winter-white skirt trimmed in teal from the Family Shop. I asked Grandma Tori to hem the skirt shorter, and she said, "Why don't I just make you two out of it? Your skirts are way too short, and I don't know what this world is coming to." Everyone was wearing miniskirts just like in *Ingénue* for the modern girl.

I bought Tommy Lee Aramis dedicated to the classic man at Kings Department Store in Bristol where everyone went shopping. Mary Katherine and I went to Kings for special occasions, and we always had lunch at the counter. It was the city thing to do.

Tommy Lee always worked at Johnny's Flowers during weekends and holidays when he was off from school. His favorite deliveries were funerals. He said, "I waltzed in carrying two sprays at a time and was always greeted by the little women who were helping out in the kitchen. I cheered them up, dressed in my madras shirts, matching pastel socks, khaki pants, and loafers. I stepped out of my loafers and got on the sofa, took down a picture, and hung the most beautiful spray, something no one ever did." They liked his arranging so well he was always invited into the kitchen for a meal brought in by friends and neighbors. "A real feast," he said.

He would then thank them, smile with his eyes like Jesus, and throw his hair back like Glen Campbell before going on to the next delivery. "I'm sure I made their day, because they would all start crying," he said.

His grandmother, Mommy Walker said, "Tommy Lee, you are being sacrilegious saying you have eyes like Jesus." I noticed she always smiled like she thought it was true. She loved that boy, and she'd say, "He will have to make a living with his head because he sure couldn't do it with his hands." His family wouldn't even let him start the fire in the furnace or mow the yard.

Mother began dating JR Rainey, brother of our physical education teacher. He was polite and seemed to be crazy about Mother. She had waited so long for love since Daddy's death, and I was so in love with Tommy Lee that my life revolved around romance. I wanted her to have the same feeling I had. Grandma Tori said he was "born with the bark on" and that it was "a crying shame that Mother couldn't see it. He will drown in his own poison and take us with him."

Scarlet did not like him from the first and seemed to have a sense that would not let her budge about him. Her dislike was so strong that I called our first family meeting of three sisters to discuss whether Mother should marry JR. At age seventeen, my point to Gee, age fifteen, and Scarlet, eleven, was that Mother had been there as our breadwinner for ten years and deserved to be happy again. Scarlet jumped upon the sink, rolling her big brown eyes, something she had taken to doing, and Gee and I were standing in front of her. She was scared, and the fear showed, but we all put our hands one on top of the other together in a pact and said, "Yes, Mother deserves happiness." She was still beautiful at age thirty-seven, and it had been ten years since Daddy had died.

The wedding took place that spring. Mother wore an aqua silk shantung dress with a jacket and pillbox hat, styled like Jackie Kennedy. Reverend Anderson at the First Presbyterian Church presided over the ceremony, and Edwin and Maureen stood up for them all dressed in their Sunday best. I wore a red sheath dress and matching Mr. John hat and T-strap heels. Gee wore a double-breasted evergreen tweed coat over a matching dress with a white corsage. Scarlet wore a red velvet dress with sheer white tights and black patent Mary Jane shoes. Grandma Tori wore a black fitted dress and a black coat with a mink collar and black shoes and gloves. She sat to herself and had a pinched look and did not smile. In all of the pictures, she looked the same.

Grandma Tori acted as our chaperone while Mother went on her honeymoon. We were hard to handle, because Tommy Lee and his friend Jason came over and wouldn't leave. Jason was sweet on Gee, but he was too old for her at twenty-four. He was a gentleman she said and was flattered that he showed her such interest. They kissed outside on the porch. I could see Grandma Tori was unhappy and maybe even a little afraid of these big boys. I knew they were harmless, and I wanted Tommy Lee to be with me. We stayed in the house but once locked the bathroom door so we could kiss. Grandma Tori would have none of that and told them to leave because it was the dead of night. "Besides," she said, "you boys are wet behind your ears, full of yourself, and up to no good." She looked stern and said, "Leave right now." They left quickly, thinking she had gone mad, going on about, "Every tub must sit on its own bottom and answer God at the final judgment."

JR and Mother returned, and our house was forever changed. It was different from the minute he walked in the door. He became distant and different as daylight and dark. He and Mother seemed to be in a life of their own and the all-female atmosphere was there no more, never to return. I did not like the way he looked at me and said, “You have the most beautiful legs I have ever seen.” Mother paid this no mind, and Gee said he liked to zip her dress and rub his thumb down her zipper. We were seeing a different JR, and Grandma Tori had been right. He was a wolf in sheep’s clothing.

It was May and time for the prom. Tommy Lee would be coming in from college to take me, and I bought a pattern and designed my own gown. It was white satin, fitted at the waist with a scoop neckline accentuating the bustline and a train attached at the shoulders that touched the floor. I wore long white gloves with pearl buttons, and my only jewelry was a pair of pearl earrings. Tommy Lee wore a tux, and I had the time of my life. We danced to “Barbara Ann,” “Hully Gully,” “Hippy Hippy Shake,” “The Twist,” and, of course, our favorite, “Last Date.” After the prom, we went to the Pink Room for more celebration, but I had to be home by midnight.

That summer, Gee and her new boyfriend, Luke, were inseparable. We all went to Hungry Mother Park and Caney Creek Swimming Pool, and our lives seemed perfect. Luke and Gee looked alike. They were both dark with black hair and dark, almost black eyes. He had long hair, kind of like the Beatles, and she had long hair to the middle of her back. These twins were water babies, swimming, diving, and kissing. Luke was the only boyfriend Scarlet liked, and she only tolerated Tommy Lee, who teased her unmercifully.

At Hungry Mother Park, we were out in the water, and Tommy Lee slipped his hand in my swimsuit. No one saw us out in the water so deep. It was very intense with the sun dappling on the water and our bodies so close. I wanted this magical feeling to last forever. Now I knew what God’s special purpose was. I could hear my own laughter, which sounded golden, as we melted into the water.

I ended up with bronchitis, and it lingered as long as the summer days. I was unable to sleep because of my coughing and wheezing. Finally, the doctor advised Mother to mix apricot brandy with honey and serve it in teaspoon sips until I was well.

Mother was a teetotaler, believing that her religion forbade alcohol due to many verses in the Bible. The one she frequently referred to was Romans 14–21: "Whereby thy brother stumbleth, or is offended or made weak." She knew they used moonshine all her life for medicinal purposes, but you didn't have to go to the ABC store to buy moonshine. The most important thing to Mother was what people would say. Even Grandma Tori reminded her that the Bible said, "A little wine for the stomach's sake" in 1 Timothy 5:23.

Mother said, "Who is going to go to the ABC store? Everyone will be talking." Maureen spoke up and offered to go to the ABC store, saying she didn't care what anyone thought. I admired her because she was the daughter of a Methodist minister.

Maureen was modern and unlike any woman living in the bottom. She was well read, receiving magazines every month by mail, like *Glamour, Redbook*, *McCall's*, and my favorite, *Cosmopolitan.* Every month I read each one cover to cover. We were so lucky to have Maureen to see us through times like this.

The bronchitis would last all summer. Gee learned to water-ski, and Scarlet tried but did not learn to swim or water-ski. I stayed on land at the lake and fancied myself as just a bathing beauty with a good tan, in love and tipsy on my brandy. This slowed down the romance with Tommy Lee, but he would sit on my bed and listen to me laugh as he read me poetry. Except when he read my favorite by Amy Lowell, "Patterns." Then, I cried. It was sexy and tragic as was another favorite, "Annabelle Lee" by Edgar Allan Poe. Tommy Lee was fascinated with me lying in bed. He wanted to touch me but couldn't, and he kissed me over and over, saying, "You are beautiful like the poems." He also had a dramatic way about him, and his voice was melodious and perfect, giving me a feeling that he was my "heavy-booted lover" As noted in "Patterns."

> I would be the pink and silver as I ran along the paths
> And he would stumble after,
> Bewildered by my laughter.
> I should see the sun flashing from his sword-hilt and the buckle on his shoes.
> I would choose
> To lead him in a maze along the patterned paths,
> A bright and laughing maze for my heavy-booted lover,
> Till he caught me in the shade,
> And the buttons of his waistcoat bruised my body as he clasped me,
> Aching, melting, unafraid.
> With the shadows of the leaves and the sundrops,
> And the plopping of the waterdrops,
> All about us in the open afternoon—
> I am very like to swoon
> With the weight of this brocade,
> For the sun shifts through the shade.

Entering twelfth grade, I decide not to go out for cheerleading, wanting more time with Tommy Lee. I applied to Radford College, an all-girls college in Radford, Virginia, and Montreat, a Presbyterian college in Ashville, North Carolina. I was accepted at both and in the top 25 percent of my class and going on scholarship due to my weak respiratory system and being allergic to everything.

My guidance teacher, Ms. Flowers, arranged all the paperwork, physician statement, and application for approval. I had almost died from a penicillin shot after having a systemic reaction. Living close to the coal temple three streets up by the railroad track did not help, as well as living on the river with all the mold spores. Ms. Flowers showed such interest in me, more than anyone. She said, "You will be successful because you always do more than required, and you will go far because you are a voracious reader."

Everything was so uncertain at home. Mother and JR never talked to me or mentioned my college plans, but she paid the entrance fee at both schools, just leaving the planning up to me. Maureen planned everything for Mary Katherine. It left me feeling like I was on my own.

Tommy Lee invited me to the Christmas Party at his college. He got a date for Mary Katherine with Paul Thomas, a student and drummer from the King Bees at St. Paul. Mary Katherine's parents convinced Mother that we were mature enough for a college party. We chose the fabric for our dresses, pink velvet for Mary Katherine and black velvet for me. Our seamstress, Ruth, finished them just in time.

The boys took us to High Knob in Wise, Virginia, before going to the campus. It was a "Virginia Is for Lovers," must-see place and had an elevation of 3,800 feet. We know the boys were looking for a little making out, but it was so cold and we counted ourselves lucky they had to take us back to the dorm. We stayed in one of the girls' dorms, feeling part of college life. It was exciting, and we pulled out all stops, as described in *Ingénue*, acting the epitome of sophistication. Mary Katherine was the cool, aloof blonde, and I was the vivacious redhead.

After that trip, Mary Katherine confided to me that she was in love with Coach Jim Haden. She said he kissed her in his office and was always asking her to come backstage in the gym behind the green velvet curtains. Everyone thought he was dreamboat handsome, but I never trusted him. When I worked in the kids' summer program at school, he let me drive his Ford LTD when I did not have a license. I liked that, but when he asked me to clean the boys' locker room, I was put off and told him I was an administrative employee and not janitorial. I just had a funny feeling about him wanting me in the boys' locker room.

He flirted with women teachers, cheerleaders, and young girls like Melissa Sue. Melissa Sue was a straight-A student and a cheerleader two years my junior. She was an auburn-haired beauty and had the most outgoing personality. Some said that once the Coach had his way with her, she turned wild in college. I don't know if all that was true, but she did turn wild.

One weekend I was helping Tommy Lee deliver flowers up in Frying Pan when he said, "You won't believe this, but I have to deliver an order of one hundred red carnations, and the card says, 'To Meg Johnson, Love, Coach Haden.'"

I looked at the card. As soon as Tommy Lee dropped me off, I went straight to Mary Katherine and told her everything. On Monday morning, Coach Hayden got me out of class and read me the riot act.

He swore she sent them to herself and for me to tell Mary Katherine I believed that she did. Of course, I told her I believed Meg had a crush and wanted to start trouble. Anyway, who would send carnations? I have always wondered about that. Everyone knew Coach Haden was into young girls, but the school board did nothing about it. Mary Katherine was head over heels, and there was no turning back, so we began planning ways for her to see him after school.

Tommy Lee asked me to marry him just after Christmas. We were getting so hot, and it was harder not to go all the way. We were at the Pink Room when he proposed. I was in seventh heaven, and now everyone would see how much he loved me. I saw this as the best option versus going to Radford College or Montreat in Ashville, which would be so far away from him.

It did not faze me that he had flunked out of UVA at Wise and was in Roanoke Business School to keep him out of the draft. His father was furious, but I had no doubt he would get his degree. He had overcome being on social probation for burning the dean in effigy and drinking in the dorm. In addition to social probation, he had only twelve credit hours to show for two years of college, but I never once considered anyone but him. I did not tell Mother any of this. Finally, he was set to transfer to Pikeville College, a Presbyterian school in Pikeville, Kentucky, for the fall of '67. I knew then it would work out perfect for us, because we could go to school together.

Since Mother had married JR, she had let up on me and was becoming more agreeable about Tommy Lee and allowed me to go to Pikeville for the weekend. There was a party, and I was supposed to stay with Vivienne who was dating Hunter Owens. It was my first real grown-up party. The lights were low in their apartment on high street. There wasn't much food, but they had a big punch bowl of "purple Jesus." I didn't know it, but it consisted of moonshine, ginger ale, and grape juice. I tasted it and thought it was really good, but I only took one sip, feeling I would be condemned by God and wondering why they had to name it after Jesus.

The record player was playing the Platters, "Twilight Time," "With This Ring," "The Great Pretender," and "The Magic Touch." Those were the most romantic songs I had ever heard. I was having the time of my life and felt so sophisticated, being the only high school girl there. We danced, and I did not stay with Vivienne. There was no heat at Tommy Lee's, and I didn't care. It was our secret and the best night of my life giving him my God's special purpose.

We told no one except Grandma Tori about our plan to get married. She had wanted me to get married for a while now. Every month she asked me if I had come around that month. I had figured out that she was referring to "the curse," and I would answer yes. So we decide to elope on April 4, his little sister, Darcy's, birthday. We went to the courthouse in Lebanon, Virginia, and found that you have to be twenty-one in Virginia to get married. So we planned it for April 22 in Boon, North Carolina, where you only have to be eighteen.

I wore a new sheath dress of shimmering off-white silk with antique gold trim cut in on the shoulders that showed the collarbone. My off-white spring swing coat had two large buttons and came just below the elbow. I wore long matching gloves and taupe T-strap high heels. Tommy Lee wore a black suit and silver tie.

His parents thought he was at college, and Mother thought I was in school because we left after Mother had gone to work. Grandma Tori gave me her wedding band, and we traveled across White Top Mountain to Boone. We were ecstatic and full of sexual energy, knowing that we belonged together. We were soon to be Tommy Lee and Laurel Victoria Durand, French for strong and enduring. That was me.

We arrived at a Presbyterian Church on Main Street in Boon. We walked in, and the minister asked us if our parents knew we were getting married. We answered, "We have eloped. They would not have approved."

The minister was happy that we were Presbyterians and had been raised in church since we were small children. He performed our marriage and directed us to Hill Winds Inn for our official honeymoon.

The honeymoon suite was perfect. It had a cherry four-poster bed with lots of pillows and lace curtains with sheers that gave the room a blush color. Tommy Lee picked me up and carried me across the threshold and tossed me on the bed. He undid his tie and unbuttoned his shirt while looking at me with that devilish grin and his crystal-blue eyes. He slowly took off my heels and panty hose and then each layer one by one, dropping them to the floor. He kissed my foot and up my leg, which he said "went all the way to heaven." He kissed me urgently, and we made love as husband and wife.

Even though we went back home the same day, it was the most perfect day of my life. I remembered a verse from the Song of Solomon that said "My beloved is mine, and I am his" in the biblical sense. We were on "the mountain of spices." Tommy Lee took me home and left me to go back to school. This most precious secret had to last four more weeks until I graduated my senior year.

Mary Katherine was valedictorian, and I was fifteenth in our graduating class. She gave an impressive performance in her speech. She was so beautiful and set to go to Virginia Tech but was unhappy to leave Coach Haden. Her parents were aware of the relationship and knew there wasn't anything they could do but put pressure on her to finish college. We parted knowing we were both in love, and that was all that mattered because love always prevailed.

The week after my graduation, all hell broke loose. Tommy Lee and I were on the sofa, and Mother walked through the living room and then turned, looked at Tommy Lee, and said, "You act like Laurel belongs to you."

He took my left hand and held it up, flashing the gold wedding band. In a possessive, mocking voice, smiling ear to ear, he responded, "She's mine now."

Mother ordered me to pack and leave and said I was disowned from the family. Gee and Scarlet were crying, and I was crying. Grandma Tori was fussing around silently, but clearly she was upset, although not crying. Mother was upset because Grandma Tori had betrayed her by helping me with the plan to elope and then keeping it from her. I packed my suitcase through the tears, and we left for Hoot Owl Holler to Tommy Lee's parents' home. I cried all the way until we reached Lover's Gap and then realized I would have a home in Pikeville, Kentucky, when we went to school in the fall.

When we arrived at Hoot Owl Holler and drove up the driveway, everyone was in bed. Tommy Lee had a private entrance to his bedroom, and it had twin beds. We pushed the two together, and I undressed and put on my white lace teddy. We slept in each other's arms and were awakened the next morning by Darcy with her little blonde angelic face peering at us.

She ran into each room and announced that Tommy Lee had a girl in his bed, and the entire family came in staring at us as we sat up in bed. Tommy Lee announced that we were married. His father was happy, and his mother glared at me and demanded to see the marriage certificate. I was nervous with her being so bossy, but I had been taught to be respectful of elders. I got out of bed, feeling underdressed in my white teddy, and got it out of my luggage. She took it from my hand so quickly that I did not know what was happening and did not realize she had no right to it. She took it to her safe, and I never saw it again.

Mr. Durand insisted we all go to my mother's home to celebrate. I was nervous and did not tell them I was disowned. The day went great, and Mother did not act up as I expected. Mr. Durand told her this was the best thing that had happened to Tommy Lee and said the marriage would settle him down.

Tommy Lee and I found a one-bedroom apartment on High Street, the same street as Pikeville College in Pikeville, Kentucky. I felt I was in a dreamworld and had a brand-new life. I registered for college and began trying to be a housewife without a clue. The first time I touched raw chicken before putting it in the flour I had to run to the bathroom and be sick. My gravy was so thick you could pick it up out of the bowl with a fork. I had one little cookbook given to me by Maureen called *Clinchco, Virginia, Community Recipes*, and it was a lifesaver. Pretty soon, the cookbook had flour, cocoa, and other ingredients all over it.

Tommy Lee found a full-time job at the hospital lab as a technician and was taking fifteen credit hours at the college. We had an old Royal typewriter, and I read a lot of books and typed papers for him. I began to notice that every time we were at a function or downtown, girls stared at us. I felt something different about him but couldn't exactly put my finger on it. I didn't like that feeling one bit.

By June, the curse hadn't come, and I told Tommy Lee that I wanted to go back to Virginia to see Dr. Bower, who delivered all of Mother's children except Jimmy. So we went to Richlands Hospital and saw Dr. Bower. He said we were expecting a baby around New Year's. Tommy acted excited, but I knew he was scared. I was in shock. Mother cried when I told her, and Tommy's mother paid a visit to my doctor, wanting to know if I was pregnant when we got married. He told her he would not divulge any information from my medical file. She started off as such a controlling biddy, and we were not going to get along; I felt it. All the while, I gave her respect as I had been taught.

After receiving the news, Tommy Lee and I settled in and moved to a new apartment on High Street, closer to the lab and school.

Four of Tommy's friends from Grundy were in college there and lived close by. They could be pretty wild when they got together, drinking beer, measuring their manhood, and other sophomoric behavior. One morning Hunter Linton knocked so loud on the door of our shotgun-style apartment and then ran straight through to the bathroom. I sat up in bed and watched him open the window at the bathtub and jump. This was High Street, and steps went from the top all the way to the bottom. When Hunter jumped, I could not believe it. A few minutes later, there was another knock at the door. It was Mr. Linton who said he was trying to catch up with his son to tell him his grandfather had died.

We were always having visitors. Early one morning, I opened the door and found a pretty, dark-skinned girl maybe about twenty-four with short dark hair. She was dressed in hospital scrubs and had a quart of milk that she was drinking straight from the bottle. She was crying and wanted to talk to Tommy Lee. It turned out that they worked together at the lab. Her name was Marlee, and she was engaged to Bobby Richards.

I already knew about Twyla, his Miss Haysi High, but didn't say a word because it seemed that Marlee had heard that Bobby was dating a girl from a prominent family in Lexington. She told Tommy Lee that she heard that girl was pregnant and had taken quinine and was hospitalized. Marlee said the girl would survive, but she was distraught over his unfaithfulness. Through her tears, Marlee was describing the apartment she was getting ready and the many gifts they had already received.

I was a little jealous because they seemed close, and Tommy didn't introduce us. She was having this breakdown on my husband. After she left, I asked him why he didn't tell her about Twyla, and he said, "It's a man thing about friends and their relationships. You don't interfere."

I told him that I was going to tell Gee so she could tell Twyla, and we got into our first argument. Twyla found out about Marlee and about the Lexington girl. Marlee moved on, but Twyla was so young and in love that she gave her body to any boy or man and was always looking for love, even with her neighbor, who had a daughter her age.

On December 3, I went for my regular checkup with Dr. Mulligan at Methodist Hospital #2 in Pikeville. He said, "Because you are so young, I need to induce labor. Go home and pack your things and come back. I will break your water and give you a shot to make the labor go quicker."

I had only gained sixteen pounds and was still craving crushed ice, which I later found out was a sign of pica.

Tommy Lee got me a to-go cup of ice, took me to the hospital, and left me. I didn't know he was supposed to stay.

I called Mother in Virginia, and she said, "For God's sake don't cry like most of those women. They act like they're climbing the wall. Be strong like a lady." I wasn't scared until then.

After the shot, I was given a saddle block and general anesthesia, resulting in a forceps-assisted delivery. I didn't remember anything until the next day when I awakened and was numb from the waist down. They told me I had a baby girl, although I had not seen her, and I began crying hysterically. *Where was Tommy Lee? Where was Mother?* I wondered.

I was upset with Tommy Lee because he went to the college basketball game and wasn't there for her birth. I was alone when she was born at 1:55 a.m., and I was glad I was out of it and didn't remember anything. His parents showed up the next morning, and his mother got all histrionic, scaring me because I had no feeling in my legs. She called Mother and gave her all the details of my condition. This only added to my feelings of being upset because Mother was not there. She was with her husband, JR, and obviously he wouldn't bring her. Tommy Lee finally showed, smiling from ear to ear with a pillow corsage of baby-pink roses. I had never seen a pillow corsage, and it eased some of the feeling of being left alone.

They brought my baby girl to me later that afternoon, and I held her in my arms. She was beautiful with lots of black hair and midnight-blue eyes. I counted her fingers and toes as I looked at the abrasion on her right cheekbone and the left side of her head from the forceps delivery. She also had a yellow color, and they hung her upside down in the nursery. The feeling was precious with a fluttering in my heart that this baby would be raised with all she needed to know about life and how to make it in the world, unlike me. I would keep no secrets from her and did not believe the old saying that children should be seen and not heard.

Everyone wanted to help me name her. Tommy Lee's mother wanted Tamara Leigh after Tommy, and Tommy wanted Selena Leigh. I did not want Selena after reading *Peyton Place,* not because I didn't like the name but because I did not want her name to be compared with any character. His mother's suggestion was overbearing, and everyone knew Tamara was his old girlfriend, who he claimed stood in the picture window nude as he would drive by. I looked at my baby and named her Laura Elizabeth, and she would be called Laura Beth.

His mother said, "Are you sure?"

I said yes, and Tommy Lee made no comment. Since no one was there when she was born, I considered her my child, and no one would ever override me when it came to her or her care.

I had Mother's intuition and had read every book in the library on babies, including titles by the famous Dr. Spock.

Dr. Mulligan explained that I should not breastfeed and said the nurse would give me a shot to dry up my milk. I didn't question him because he treated me like his little girl, and I trusted him completely.

I had just put on my gold velvet robe trimmed in gold satin with my initials embroidered to match. A girl walked in who looked just like Twiggy except she had long dark hair. I recognized her as one of the singers in the band the Reasons Why. She said she had come to see Tommy Lee's baby. I was seething, wondering why she did not ask a nurse to avoid coming to my room. I gave her a look of disdain and told her, "As you can see, she is not here; maybe her daddy will show you."

I later learned she was the girl Tommy took to prom after we were married. She was also the daughter of the lawyer I worked for during my last five months of pregnancy, and Tommy Lee had gotten me the job. I was devastated and pushed my feelings to the back as far as I could. My heart was beginning to fill up with a quickening hurt that wouldn't go away, and the beginning of a slow leak of my love for Tommy Lee flowed out of my soul.

Once we were home and settled in, all my attention went to my baby girl and me. We went to Tommy Lee's parents' house for the holidays. I quickly lost the baby weight by Christmas, which was only eighteen days. My high school figure was back, and I was noticed by his friends who told me I looked like a movie star.

I put pressure on Tommy Lee to buy me new outfits from the Family Shop in Grundy even though I knew we couldn't afford it. His guilt went wild, and he purchased me four new outfits and I wasn't even there. He chose a beautiful winter-white knit, formfitting dress and two pairs of the new style, above-the-knee culottes in wool plaid with matching blouses and pullover V-neck sweaters. The tailored slacks were a perfect fit and were matched with a long-sleeved, lightweight wool Poor Boy sweater. No one would believe I'd had a baby eighteen days earlier. I went to the beauty parlor to get my hair frosted and sat for hours having my hair pulled through the skintight cap with a crochet needle. It hurt so bad that tears flowed from my eyes, but it was worth the pain. My blondish-red hair was styled in a bouffant like Sandra Dee in *Portrait in Black*.

The last year of school Tommy Lee started hanging out with an OR nurse named Ruth, who was old enough to be his mother. Scarlet was down helping me with Laura Beth so I could continue college. Ruth invited us down to her house, and we met her husband, Leo. They had a big cookout in their backyard, and we met their daughters, Betts and Shauna.

Betts was married to a Pikeville policeman, and they had a baby daughter. Shauna was also in school at Pikeville College. She was my age and had all sorts of stories about Tommy Lee and his friends. It was evident that Tommy Lee had many girlfriends in Pikeville. My heartbreak continued as I bore the news in silence. Scarlet and I also learned that on Saturday nights he sometimes went with them out dancing when we thought he was working in the lab at the hospital.

Ruth wanted me to check up on him and go through the car to see if I could find any evidence. She said, "I always do that with Leo, looking for a hair or anything to use against him."

I told her I wouldn't do it and that I didn't believe in checking behind his back. I thought my marriage vows would be broken if I did that, even knowing he had not kept his. The truth was it was not in me to check up on him. Even more importantly, I worshiped Tommy Lee.

At the same time, I didn't question him about why he had not taught me to drive our new car or why he chose a straight shift. It was never discussed. Driving through town was a little scary with the one-way streets where we lived close to the college, and I was accustomed to walking everywhere.

Telltale signs of his devil-may-care attitude were raising their ugly head more often. Once he took me to the Piggly Wiggly to get groceries and waited until we were there to tell me there was no money in the bank. I became so upset and began screaming all over the parking lot for him to tell me what he had done with the money. He claimed he bailed Brian Music out of jail for breaking a shower door in a motel during a party. He was taken to jail and charged because he was over twenty-one. He was looking out for Brian and not for us. I went home empty-handed, trying to figure out what to do. I was forced to spend all the money from Laura Beth's piggy bank on her formula.

My life consisted of my baby girl, school, and the honeymoon cystitis. (That's what Tommy Lee called it.) He kept sending lab technicians to our apartment to take my blood and urine and then "bump" into a doctor in the hall at the hospital and show him the results and come home with my prescriptions. I finally had to go to Dr. Mulligan. He never told me what the problem was or where it came from, but he did say that freezing my cervix, which was also called cryocauterization, was necessary due to chronic inflammation. All of that information was written on the sheet he gave me. The ordeal was ongoing, and it made me nervous and gave me chills and sometimes a severe headache. Each time I was so scared and did not tell anyone, even Mother.

Laura Beth kept me going, and I religiously wrote in her baby book and kept all her records up to date. She loved music and danced to "Joy to the World" (Jeremiah was a bullfrog) in her crib. In my English class, I wrote about her, and Ms. Haney scored me an A every time. She advised me to write about her until she was grown and then let her read everything. I wrote about how much she loved her daddy, but the truth was, he loved her but never fed her a bottle, changed a diaper, or sang her a lullaby. She was only attached to me. He worked full-time as a lab technician, carried a full load of credits, and still had time to go dancing without me, so continuing a record of love in her baby book was true to form for me making everything appear better even if it wasn't true.

Tommy Lee would graduate at the end of the year, and that deadline was all that kept me going, hoping he would change.

Laura Beth was in her playpen in the living room in our little shotgun apartment on High Street. I was typing a paper for Tommy Lee's class, and the TV interrupted with the announcement that Bobby Kennedy had been shot in a hotel in California. About that time, a swarm of bugs circled the room, and I ran and grabbed Laura Beth out of the playpen. I was crying about Bobby Kennedy and did not know what kind of bugs were flying all around us. I did not know what to do, so I took Laura Beth and walked from High Street to the Highway 460, a good four miles, to Malin's Flower Shop.

Malin took us to her house beside the flower shop. She was a dark beauty even though she was in her forties. Tommy Lee and his friends were good friends of hers, and she treated me and Laura Beth special. We stayed for dinner; she cooked spaghetti from scratch and showed me how to make a good salad, bursting the core out of the lettuce and putting it in ice water. Finally, Tommy Lee showed up, and after checking the apartment, he said the landlord promised to treat it for termites and said they were harmless.

We went home and watched TV and all the news of Bobby Kennedy's death and funeral. His brother Ted gave a moving speech about Bobby, "Seeing wrong and trying to right it ..." I watched his funeral all day.

The morning after the funeral I was called home because Grandma Tori was in the hospital. She died after a week, and the funeral was at Rebekah Chapel on Backbone Ridge. It was a time of such grief, and we were all in shock. Grandma Tori had been the mainstay and our rock at home when Mother was working six days a week. She was in our house for twelve years. We had shared everything with her from Daddy's death to Scarlet's birth to my marriage.

The day before the funeral, I was totally out of it and stayed next door with Edwin, Maureen, and Mary Katherine. Tommy Lee came back to be with me just in time for the funeral. There were so many flowers in the small church, and it was so hot I fainted.

I wanted to stay another week with my family, and Tommy Lee said his parents would bring me back. When I got back home, I walked in the door to find dirty glasses everywhere circled in mold, and the mattresses were off the beds. Tommy Lee and his friends had thrown a party. I was so overcome with hurt and anger that I ran to our room and hit the center of the bed as I cried. I accidentally hit my hand into the wall, breaking two fingers that began swelling and hurting.

All his mother would say was, "Laurel, what is wrong? Why are you upset?"

His father saw clearly there had been a party and quickly asked her to leave. She would never admit that her "baby boy" could do any wrong, so I never told her anything about our life.

When I left, Gee and Scarlet were in their own grief over Grandma Tori. Gee had been in the ambulance with Grandma Tori, and she was talking out of her mind. She kept rolling over the side of the bed and leaving room for the baby she said. Even though Gee was not favored by Grandma Tori, she loved and cherished her very much. I really don't know why she treated Gee that way.

Gee said, "Sometimes I would pretend to be sick just to lay my head in Grandma Tori's lap as we gently rocked in the glider." To love and not feel love as a child made me feel guilty for being loved and favored, as was Scarlet, but she was too young to know. At the funeral, Gee broke down and cried.

Scarlet had, in essence, lost one of her mothers. Grandma Tori had stayed with us for twelve years since Daddy died. Mother went to work when Scarlet was three months old. She had shared a room and bed with Grandma all those years even though she had her own little bed. This was the beginning of her unraveling to an emotional state that would last for many years. She went from being a favored little granddaughter to feeling like a third wheel in Mother's marriage to JR. To her, it had been twelve perfect years, and life was now gone as she knew it. Gee was going to college soon, I had left her and was married with a baby, and Grandma was gone from her forever.

In addition to loosing Grandma Tori, Gee's senior year began with a heartbreak that would last three years. Luke's father put pressure on him to have a college education and insisted that a love affair so young would not survive. His father sent him to relatives in Arizona for the summer. Gee had never felt love before, and she not only lost Luke but his family, whom she had loved so dearly.

Gee's class was fun-loving and very close, and her friends held her up as she walked through her days and nights of pain. It was 1969, and their motto was "Sex, Sin, Beer, and Wine, We're the Class of '69." It was the year the Tigers were going to the state basketball championship in Blacksburg, Virginia. Gee was going through the motions of trying to forget Luke, and for reasons unknown, Mother allowed thirteen-year-old Scarlet to accompany Gee this trip. There was a party in a motel with all of Gee's class after they won at state.

Scarlet saw seniors drinking alcohol, smoking, and going off to rooms and locking the doors. Scarlet saw Gee go into a room with Quinn and became upset. She was not mature enough to know they were not doing anything except a little partying and kissing. The truth was Gee was trying to forget Luke and became sick after drinking alcohol and ruined her new herringbone pantsuit. The alcohol did not erase from her mind that no one except Luke would get to her again.

Her senior year was also saved by her friend Jenn, short for Jennifer, who was an only child. They could be seen all over the mountains riding Jenn's motorcycle. She was smart and beautiful and also had a wonderful family who loved her. Jenn's mother added Gee's senior picture beside Jenn's on the piano, like sisters.

They went camping at the lake with Jenn's parents, and after they went to bed, they would push the motorcycle up the road and meet their friends out at the swimming hole. Then they would walk the motorcycle back and climb back on their cots like they had been there all night. When they were at Jenn's house and went out on a date, they made it up between them that the first one home would tiptoe by her parents' door and say, "I'm home," so the other one could stay out late. Together they would spend hours getting ready to go to the Pink Room. It was at the Pink Room that Gee met Lance Moore.

During the first year JR was dating Mother, he never drank any alcohol. Mother believed that alcohol was a sin, that one drink led to two, and that the Bible said a brother could be influenced who could not handle the addiction. But slowly, he introduced it to our house and took Mother to the private Moose Club. Gee was also served a cocktail at home, and he took her and Mother to the Moose Club and had Gee served before she was of age. It seemed Mother went along with everything he wanted.

That year, Gee was nominated for homecoming queen. I was there when Gee was getting dressed. Her gown was a V-neck teal satin brocade with gold flowers embroidered all over. Her ample cleavage gave her a sexy, sophisticated look. We had to use a coat hanger to loop in the zipper because the waist was a snug twenty-one inches. Her dark hair was in a modern, asymmetrical bouffant style.

She later told me, "I was appalled because JR ran his thumb down my zipper and gave me a sickening chill." And her heart was broken that Mother sent her with JR to the football field to be dropped off. And to top it all off, the first person she saw when she got out of the car was Luke. She walked straight ahead with her head held high, and when she was crowned homecoming queen of 1969, the football captain, Brad Yates, gave her a kiss.

Gee came home in her tiara and changed into dancing clothes for her date with the young teacher, Lance Moore, from Clintwood. He was about six years older and was six four with blond hair and blue eyes. Besides being a star basketball player in high school and college, he was a talented artist.

Gee was still upset with Mother because she did not come to see her crowned homecoming queen. As they left, Mother said, as Gee had requested of her, "Take good care of my baby." Gee had told her that was the least she could do.

Lance took Gee to the Pink Room and treated her like the queen, paying for a private alcove off the dance floor and giving her a butane gold lipstick-shaped cigarette lighter. She burned her eyelashes the first time she used it. He was crazy about her, but she was still carrying a torch for Luke.

Just after graduation Jenn and Gee took off to Baltimore to get jobs. They bought tickets at the train station and had to show their new graduation IDs because they were suspected to be runaways. Getting jobs was a joke, because they just wanted to go to the beach. They got themselves fired from their first jobs. The lady they rented from gave them a new car to drive, and they acted like they had grown up in the city.

Jenn and Gee went to Washington and danced all night long. They were lucky they had their friend from back home, Big John, show up and look out for them. They just wanted to sunbathe, wear miniskirts, and see how much they could eat. The trouble was they ran out of money, and Big John took them back home to go to college at Southwest Virginia Community College.
Mother found an apartment for Gee because of the tension between Gee and JR. Gee had his number, and he knew it. He was flirty and inappropriate, and Gee was not going to put up with it. The final straw was when he called Gee a whore during another drunken weekend.

Gee had asked Mother, "Are you going to stand by and let him call me that?"

Mother gave no answer as he threw our pictures on the floor, an action that would become a regular occurrence. Jenn joined Gee along with two other friends at the SVCC apartment, splitting the rent between them.

We moved to Grundy where Tommy Lee took a job, and I transferred to SVCC. I went on Tuesday and Thursday, taking a full fifteen credit hours and scheduling more time with Laura Beth. We got a babysitter named Janey, who was a relative of Tommy Lee. She used scary tactics to keep Laura Beth in line, introducing her son Billy as the boogeyman and telling her if she wasn't good he would get her.

I knew Laura Beth was timid but had no idea this was going on. During this time, I began to hear Laura Beth talking to someone in her bedroom after I had read her a story and tucked her in.
At first, I was shocked because I knew no one was in there with her. Then each night I would stop and listen to conversations, and I came to the conclusion that she had an imaginary friend named Bucky. Bucky was a boy but wore girl's clothes and liked to eat alligators and fire. She started saying Bucky did it when she did something wrong. Of course, I referred to my Dr. Spock book and found that this was normal for some children.

During her first year at college, Gee was nominated for the queen's court. Because of JR, she could not go home, so Mother mailed a dress that our seamstress had made for her. Gee hated it, but she looked great with her long black hair and suntanned skin. The floor-length white brocade dress was a fitted sheath cut in off the shoulders, showing her bustline. I wore a long yellow-and-white organdy gown that had belonged to Tommy Lee's cousin.

Percy Sledge was the entertainer, and we all danced to "When a Man Loves a Woman" and had a big time. Gee would not accept any offer for a date, and Dr. King, the dean of the college, walked her down the aisle to the queen's court. Across the table was Matt, who was with a date; Gee had no idea he was to become her husband.

The next day was a Sunday, and there was a knock at the door. It was Matt. None of Gee's roommates were there. He asked her to go to the racetrack, and they began a summer romance. Gee shared everything about him with me. She said that the first time she laid close to him she noticed his arched eyebrows and blue eyes, his white and straight teeth, his curly dark hair, and his perfect physique at six feet tall. He was in love with her and was ready to marry, so after a five-month, whirlwind romance, he asked her to marry him. He went to the finest jewelry store and picked out a flawless diamond. He drove to my house on Slate Creek to show it to me to see if Gee would like it. I said yes, and he told me he would love Gee for the rest of her life. So the wedding was planned for December 27, 1971, at the Presbyterian Church where we grew up.

Scarlet was fourteen years old and had met Richard Claiborn Dante III, called Trey, who was the senior quarterback from Ervington High, one of our rivals. They had met at the Dixie on a cold night. Trey was tall and lanky, wore contact lenses, had braces, had straight hair down to his shoulders, and wore his jeans so they hit just above the ankle. He admired Scarlet's kneesocks and short skirt, but it was really her legs. He told her his feet were cold, and she pulled off one sock and shared it with him. He wore it home. He was an unlikely match for her. He was a brainiac and had been selected as one of the students from the county to meet President Nixon along with other honor students from across the United States. They just clicked with their opposite characteristics, adding a new spark to both of their lives.

Scarlet had changed overnight from a beautiful little girl to a woman-child. She had very large mahogany-brown eyes and thick, long, straight chestnut hair that hung to the middle of her back. She was voluptuous and looked sensuous. A rebel was forming, as she still felt like a third wheel at home with Mother and JR. She had lost Grandma Tori, Gee, and me. She had not learned to tie her shoes, curl her hair, or tell time. We did everything for her, and then she was alone. At school, she was compared to her sisters, our grades and our ladylike behavior. I was the most popular and in the National Honor Society. Gee had been a majorette and homecoming queen.

Scarlet decided to be different. She craved the attention Mother now gave JR, and she rebelled against house rules. Her opinions were not allowed to be expressed as Mother followed her standard pattern of "my way or the highway." Scarlet had no sexual experience but acted like she did. Her eighth-grade class voted her president of Student Council. She quickly got busy and rallied for girls to be able to wear pants, a privilege granted in 1973 and a first in the history of the school. She began dressing in camouflage pants and insulated underwear shirts like the young men wore coming back from Vietnam. It was rumored she was buying a matchbox of Mary Jane with her lunch money because it was the thing to do. She denied it.

More trouble for Scarlet was looming at home. Mother became pregnant at age forty-two. Scarlet did not want to eat at home after that, so Mother allowed her to buy her dinner at the drug store, as she refused to eat with her and JR. She felt alone and misunderstood and began smoking and became more withdrawn. She painted her room with peace signs and little hippy men. Her light fixture was a red lightbulb. Mother would have never allowed Gee and me to do that, so it was clear Mother was in her own world and did not know what to do with Scarlet.

That summer Scarlet stayed with me at college and babysat Laura Beth. She confided that a note had been given to her by a male teacher, and she was flattered and had answered back. It was discovered, and Mother had to go to school to see the guidance counselor. The school wanted to put the note in Scarlet's permanent folder, but Mother flew into them like a wet hen. She informed them that, and I quote, "Scarlet is the child and the student, and you have dirty minds. It will not be put in her folder." Mother then grabbed the note, took it home, and burned it. All she would say was that it was the innocent writing of a young girl and that they had made it dirty.

At home, JR began a series of inappropriate sexual advances that kept Scarlet in fear. The last straw was when he leaned over her bed when she had her friend sleep over. He was drunk and awakened them, accusing them of flaunting their breasts. Her friend never returned, and she did not confide in Mother.

Gee thought she had been reading too many *True Story* magazines, but I believed her. I had to protect her.

One evening there was a knock at the door. Tommy Lee, Laura Beth, and I were on our way to his parents' house for dinner. I went to the door, and it was Matt with Scarlet leaning on his shoulder. It was clear that she was under the influence of something. He found her at the bowling alley in Grundy and did not know who she had been with or any other details. He said he could not leave her there, so he brought her to me.

I went on to dinner and left her asleep because Tommy Lee would not go without me. I have always regretted that I did not try to get to the bottom of what had happened at the bowling alley. I didn't know who had brought her there or who gave her something to make her so out of it. I was twenty years old and had never had anything like that to deal with. I did not use alcohol or pot, and it didn't help that Tommy Lee insisted I go with him and leave her alone to sleep it off. She must have thought she had no one in her corner when she woke up to an empty house. I should have talked to her and tried to help her with the uncertainty and confusion in her life.

It seemed what helped her most was that Trey Dante began spending a lot of time with her. He helped her with homework and wanted her to overcome not caring about her grades. She did it for him, and they became very close. She took him to

Grandma Tori's gravesite, and he said he would always be there for her. She believed him.

Gee knew Scarlet had been having a hard time since losing Grandma Tori, but she was a face-the-music kind of girl and moved along with a lot of energy. She was caught up in her plans for her wedding and had to change the wedding date from December 27 to November 27 because Mother was scheduled for her third cesarean on December 16. Gee was furious and hurt because nothing was ever about her, and this added to her being deliberately suspicious about situations and people in her life.

Knowing Mother would be in the hospital for at least a week, I paid a visit to Maureen and Edwin next door. They had always been rock steady for me when I needed a shoulder to lean on and offered advice that carried no power of reprisal. Maureen and I went into their bedroom, and I explained my fear of Scarlet being left alone with JR while Mother would be in the hospital.

Maureen had a knowing look and said, "Laurel, Scarlet is invited to come and stay as long as she wants."

I fell into her arms and cried. I don't know why I could not discuss this with Mother. We never discussed anything with her.

Maureen went on to say with a chuckle, "I am going to burn that insulated underwear shirt the first chance I get."

I smiled, giving her my approval.

I was able to handle situations for Scarlet and Gee, but there was no one for me so the scene was set. One of my professors, Luther Collier, began giving me a lot of attention.

Since I was a health and physical education major and he was chair of the department and my advisor, he set himself up to be my go-to person without me even knowing it. I had him for golf, tennis, and health. I was chosen to be on the golf team, and we played a different golf course every Monday. There were six guys and two women who played.

I knew he was married and was a little flirty with the female students. I did not think of him in a romantic way. I liked the attention, and he was older and I trusted him. I compared him to my husband, who was handsome and unfaithful, versus Mr. Collier, who was not handsome but was confident and reliable. I thought. He was a favorite professor, students loved him, and he was strict and fair so his classes filled up early each semester.

It was fall semester, and I was walking up the hall between classes when I heard a whistle and turned around. Mr. Collier was carrying a cup of coffee. He smiled and said, "You are the best-looking female on campus." I was flattered, as I had been feeling down because Tommy Lee was showing me no attention. In fact, he seemed preoccupied and aloof and did not want to talk about our problems.

I was a naïve woman, more of a girl, and was unable to think for myself through marital problems in a mature way. He had made promises to me that he couldn't keep when he painted the picture of us as Mr. and Mrs. I was impressed to be singled out and admired, and it gave me a little push to put Tommy Lee and our problems in the back of my mind.

Tommy Lee and I got caught up in the excitement of the plans for Gee and Matt's wedding. Even though she knew Tommy Lee and I were having problems, she did not want JR to walk her down the aisle and asked Tommy Lee to give her away, avoiding trouble with JR, who would have been furious if she had asked Edwin.

On the morning of their wedding, Gee was in the bathtub crying, thinking about the big decision of getting married. She was not naïve like me and said she clearly knew Matt was the one, but she doubted herself in a jag of brief, last-minute jitters mixed with excitement.

Mother walked in all dressed up in a black silk dress with a long beautiful white collar made of lace tatting that formed a pattern of rings and chains. Even though she was pregnant, she was beautiful with her black hair coiffed like Jackie Kennedy. Gee continued crying, and Mother told her in no uncertain terms that she was getting married. I was so unhappy in my marriage that I begged Mother not to make her get married. Gee finally got out of the tub and said, "I really love Matt, and he treats me like a woman. I just have a bad case of vapors."

I watched as she put on her white velvet empire wedding gown. It was chosen for a Christmas wedding, and she was unhappy that it had to be changed to November. Her veil was embroidered in Chantilly lace and attached to a velvet bow, allowing her long black hair to cascade down her back.

Scarlet and Jenn were her bridesmaids, and I was her maid of honor. Our burgundy satin, scooped-neck, empire-style gowns matched Gee's. She carried a winter bouquet of burgundy-and-white roses and winter greenery with stock and berry stems interspersed with mistletoe and all wrapped in satin ribbon. We wore short, white lace gloves and carried one long-stem white rose. Scarlet cried throughout the wedding, losing Gee after losing Grandma Tori and me. The church was beautiful with white flowers and two candelabras at the altar. Reverend Johnson, our childhood minister, performed the ceremony. After the reception, we danced the night away at the Pink Room, except for Scarlet who was too young to go. No one knew then the impact this would have on Scarlet's life.

Gee and Matt went to the Greenbrier in White Sulphur Springs, West Virginia, for their three-day honeymoon. They had a winter wonderland honeymoon with a view of the outdoor Christmas trees and lighted sculptures. Gee ordered breakfast in bed and champagne, and they vowed to return there every anniversary.

Gee and I settled back in school, and she decided to teach me to drive because she was upset that Tommy Lee had not already done so. We began practicing in the college parking lot. Tommy Lee did not offer to take me for the test, so Gee asked her previous landlord, Zack, to take me for my driver's test. He worked in sales at Sears and borrowed a Plymouth Fury III because his Barracuda was a four-speed. I was really nervous, and the day of the test was the first time I'd driven the Plymouth. He picked me up at the college and took me for the test, asking me not to tell my husband that it was him. I didn't notice the bottle of champagne in the backseat. I was nervous, but the officer told me what to do. I had a hard time parallel parking, but Gee proved to be a good teacher, being able to drive anything herself.

The officer told me that I'd passed the test and asked me if the champagne was for him. I was so happy that I passed but shocked that I hadn't seen the champagne. I said, "If it helps get my license, you can have it." I think Zack left it for him, and I was ecstatic with my new freedom.

On December 16, 1971, we were all in the waiting room at Richlands Hospital. JR was careful to sit on the other side of the room away from us. The room was tense, and Gee whispered to me and Scarlet, "If anything happens to Mother, I will kill him." I shuddered, but it was becoming clear he had shattered our family as we knew it.

At one o'clock that afternoon, Benjamin Ezra was born. Dr. Bower announced that Mother and baby were doing as well as could be expected at the age of forty-two. We were Benjamin's big sisters, now twenty-one, nineteen, and fifteen, and were at that moment fragmented with love and concern and silently relegated as "the other family" by JR, finding fault with everything about "the girls."

JR's behavior was becoming more controlling, and he made Scarlet feel like an outsider. He had her give away her little dog because of the baby. It was conflicting, because she bristled at his inappropriate comments and advances. The new family of Mother, JR, and baby Benjamin caused her to feel the loss of love from Mother. She wanted to rebel and go her own way.

JR did not even get a Christmas tree for Scarlet, and Edwin was furious. He and Maureen had always shared in all our holidays, and they knew Scarlet was stuck through no fault of her own. Gee and I were also stuck because we couldn't go home, but it was dire straits for Scarlet. Edwin came marching in with a tree, and JR didn't say a word. Scarlet was happy and felt the love from our second family next door.

We all went over for Christmas, but JR got drunk on his favorite choice gin, knocked our three pictures to the floor, and stayed in the basement. Mother was frail after having the cesarean birth, so Gee and Matt brought a ham and she and I cooked our Christmas meal.

After the New Year's holiday, on the following Monday, the weather was warm, and our golf team played the Saltville

Golf Course. I was coming out of the ladies' room as Mr. Collier was going to the men's room. Before I knew what was happening, he leaned over and kissed me. Shivers ran all over me, and I was surprised. I felt sexy, scared, and mysterious. I knew it was wrong. I cared about doing the right thing, but I was so confused by men and love, and I was getting even with Tommy Lee. It was a secret, so it couldn't hurt anyone.

After all of Tommy Lee's affairs, and the last one with Tina at Wytheville, I wanted power over him, and secretive power was even better. After that, Mr. Collier began to ratchet up his attention to me, saying sweet and admiring things. He told me how intelligent I was, that I was one of his favorite students, and that he would like to protégée me through my last two years of college.

I explained the protégée part to Tommy Lee, and he encouraged me to go for it. He was so in love with Tina, and three-year-old Laura Beth had confided in me that they met Tina and ate peanut butter sandwiches while pulled over beside the road. I was furious that he took her and began to listen more and more to Mr. Collier. I was not convicted by God for loving the attention from him, and I don't know why. I knew it was wrong.

I was unable to address the issue of Tina with Tommy Lee, because he would clam up. I felt I had already lost anyway. I did not go to anyone for advice and just buried it deep in my soul, but my mind knew better. When we got married, I thought that I was living a fairy tale with the man I idolized and that he would love me forever. He was bigger than life, taking up the entire room. He was like a movie star and debonair like Troy Donahue. I did not know what to do about it.

He always denied all the other rumors except Tina. Instead, he told me he was in love with her. I had already given him his last chance before we left Pikeville. Over the four years of our marriage, he never hesitated to have sex whenever it presented itself, maybe because he wanted every fresh, innocent girl he could make a conquest. I never knew him to go after an experienced girl, and each time it seemed to give him excitement and anticipation of even more.

Everything pure between us was lost, because I was the only one true to the marriage. I never told his parents or my mother. I knew those things were sacred between husband and wife, like a binding force of religion and how things should be, leaving your parents and becoming one with your husband. I heard women talk that we must suffer in silence and keep our powder dry. I had joined the other women in my family in the pattern of denial passed down in my family. Without realizing it I had married someone just like Daddy, and how could that happen since I was only six years old when he was killed? A wife and baby did not interest Tommy Lee anymore, and all the advice I heard while listening in my circle of women was "men will be men."

Maureen sensed the tension and began sending me magazine articles on birth control. She was afraid I would become pregnant, so I went back to Pikeville, and Dr. Mulligan put me on the pill. Some said it was against God, but I didn't care. I was glad to control when I wanted another child and felt a sense of power and relief. I became immersed in my own life of school and being a good mother to Laura Beth. The pill helped me to feel independent and on my own in a way that I did not fully understand. I made straight As and loved playing golf on Mondays. I set up an independent study class of required reading with written critiques and set a goal to finish my associate's degree by the end of spring.

People start gossiping about me and Mr. Collier, but it didn't matter to me. Professors flirted with their students all the time, and that was the way it was in college. He encouraged me to apply to East Tennessee State University, and I was accepted for summer semester as a junior. By that time, it was rumored that we were having an affair. I had to admit, I was attracted to his advances but had no desire to go further. He put his arms around me in golf to help me with my swing, and I relished in the attention.

He picked up the bounced check for my golf shoes when Tommy Lee used the money at Wytheville with Tina. He seemed to always be there when Tommy Lee let me down. He surprised me with a new set of navy-blue golf clubs and a matching white bag trimmed in blue as a graduation present. He was looking out for me. I had never had that before, and it gave me confidence, freedom, and hope for my future and for Laura Beth. This future did not include him, but I knew I wanted to get away from Tommy Lee. East Tennessee State was my ticket.

As I was getting ready to move to Johnson City, Tennessee, to begin my junior year at East Tennessee State, Trey went off to Virginia Tech and broke Scarlet's heart, the same as when Luke left Gee. It was during this time that Bobby Joe Kiser returned from the army. He was two years older than I was and nine years older than Scarlet. I had been a cheerleader when he played football. He was cocky and handsome with light-brown hair and blue eyes. He was also a charmer and usually dated girls older than he was.

Upon his arrival home from the service, he immediately noticed Scarlet, and she was flattered by his attention. With her heartbreak in full force over Trey, her first love, leaving for Virginia Tech, she continued to mail Trey a letter every day. Bobby Joe began taking her to the post office to mail her letters and was there to see there were no letters for her. He was taken with her looks and rebellious spirit, and she knew it. She loved the power she had over him and that he was a man and not a boy. She bragged to her friends that she could make a phone call from school, and he would send her long-stemmed roses. They didn't believe her, but to their surprise, the roses were delivered that day.

One night when Gee was dancing with Bobby Joe at the Pink Room, she asked him to be good to her little sister. He replied, "I'll be good to her. I'm going to fuck her."

Gee told him to go straight to hell. She then called me crying, telling me Scarlet was headed for a lot of trouble. We knew Scarlet could not handle the hand she had been dealt from Mother, JR, and Bobby Joe, and there wasn't anything we could do about it.

I ask Tommy Lee to find me and Laura Beth an apartment at East Tennessee State, and he and a friend went to Johnson City and came back with the key to our new life. Laura Beth and I would be moving, and Tommy Lee would stay and work. He was fine with the idea. We did not discuss breaking up.

Scarlet would go with us for the summer. This would help us and would get her away from JR and Bobby Joe. East Tennessee State was a huge campus to me, and I was excited and intimidated. I was on full scholarship and a tight budget with a student loan of a thousand dollars and a hundred and fifty dollars a month from Tommy Lee. But with this meager beginning, I jumped in feet first, determined that I could do it.

We settled into our apartment, and one evening Tommy Lee showed up, almost drunk. He bragged he had a case of beer in the car. I put Laura Beth to bed and Scarlet stayed in the bedroom with her. I sat in the kitchen with Tommy Lee.

"I am in love with you all over again, and Tina is the out of the picture," he said.

I didn't know what to think, because our neighbor had told me that as soon as Laura Beth and I left for university, he had a party every night. I was also confused that I had held on so long for him and now just felt numb inside.

He sat at the table smiling that Tommy Lee smile and picked up a butcher knife and laid it on the table. He kept drinking beer and told me, "I can rape you if I want to."

With my extraordinary naiveté, I believed him and felt very unsafe. I knew he would do it. We stayed up all night, and Scarlet did not sleep either, also afraid while listening in the bedroom with Laura Beth, who, thank God, was sleeping. We passed the night there at the kitchen table until early the next morning when he began rambling about his father sending him down to bring us home. He looked at me with tears in his Jesus eyes and said, "I'm sorry." Then he turned and walked out the door. I got dressed and went to class. Tommy Lee never professed his love for me after that. He acted cocky and glib with that smile and go-to-hell look.

Scarlet and I were very careful that Laura Beth's diet came first. So we never drank milk and fed her first, saving all we could for her. I don't know what we would have done without Mother sending food every month. She sent canned food that she had preserved and other canned goods from the store.

Life was hard, but we were determined and never once thought of quitting. Not one ounce of assistance came from Tommy Lee's parents, and he only paid the hundred and fifty dollars per month to us. I heard about selling blood for twenty-five dollars, but when I went down to the blood bank, they did a test and said my red blood count was too low and turned me down. Scarlet wanted to sell hers, but she was underage.

We had no car, so I walked to campus every day. Being a health and education major plus all the walking had my curves accentuated, and there was not an ounce of fat on my frame. I was noticed by the men on campus, but my mind was on finishing school and taking care of Laura Beth so I refused all requests for dates and didn't tell them I was still married.

One day while I was in school, Scarlet and Laura Beth were walking up the street and a car came by them, driving very slowly. It was Mr. Collier, and he was looking for me. Scarlet and Laura Beth knew him from the college, so they went with him to McDonald's. Laura Beth gave him our address even though she was only three years old. So when I got home, he asked me to go for a ride. I accepted. He informed me he had moved back to Tennessee and that his wife had moved in with her parents and filed for divorce.

Luther and I began a love affair without a second thought, and naturally, I felt Laura Beth and I had a rock to lean on. Scarlet liked him and told me that he would take care of both me and Laura Beth. Her approval did not come easily where men were concerned.

I decided to see a divorce lawyer after arguing with Tommy Lee every day on the pay phone on the way to school. I felt like I was another person and not the one who had married him to begin with. I went to the university library and read everything I could get my hands on about divorce and children after seeing the lawyer. I wanted to protect my little girl at all costs. We could not count on him for emotional or financial support. I had to plan as if I were alone. He bounced our support check, and Luther just happened to be there and had a hundred and fifty dollars in cash. He paid the landlord our rent and gave me an extra fifty.

I found out from the attorney that because Tommy Lee had acted violently toward me outside a club in the presence of Matt and Gee, there was a precedent case involving an out-of-state college student. We had just moved to East Tennessee State. Gee and Matt came down, and the four of us went to the Eagles Nest. Tommy Lee accused me of flirting with the band when Gee and I went up to thank them for playing her favorite song, "I'm So Hurt." When we got out to the parking lot, Tommy Lee was livid and acting jealous. He manhandled me in a rough and flippant way. I decided right then and there that our new song was, "It's Too Late" by Carole King.

I was awarded the divorce, custody of Laura Beth, and a hundred and fifty dollars a month for child support. In Tennessee, a divorce was final in thirty days, which was something I did not know. I was glad not to wait and put up with his acrimonious behavior.

Tommy Lee began acting glib when he picked up Laura Beth, telling me as they were leaving, "You will never see her again. We'll board a plane to nowhere and never come back."

I always believed him and was on pins and needles until he brought her back. And then it would happen again and again. Some of the personality traits that I had once loved about him now turned into weapons against me. The self-confident, witty, and cocky smile would turn into sarcastic, glib words and gestures that stung me to the core of my being.

Laura Beth and I shared the bed in our one-bedroom apartment, and when Scarlet was there for the summer, she would sleep on the sofa. On weekends, when Scarlet went home, Luther would visit. We hung out in the living room after I put Laura Beth to bed. She would sit on the end of the bed waiting for me even to midnight despite the fact that I had tucked her in early. There she was, saying in her soft sweet voice, "Just waiting for you, Mommy."

When Scarlet was planning to leave to go back to school, I put Laura Beth in Mother Goose Nursery, taking a taxi each day. She hated Mother Goose Nursery, and it broke my heart to leave her crying. I would later find out that there was a little boy there who would tell her, "Your mommy will never be coming to get you."

And Mae, one of the caregivers, would rock her gently and at the same time have a ruler in her hand, which gave Laura Beth mixed signals about love and discipline.

We settled in and were comfortable knowing Luther was visiting us about once a month. Once he bought me hot pants, which were the new style. They were cobalt blue velour with a silk top to match. He asked me to wear the outfit without a bra. I felt so daring with my perky breasts and tan legs, and we went to Howard Johnson's for dinner. Tommy Lee had never made me feel sexy like that. Luther always took us out to dinner for fine dining. We dressed up, and Laura Beth acted like a miniature lady using her manners and saying big words like *adamant*, *prerogative*, and *ebony*. People would come to our table and compliment the little four-year-old acting so grown up.

One evening there was a knock at the door, and it was Bobby Joe. He had a pizza and asked if he could come in to visit with Scarlet. I had no idea how he found us, but I allowed him to come in. We were delighted to have pizza for a change. He asked me if Scarlet could go to the lake where his family was camping. I told him that our mother had left her in my care, and I didn't have the authority to allow her to go.

I was a little afraid of him, the bad boy who wanted the older girl, usually three years or more and girls with experience. I knew he could act like a jerk, because I remembered high school when I would not have anything to do with him. Maybe he was scared and did not want his heart broken, but he covered it with making the girl feel special and treating everyone else awful. But I had the feeling he could turn on a dime and treat a girl bad like it was a hobby and then move on.

Besides, why did he want a girl/child of fifteen to his twenty-four? I had a creepy feeling but didn't let on that I thought he was a hothead and would not have been able to handle him. He took it well as I explained I could not let her go because of Mother, and he left without being asked.

Scarlet began playing tennis close to campus and was quite good at it. She made friends easily, and I allowed her to go to a frat party with one of my friends, Carol, who was an elementary school teacher. Scarlet looked so mature telling everyone she was a teacher from Honaker. As it turns out, there was a lot of drinking, and she could have gotten in serious trouble even if she was with my friend. That was bad judgment on my part and scary. She wanted to stay with me and go to school. I wanted to keep her, but Mother wanted her to come home. I knew deep down that I may not be the best guardian for her at twenty-two.

At the end of summer, Scarlet left, and Luther came more often. He found out I was taking Laura Beth to Mother Goose Nursery in a taxi, and Luther brought a 1966 white Thunderbird to keep there for me to drive. I loved not having to walk in the rain and snow, and Laura Beth and I could go see Matt and Gee on weekends. No one had ever done anything like that for me.

During Christmas break, we were still encouraged not to come home, because JR always caused a scene. We left Johnson City in the pouring snow to spend Christmas with Matt and Gee in Virginia. The roads were slick, and we slipped and slid as I made the two-hour drive. We were excited, and Laura Beth loved going to their house because they had no children, and she was the center of attention. Their home became our home because we had no place to go. We were so lucky Matt loved us too.

I had just enrolled for my last semester when I got a call from Mother. She had to have serious surgery, and JR wouldn't allow anyone to keep three-year-old Benjamin except me. I didn't even think twice about dropping my classes to take care of Benjamin for one semester. I was raised not to put myself first and felt it was my duty. My department head had just asked me to be her assistant, which was a great honor. However, I had to tell her that I was keeping my baby brother. It seemed no one cared about me and my education or the hardship I endured being a single parent while working frantically to finish my degree. No one gave me any extra money during that time. While I had Benjamin, Luther bought him new clothes, including a raincoat just like the big guys. He was so cute with blond hair and blue eyes, and I took good care of him. No one acknowledged me in any conversations about taking care of him, not even a thank you.

Mother had a tough recovery, and Benjamin was a handful. JR was acting out and drinking, even getting a DUI and losing his driver's license. This made him worse, and he began to get violent with Mother first and then Benjamin. She became afraid of him and began to hide from him, taking Benjamin with her. The last time I saw him he was passed out drunk on the floor holding a shotgun. She called me at ETSU to come home. It was a three-hour drive, and I endangered Laura Beth and myself by going, but I had never told Mother no. She and Benjamin had bruises, and Benjamin had a man's handprint in the middle of his back. I took the gun next door to Edwin for safekeeping. JR had come into our home and caused so much pain, hating "the girls" so much it fractured the family like a ripped picture that could not be glued back together.

I received the news that JR had moved out after Mother put a padlock on the front and back doors. She and Benjamin went in through the basement, turning all lights off early every evening. JR would bang on the front door. They were quiet, and she called it a blackout. He finally quit coming. He had hurt Mother and Benjamin in another drunken rage. She was slowly trying to put her life back together but sank into a deep depression. I was called home by Gee and Scarlet who said that she had "gone around the bend." The day I arrived she was "out of this world," as she put it. I called Reverend Johnson, and he prayed with her and anointed her with the holy myrrh oil from the Holy Land.

Mother slowly recovered. "God spoke to my broken heart," she said. She explained that she'd told the devil, "Get behind me," and after that, he would no longer speak to her head. God looked at the heart, and her walk with God would no longer be hindered with things of the world. We were stunned by Mother's new life, but at least she was looking forward instead of being stuck in her black hole of depression forever.

By the end of spring, Luther made his move to let my family know he loved me and Laura Beth and promised to take care of us. He took the entire family out to dinner and made a big deal about showing Mother his financial statement. She was impressed and did not see any reason I should not accept his proposal of marriage. The only problem, I later found out, was that the money belonged to his mother. Our life began on this charlatan's promise to my family, and the web of deceit that would follow almost killed me.

Laura Beth and I were getting ready for our trip to Chattanooga to meet Luther's mother when I received a phone call from Scarlet. She was crying and told me she was at Mother's and no one was at home. She said, "I am pregnant and need to know what to do."

We began crying together, and I asked her if the father was Bobby Joe. She said he was.

"You must stay there and tell Mother," I said.

Mother showed more understanding than I thought she would, saying to Scarlet, "You know I love babies." And Scarlet's plan to escape from JR had backfired, because he was already gone.

Scarlet would tell me that she heard Mother telling a friend that none of her girls would ever get in trouble. Scarlet wanted out, and she knew she had a man in Bobby Joe. Mother went next door to Edwin and asked him what she should do. He told her, "You can press charges because Scarlet is just sixteen, or you can force Bobby Joe to marry her." He advised the marriage. However, Bobby Joe bragged that he could leave town and wouldn't have to marry Scarlet.

The marriage was hurriedly arranged. I cancelled my trip to Chattanooga to attend the wedding. In the haste that followed, Scarlet did not get to choose her dress because Mother did not think of her feelings; she just wanted her married. Mother, Gee, and I chose a white sheath dress, and Scarlet rebelled by having it hemmed very short into a minidress. She looked beautiful with her long hair down to her waist framing her not-yet-a-woman face. They were married at the First Presbyterian Church by Reverend Johnson, who had also married Gee and Matt.

The weekend after Scarlet's wedding, Luther, Laura Beth, and I arrived late in the evening in Chattanooga, and as we crossed Missionary Ridge, it was the most beautiful view of the city lights below on the Tennessee River with Lookout Mountain on the left and Signal Mountain on the right. It was the first time I had fallen in love with an area at first sight. We were going to Swedens Cove about thirty minutes outside Chattanooga. Luther called it the Cove, even though there were several coves I would later learn.

We arrived after dark, driving the winding two-lane county road, and pulled in the driveway. We were greeted at the back door, if you could call it a greeting, by Alma, who had lived there alone since the death of Luther's father at the age of forty-nine. She laughed a nervous laugh, and her eyes looked piercing and cold. We had dinner on the way, so I asked to be taken to our room. Laura Beth and I shared a room with its own entrance. Luther was put across the hall in his old bedroom and closer to his mother.

When we awakened the next morning, I noticed a bundle of switches lying on the floor tied together with burlap string. I was taken aback and quickly moved it before Laura Beth saw it. I showed it to Luther, who did not act surprised.

"Mother has a masters in psychology and is always using subtle ways to show her disapproval," he said. He also mentioned that her favorite book was Freud's *Abnormal Psychology.*

I didn't call this subtle, having studied four years of psychology. I threw the bundle of switches in the stream out back on the property and decided not to mention it to her.

I later went to the local library and looked up superstitions and found some obscure reference in the 1500s regarding contemptuous and worthless women. She wanted me to think this was her impression of me.

Luther was her only child, and I realized the need to keep her at bay. She cooked a big country breakfast, including ham and red-eye gravy, which looked disgusting. It was made from fat off the ham, coffee, water, and butter. After breakfast, Alma invited Laura Beth and me to go for a ride around Marion County. Little did I know this was a ploy to split me off from Luther. Once we were sequestered in the car, a series of questions began, fired in rapid succession. She used a nonassuming tone of voice and asked questions about my marriage and divorce. I was careful and gave short answers. I was angered because we had Laura Beth with us. She was nosey, but I had been raised to respect elders and that withholding the truth was the same as telling a lie. When we got back, I had a talk with Luther.

“Don’t let her get to you,” he said. “Prove you are smarter and quicker than she is, and she will leave you alone. She likes to put the monkey on other people’s backs; it is one of her favorite sayings.”

Luther promised me that we would get our own place. Our short visit was just to introduce us, and we would live our own lives. We went back to Johnson City after taking Laura Beth to Rock City and Ruby Falls to make plans to move. Our wedding date was set for July 22, and our new life was just beginning.

Luther called the next week with excitement in his voice. “I am looking at some property on the mountain at Monteagle, about thirty minutes from the Cove. It’s a two-story house back in the woods and needs a lot of work." He wanted to come and get us the following weekend to go check it out.

The first time I saw it, I fell in love. It was a two-story Colonial, built around 1930, with a covered gable roof entrance supported by two round pillars. There was a large living room with a mountain stone fireplace, a formal dining room, and large, arched doorways throughout the bottom floor, which was all hardwood flooring. The walls were swirling thick plaster that had not suffered any damage. The eat-in kitchen had old plumbing and needed new appliances, and a powder room was off the living room and kitchen in the hallway. Out back was a screened-in porch, and off the living room was a glass/screened-in sunroom. Just off the living room and dining room was a small foyer with a winding staircase to the upstairs where there were three large bedrooms and a bath.

Luther said, "You are beaming. It will be fun and an adventure to work on it together."

I agreed, knowing Laura Beth and I needed to be taken care of and have a home. We made plans to go back to Johnson City and get our things, and I decided to finish my last twelve credit hours at the University of Tennessee at Chattanooga.

We moved into the house and began all the work of plumbing, painting, and landscaping. I had never done manual labor, but I was soon wearing coveralls, putting up fences for horses, and learning to paint. We painted the house yellow, and I personally stripped and stained the beautiful winding staircase. We did the three bedrooms upstairs and the dining room and living room. The kitchen needed the most work, so we left it for last. I drove the pickup truck down to the Cove and went to the barn and shoveled manure, loaded big river rocks from the stream, and dug up crept myrtles, lilac bushes, and old-fashion roses in order to transplant them into the huge yard in a rock garden. Luther made a long flower box just beside the driveway that went around the house of two entrances.

We went shopping in Chattanooga to Haverty's Furniture, and for the first time, I chose beautiful furniture, window treatments, and a canopy for our bed. We painted our bedroom lilac, and the light streaming in gave it a heather hue. Laura Beth's bedroom was pink, and we purchased two matching wrought iron beds and trimmed everything out in pink and mint green. The guest bedroom was jade green and called the antique room due to the antique furniture and flower garden quilt given to us by Luther's mother.

I was happy pledging my love to Luther and anticipating the wedding. We went to Nashville to go shopping for my wedding dress. It was a floor-length design, sweetheart sheath, two-toned blush and ivory chiffon with a neckline organza choker embellished with pearls that was attached to a sheer décolleté overlay. The gown also featured a sheer long sleeve with pearl-embellished cuffs matching the choker neckline. We chose ivory silk high-heel ankle-strap shoes that went perfect with the gown.

We selected matching gold wedding bands with a small Greek key design in black edging. I had no qualms about shopping with Luther for my wedding purchases and did not consider it bad luck. I didn't even notice that he was choosing everything. I chose not to wear a veil or headpiece, having been married already and being the mother of a small child. Laura Beth's dress was ivory silk with a low waist and pearl smocking on the bodice and matching headband. Luther wore his black-and-red tuxedo that had been custom made for him.

We finished the house, and my immediate family was coming from Virginia. Because Scarlet was pregnant, we picked her up at the airport in Chattanooga. She was tan and beautiful, dressed in red short shorts and a matching cut-in, off-the-shoulder top and T-strap sandals. Except for her small round tummy, she looked like a movie star. Matt and Gee were bringing Mother and Benjamin, who was four years old. Luther's mother made the wedding cake and gave us a quilt she made in 1938, which was embroidered with each month of the year. I felt we were beginning to get close, but that would prove to be wrong.

The wedding was at our new house in the living room in front of the mountain stone fireplace. I arranged white roses on the mantle and lit white candles. The minister from Monteagle Mountain Presbyterian Church performed our wedding ceremony. I explained to him that I felt like Ruth in the Bible. I was leaving my family to come with Luther, trusting him with my baby girl and our future. I asked him to read from the Bible, Ruth 1:16:

> And Ruth said, Intreat me not to leave thee, or to return from following after thee; for whither thou goest, I will go; and whither thou lodgest, I will lodge; thy people shall be my people, and thy God my God.

I felt a strong presence from God that Laura Beth and I would finally have stability and love and a new beginning in our beautiful two-story mountain home. It was a great day, and we left that evening for Nashville on our short honeymoon. I didn't want to leave Laura Beth for very long in a new environment. Mother stayed to make it easier. When we got back, there was a new Buick Riviera, my wedding present, which oddly got traded down within a few months. Not being materialistic, I didn't see a red flag about the car. Mother did.

On August 4, we got the news from Virginia that Scarlet had delivered a three-pound baby girl two months early. She had a fifty-fifty chance of survival and was in an incubator. We made a quick trip to see her. Her name was Rachel Patricia. The nurse held her up for us to see, holding her in one hand. She had no eyelashes or fingernails and still had white fuzz on her face. But the doctor was now giving her better odds. She was a fighter. Scarlet had gone into labor ten days after she flew back from Chattanooga for our wedding. The doctor advised Scarlet not to have any more children due her young age of almost seventeen and the early labor.

In late August, Luther announced that he had new jobs for us. Even though I was a secondary education major, I was to teach third grade in the fall at Coalmont Elementary, and he would be principal. Laura Beth would go to kindergarten, so we would all be together. I knew nothing about elementary education and was very concerned. If it hadn't been for Ms. Smart, the first-grade teacher, I would have never made it. She encouraged me and tutored me on the new math, and I enjoyed the eight-year-old third graders. I worked very hard on my lesson plans to stay ahead of any new practice. We were the smart-looking couple with modern ways in the small town of Coalmont, Tennessee.

As we settled in to our jobs and new home, I did not cook one meal. Luther set up a charge account at the local diner and restaurants, and we had breakfast and dinner there or went out to other restaurants in Suwanee or Chattanooga. I didn't think it strange, because he made it feel so special and normal. We were treated first class, and Luther acted proud of his family in public, almost as if we were a cut above. I felt privileged, not snobby, but taken care of and normal.

Tommy Lee called, and we discussed that he was behind on child support. He wanted me to know that he had met the only woman who could keep him home. He said he'd seen her walking down the street in Grundy, and she had the prettiest legs he ever saw. Her name was Coretta Blue Blakely, and she was about eight years older. I doubted she could keep him home and wondered if she thought he was that great a lover. I told him I was glad for them but wanted to know about the support. He wanted to arrange a visit for Laura Beth to fly to Virginia, traveling alone. I told him no, and it wasn't because of the overdue child support. She was a timid child, attached to me and afraid to ride the Ferris wheel, and there was no way I would put her on a plane, contempt of court or not.

Just before beginning kindergarten, Laura Beth began to say she wanted the same last name as me. I ignored it at first, but she said it over and over: "Mommy, I want my name to be the same as yours."

Luther jumped on it and said, "We should see our attorney about the child support issue. I would like to adopt her."

We found out that if Tommy Lee was at least six months behind, we could run an ad for four weeks about the adoption and take it before the court to file adoption. It went fine, and we didn't hear from Tommy Lee for another six months. He had moved to northern Virginia with Coretta and her twin boys. He was furious about the adoption, but there was nothing he could do. And Laura Beth was happy with her new name.

Back home in Virginia, Matt and Gee's first baby arrived on December 8, 1974, a bouncing baby boy. His name was Hunter Matthew, and he weighed eight pounds and five ounces. According to Matt, he had shoulders like a linebacker.

Gee wrote a long letter to me telling me about the love in her heart for her baby. She thought she was not ready to have a child, but once she held him, she said there was a place in her heart that filled with love that would have stayed dormant. She would never have known the happiness she would have missed. I was so happy for her and could not wait to go see them.

The adoption was finally final, and we spent the first Christmas in our house. We decorated the house with fragrant pine and mistletoe that Luther had shot out of the tree and a beautiful cedar tree. I received a diamond ring hidden in the mistletoe on the mantle above the mountain stone fireplace. Laura Beth loved her new doll, Baby Go Bye-Bye, and china tea set. The day after Christmas, an ice storm rolled in, and it was a winter wonderland with the sun glistening everywhere. We had electricity but were worried because the lines were frozen with ice. We kept the fireplace going in case there was no heat. Our heather bedroom was a warm and toasty respite, wrapping me in a blanket of love.

I suppose it had been gradual with Luther and me. We were never apart, not for anything. He had an opinion on everything concerning Laura Beth and me. I began to notice Luther being unreceptive to making friends. I was invited to a ladies' Valentine tea, and we were invited to other social functions as a couple. He said he was happy with just the three of us and planned trips to Nashville, Atlanta, and Chattanooga. Laura Beth and I had not traveled at all, so we enjoyed the weekend trips and were learning so much that I didn't take notice of the isolation that he had planned.

In the spring, we went to Eastgate Mall in Chattanooga for spring and summer clothes. Luther took me to Loveman's, an upscale clothing store, and chose a new wardrobe. He had the sales lady bring me outfits to try on and then I walked out to model for him. He chose what we would take and then took me to a hat shop and chose hats for the suits. Then we were off to the lingerie shop, where he chose my underwear, nightgowns, and robes. His taste was classic with an occasional hot-pants suit or palazzo pants added in. He liked to take pictures of me in our bedroom with his new Polaroid SX-70 camera. He kept the pictures in his top chest drawer. I didn't think anything about it, and it was exciting to pose for him. I would learn later that those pictures would cause me a lot of grief.

Luther bought horses for newly fenced-in pasture, and we enjoyed learning to ride. His was a Tennessee walker named Midnight, I had a palomino named Cinnamon, and Laura Beth had a brown-and-white pony named Bambi. She had a close call when she accidently switched him, and he ran away with her all the way to the fenced property. She was only six years old and used great judgment when she grabbed the limb of a tree and held on for dear life to prevent the sudden stop that would have thrown her over the fence. I was running after her and got there just in time to lift her out of the tree.

It was almost the end of the school year when I noticed we were getting notices from the bank. Luther was very defensive when I asked him about it. "I am head of the family," he said. "Trust me and don't worry about it."

He always had a reason and was into deal making, buying, and selling. He would bundle bank loans and buy new cars, and it seemed to work out. I was very upset about his unwillingness to discuss or involve me in any business discussions about our life and future. It became clear when we argued late one night after I put Laura Beth to bed. I was so upset and went for a drive from Monteagle to Suwanee. When I returned, he said he had me followed by a state trooper, and I believed him. From that moment on, I knew my life was a make-believe world. I felt betrayed, and the uncertainty permeated my being. I also knew I could not have another failed marriage.

Alma decided to buy the property behind us and moved a one-hundred-year-old log cabin that belonged to the Collier family to that property. I was very unhappy with that decision. We would wake up on a Saturday morning, and she would be in the yard below our bedroom window chopping on a tree stump, working like a man. Luther told me to ignore her, but I was feeling trapped and controlled by both of them. She was nosey and too involved, and he was a control freak and a liar. In fact, he would lie, and she would swear to it. It was a sick relationship between the two of them. They played mind games on a regular basis.

School was out, and I told Luther, "Laura Beth and I are going to Virginia for a visit with Mother." I didn't tell him I had that run-away attack giving me anxiety and fear. He didn't want us to go, but I was set on it, and for the first time, I defied him and packed our bags and left. Once I was there, I had no plans on going back, but I didn't tell anyone. I had the summer to decide what to do, before Laura Beth went to first grade. Except Luther followed me, and we fell into a pattern of acting like nothing was wrong, forced to keep up a front about our marriage. Mother was happy to have us there to help out, and Luther and Matt painted her house.

While there, I began having stomach cramps and decided to go to Mother's gynecologist. He did some test and told me I needed a biopsy and another test that included putting dye in my fallopian tubes. That test was very painful. He called us back to discuss the results. It seemed that when I was married to Tommy Lee, I became infected with a sexually transmitted disease, most likely gonorrhea, which had formed scar tissue blocking the fallopian tubes and causing infertility. He recommended that I have surgery for lysis of adhesions. I was shocked but finally understood the ongoing medical problems early in my marriage to Tommy Lee.

During this time, Luther had developed a relationship with the vice president at Mother's bank. I don't know how he did it, but he was able to obtain a loan by adding on to a one-thousand-dollar loan Mother had taken out for some of my expenses at East Tennessee State. The bank didn't even call Mother.

As soon as my surgery was over and I was released, Luther insisted we were going home. Mother begged him to stay until I was able to travel, but nothing would do him but to take us home. I knew money was running out and felt guilty staying at Mother's all summer, so I agreed to go. What I didn't know was we were not going back to our home at Monteagle but back to the Cove to the little house beside Alma. Luther had moved us before he came to Virginia and had put the Monteagle house on the market because he was in danger of losing it. He also sold our horses. Laura Beth was devastated that her Bambi was gone.

Luther had already taken a job as principal in Trenton, Georgia, just across the Tennessee line in Dade County. He had enrolled Laura Beth in first grade in Trenton. They made the forty-five minute drive every day. I was unhappy that Laura Beth did not live in the town she went to school in, making it hard to have friends and participate in school activities.

I was beaten down by living in the Cove. Alma's house was next door to ours, and she was always peeping through the curtains in the windows on our side of the property. She would also walk in without knocking. If I didn't hear her, she would even walk back to our bedroom. I started locking the doors. She was spying on me and talking to Luther about it.

She said, "Laurel can't sew, knit, or crochet, so what can she do?"

Alma was an expert at those things because her mother had been a tailor. She was also an expert on Freud's abnormal psychology. She started analyzing everything I did and the way I dressed and wore my hair. She focused on my fathers' absence in my childhood and her educated opinion of how it impacted normal transition during the critical developmental stages of a young girl. When she questioned me about my childhood and my father, I felt like she was watching my mouth move as I answered rather than looking me in the eye. Her voice sounded hypnotic as she would make suggestions to get me to talk about my "suppressed memories."

She told Luther, "Laurel will always have relationship problems due to suppressed trauma over her father's murder."

One day I had reason to go into her attic, looking for some old college books belonging to Luther. There were a lot of boxes of books up there, and the last box was open, and right on top was a new big book on witchcraft. I was startled and picked it up. I wondered who it belonged to and assumed that because it was on top it must have been put there recently. The page was turned down at the topic "Classic Witchcraft, a.k.a. Cunning Craft."

I sat down and began reading about this sect of people. It said this practice was for cunning men and women with a bag of tricks: midwifery; healing with magic, herbs, and other folk remedies; providing abortions; love potions and poisons; divination; and casting of curses and blessings. I thought back to the bundle of switches from our first meeting. Just as

I was reading on, I heard Alma at the bottom of the stairs and quickly put it back and grabbed a couple of books on health education. I made an excuse about being in a hurry and went home. I was in a state of disbelief. I didn't share this with Luther or anyone else.

I continued having some female problems and began to go each month to get a shot to start my period. Each time they did a urine test to make sure I wasn't pregnant, and I thought nothing of it, knowing what the doctor had said about my infertility. It became a routine thing until December 1975. I was waiting for my shot when the doctor told me there would be no shot because I was pregnant. I almost fainted, and it was a good thing I was leaning against the wall. Laura Beth had just turned seven, and a baby was on the way.

Luther and his mother hovered over me until I could not breathe, talking about the baby all the time. "We want a boy," she said. "There is no boy to carry on the name with Luther being an only child. Why, I would rather have one boy than two little split-tailed girls."

I thought that was a horrible comment and had a realization not to trust her. She was strange all the way around. I had never known a woman who was totally antifeminine and mocked those who were. She was such a fan of Freud that it did not make sense. He believed nature determined a woman's destiny through beauty, charm, and sweetness, and she acted more masculine and had always had a career.

My unhappiness was becoming unbearable in the Cove. My only solace was lying out in the sun, feeling the rays seep into my skin, providing a feeling of comfort, and at the same becoming tan and healthy looking. Even so, at every checkup the doctor questioned me about my depression. I tried to keep him at bay, knowing I could not go into it, or I would have a complete breakdown.

I discussed with Luther the fact that I couldn't live in the Cove a day longer. He finally came home and said he found a house in Trenton, Georgia. It was built by a contractor for his family, and he was willing to finance it for us. I tried to not fall in love with it, beginning to know that nothing with Luther would last. I could not help but think about the Monteagle house and all the love and hard work I'd put into it when I began my new life with Luther. Deep down, I knew we may lose this one also.

It was modern with three bedrooms and had two mountain stone fireplaces upstairs and downstairs and a full basement. The lot out back was filled with rosebud and dogwood trees that made an umbrella in the spring of pink and white. The family room on the back had windows all the way around, giving a view of the splendor. We settled into our new home, wallpapered our bedroom, and painted the other two. Slowly, trust seeped into my soul, and I began to trust Luther again. We went to church and made friends with couples, which was a first for us. I was happy.

At the beginning of summer, we were in the Cove visiting, and the police from Grundy County showed up. They had a warrant for Luther's arrest. Laura Beth and Alma had gone to the barn and knew nothing about what was going on.

I was devastated as they handcuffed him and led him away. I was six months pregnant, standing there listening to Luther tell me to call Bob Alder, the family attorney. I went to the barn and distracted Laura Beth by telling her to go feed the ducks. Ava was not as shocked as I was when I told her that I would need to leave Laura Beth with her while I went to the attorney.

It was like I kicked into my acting mode, not letting myself cry or get emotional. I had a lot of experience with expecting the worst. The charge was misappropriation of funds when he was principal at Coalmont. Now I was putting the picture together of why he left the Monteagle house. Bob told me the bond was set high because they had been looking for him for about a year. Also, the bank was about to foreclose on the Monteagle house, which was in Marion County, and we would be required to have property in Grundy County to stand good for the bail.

I went to the Grundy County Jail. I had never been to a jail. It was small and dirty. I asked to see my husband, and when they took me back to where the prisoners were, Luther told them, "God, get her out of here."

It was odd seeing the man who had been my professor and then my husband behind bars. He was adamant for them to get me out of there. I was willing to do whatever I had to do to resolve this mess. They wouldn't let me stay, so I went back to try to handle this nightmare alone. I felt like I was having an out-of-body experience. I caught a glance of myself in the mirror. I had on a sundress and was tan from lying out in the sun, but my face looked gaunt and my eyes were hollow. The baby kicked, and I placed my hand on my stomach, thinking this was a bad dream and wondering how it would end for us.

This was the one time that Alma went easy on me. She took Laura Beth on outings, and they baked peanut butter cookies while I was sorting out the nightmare we were living. Bob said he found a businessman who owned property in Grundy County to go pay Luther's bail. He was a good friend of Bob's and of Luther's late father, Louis. Luther was in jail three days before bond was made. The next step was to hire a forensic accountant to go over the books before Luther's case went to court.

Bob said that it was a good thing the books were in a mess already, because they couldn't tie more than $2,500 to Luther's misappropriation of funds charge. We had to get the money from Alva to pay the school board restitution, the accountant, and Bob's attorney fee. Luther refused to discuss it and acted like it didn't happen. It was a good thing he already had a job in Georgia with the school board. Maybe that was why he went to Georgia and applied for a job before everything hit the fan.

Alma had a nervous breakdown, and I put a bed in our family room and took care of her for the following two months. I don't know how I got through the summer. I was beginning to fit right in to my make-believe life again. I was popular among the mothers, went to church, and befriended Reverend Donner who had a daughter Laura Beth's age. Luther played the perfect husband and sang in the church choir. This was the first time we'd had any semblance of a social life, but the façade was fake, which put more pressure on me.

I awakened at eight o'clock the morning of August 25 with labor pains. Luther stopped on the way to Memorial Hospital in Chattanooga to buy powdered donuts and coffee, his usual routine. I was ready this time, because I had taken Lamaze classes. I wanted to remember this birth and for it to not be difficult like with Laura Beth. I had my focal point to put on the wall, a picture of an ancient ankh symbol for life. I was drawn to it and felt protected by it, so I had Luther put in on the wall at the end of my bed. I focused and used all my breathing techniques so I would remember my baby's birth unlike my experience with Laura Beth, which was a total blank.

Beauregard Louis Collier (Beau) was born at 9:50 a.m., and by lunch, I was hungry. It was an easy birth, and he was delivered quickly. The nurse tried to get me to hold back until the doctor got there, and I panted, "This baby is coming now." Just as the doctor got off the elevator, they threw on his mask and gloves, and he said, "Push." Luther called everyone and said the baby had a penis, which Mother expressed was "a crude announcement that it was a boy."

From the moment I got home, Alma and Luther continued hovering over me. I wanted to breastfeed but had a hard time because I was redheaded and so fair skinned that my nipples cracked. They had me spray them with Tuf-Skin, which was used by athletes. I was determined to make it work and joined the La Leche League of Chattanooga where I received all the support I needed.

Mother flew in with Benjamin to help out. Scarlet and Bobby Joe had been in Nashville and drove to see us on their way home. I asked Luther to take everyone out to breakfast because I was not up to having company. My milk had finally come in, and I couldn't handle all the fuss. I was alone and able to feed my baby boy for the first time. It was a special feeling when my milk came in, but I noticed that I needed to keep very calm when breastfeeding, especially at first.

Alma kept saying, "Laurel is unable to take care of the baby." And she always spoke within earshot. This made me furious, because Laura Beth was so perfect and well-adjusted. I was her mother, so I must have been doing something right. Even so, Ava never let up on me.

It was during this time that the bank called for Luther about the loan he'd added to at Mother's bank. This was the first she had heard of him doing this. Mother didn't make him pay it back and paid it herself. I began having a revelation of what it was like to be a mother and to have some insight into her life and what she had been through. It had taken two husbands with irresponsible ways to bring me as close as I was to a nervous breakdown. I was trapped in my second marriage with two children, and one was only six months old.

The winter after Beau turned one Scarlet came to see us. She and I were visiting, Laura Beth was in school, and her little Rachel was playing in Laura Beth's room. I had just breastfed Beau when there was a knock at the door. I was accustomed to things being repossessed and carried Beau to the door. Sure enough, they wanted my new Electrolux because of lack of payment.

It was bitter cold, and I didn't want Scarlet to know what it was all about, so I stepped out on the porch. They came for it, and I had no choice but to give it to them. Scarlet said she knew at that moment my children and I were in trouble.

I called home and told Mother, "As soon as I am able, I want to come home and be baptized in our church, First Presbyterian, and I want Beau and Laura Beth to be christened."

She agreed to speak to Reverend Johnson about it. Luther was not keen to have Beau christened, but I was going through with my own. When Beau was just past twelve months old, I went back home. Reverend Johnson said Laura Beth was too old to christen and that because Luther did not agree, I should just make my own commitment and let the children do the same when they were of age. I was twenty-seven years old, and my life was in shambles. I did not know how much longer I could hang on with no light at the end of the tunnel.

I went home and was baptized. Luther went with me, but he was very uncomfortable because he knew I was in a different state of mind and was beginning to think for myself. I prayed to God for the courage to take the right path even if it was harder.

After returning home, I was on a mission, feeling strength from God to go back to Alma's attic and remove the book on witchcraft. I wanted no part of it, and even though I did not believe in it, a strange aura seemed to permeate the entire place. I did not want anything to compromise my plans.

Luther had taken the children and Alma to Jasper for ice cream late one evening. I deliberately planned to stay at Alma's. Once they were gone, I went upstairs. The book was just as I'd left it. I grabbed it and went down the narrow staircase from the attic and walked up the paved country road. It was dusk. I walked past the property line, and with all the strength I had, I flung it into a pasture that was so grown up I could not see where it landed. As I walked back, Luther came up behind me, driving slowly.

"What are you doing out here so late?" he asked.

"Just walking the property line for exercise," I replied. I didn't tell him I had prayed from each corner of the property for God to remove any negative spirits connected with the land that had been in the family more than a hundred years. My survival instincts were alive, and protection of my family was heightened. I was putting this part of my life behind me and any spell or omen connected with it.

Gee called and updated me on Mother's health. Mother was going through the change, and Benjamin was hard to handle. Her marriage failure had hit her hard; she was sinking into another deep depression, and the nervine tonic had quit working. Gee had overheard her. Mother had been standing in the kitchen by the medicine cabinet and was telling Maureen she was heartbroken with grief and nervous as a cat. She had started to go to charismatic prayer meetings, some of which were called Women's Aglow meetings.

The Presbyterian Church was prim and proper, and people did not go outside the church doctrine and programs. Mother said that she needed something more and explained that her church did not minister to her. She was drawn to the praise and worship and intercession, which included prayers of the faithful. The meetings were lively and vibrant, and the gifts of the Holy Spirit were supposed to be evident to anyone there. Mother had already been given the gift of speaking in tongues, and she would burst out with a voice that seemed to take over her body, sounding like a chant, maybe Indian.

Even though I revered her, I did not understand her new gift, especially when she began distancing herself from us. I would drive from Chattanooga to see her, and she would be going out the door to her Women's Aglow meeting. She was coming down hard on Scarlet about changing to the charismatic movement, and Scarlet was confused, having grown up in the Presbyterian Church.

Scarlet was nineteen years old, unhappy in her marriage, and seeking help. Mother's newfound spirituality did not answer her needs. It only made her worse. She went to a doctor, and he put her on Ativan. Bobby Joe only pleased himself, and she never knew the benefit of true sexual love in a marriage. I wished I'd known enough to make her feel better.

I was twenty-seven years old and unhappy in my second marriage. It seemed something was missing. Sometimes in the middle of the night I would get up and go to the family room, and the tears would flow. I had read about the awakening of sexual passion. I had also read that redheads were the most passionate of all. Mark Twain had once said,

"While the rest of the species is descended from apes, redheads are descended from cats." And an old Russian proverb said, "There was never a saint with red hair."

My only experiences with lovers were with my husbands, and I did not know what true sexual passion was unless I read about it in a book. Maybe Mark Twain was right, because cats are very mysterious, and I think my upbringing worked at being mysterious and enigmatic. I was sure of it. I never declared my true self, and men watched and wondered. I was captured too soon and never got the hang of the advice, "Be a saint in public and a devil in the bedroom." I wanted something more and always felt empty after making love.

When Scarlet turned twenty-one, she had "band-aid surgery" so she would not have any more children. Her little Rachel was four years old with chestnut curls, dimples, and slanted golden, cat-shaped eyes. Certain people in our church had been critical, thinking she was too young to take care of a baby. Realizing this, Scarlet went extreme, and Rachel always looked like she was in a beauty pageant.

Scarlet said the surgery wasn't that bad, and she was glad she had it. I knew I did not want to have any more children with Luther, so I made an appointment to also have "band-aid surgery." Beau was only six months old. Luther pitched a fit, saying he would not sign, and in Tennessee, it was a law that the husband had to sign permission for his wife's procedure. I was outraged, because it was my body. I called Mother.

"I am all for it," Mother said. "Tell him if he doesn't sign it, I will come down and sign his name in the parking lot."

Alma gave me a wrath, acting like I was having an abortion. I did not let Luther intimidate me about my decision once I had made up my mind, and it became a cold war at our house. He finally signed, and I went through with the surgery.

Laura Beth had just started fourth grade. I made friends with Marge, president of the PTA. I first met her in Luther's office at school. They were talking and very friendly as I walked in. He introduced her to me, and we hit it off. Marge was very pretty, tan, and fit and had a great smile. Her little boy was in Laura Beth's class, and she thought Beau was so cute. We made plans for our kids to go trick-or-treating together. She took a lot of pictures of Beau and seemed to favor him.

We both joined the spa and worked out together. We would sit in the sauna and rub baby oil on our legs and talk about everything as if we had known each other for a long time. She was my first friend since marrying Luther, and the strange thing was, he did not mind at all. In fact, he encouraged it. I had missed having a woman friend to share a cup of coffee and chat about girl talk.

It was a Saturday, and Luther had taken Laura Beth to a Brownie meeting. The doorbell rang, and I picked up Beau and opened the door. It was the sheriff of Dade County. He informed me that he had a warrant to arrest Luther. Luther had bought a new washer and dryer, and the check had bounced. The owner had sworn out the arrest, and I begged the officer to not pick him up because he had our little daughter with him. He said he would be back later in the day.

I drove with Beau in my lap, in the Ford Econoline van to Alma's house, which was about a forty-five-minute drive. I explained to her that I needed the cash to cover the check so they wouldn't pick up Luther. We went to the bank, which closed at noon, and made it just in time. She handed me the money plus an extra hundred dollars in case there were fees.

I went to the home appliance store and asked for the owner. A short, balding man came out, and when I told him who I was, he got red in the face and became very agitated. I was holding Beau on my hip as I spoke.

"I have brought the money to cover the check and any fees that may be due because of this problem," I said.

He said to me, "I would rather see him in jail for lying to me about picking up the check than to take the money."

I was beside myself with worry. "Luther has our little girl, and she is old enough to understand and will be traumatized by this if he is arrested and she is present," I said. He finally gave in and took the money but did not show any sympathy for me.

Luther blew me off about the incident and said I had overreacted. He refused to talk about it. That evening after picking tomatoes from the garden, I began to break out in hives beginning with my ears and going down my body to my knees. I had a difficult time breathing, and my stomach was cramping severely. Luther took me to the ER, and they gave me a shot of epinephrine and told me to see an allergist. The allergy test results revealed I was allergic to a myriad of environmental toxins; everything from pine trees to mold. This type of reaction was a severe, life-threatening reaction called anaphylactic shock. The allergy specialist interviewed me and then Luther about my emotional condition and our marriage. He informed us it was the most dangerous of all allergic reactions and had been exacerbated by emotional upset due to the stress in our marriage. I was instructed to carry the epinephrine shot at all times.

The next week Marge and I were in the sauna again, rubbing baby oil on our tan legs, and I begin telling her about my allergic reaction over the weekend. I was careful not to tell her about the warrant because of her relationship with Luther at school and the PTA. But I related that I was very unhappy in my marriage and thought I need the advice of an attorney. She encouraged me all the way, saying, "I wouldn't put up with it." I did not follow through at that time, but it was the first step for me to share an unhappiness that was getting bigger and more out of control.

I began getting the anaphylactic reactions about once a week, and Beau seemed to follow in my path, having to sleep in a croup tent just as often. Luther wanted me to sleep in the tent with Beau, but he never offered. It became a cycle of Beau and me sleeping in the croup tent, me giving myself the shot, and Luther and I arguing every night after putting the children to bed. I was careful to keep our differences about all this from Laura Beth. She was a happy little girl having sleepovers with her friends. She thought we were a happy family.

In addition to keeping all of this a secret, it was becoming harder and harder to operate like a normal person. With weekly attacks and Beau's croup, I was going through the motions of sheer existence. I was giving myself a shot of epinephrine in the leg at the beginning of each attack and then heading off to Chattanooga to the nearest emergency room. The only person who knew of my increasing unhappiness outside of Luther was Marge.

One evening after reading a bedtime story to Laura Beth, I came back to the family room and heard Beau crying. Luther wanted me to go in his room and sleep with him. I was standing in the door between the family room and the dining room just off the kitchen.

"No," I said. "Beau is becoming spoiled because I sleep with him in the croup tent so often. When he is well, I need to leave him in his own bed and room."

Luther came over to me and tried to pull me across the room. I held on to the door, instantly making a decision to not give in to him for the first time. He was furious and pulled me so hard that he threw me across the room. I hit the bar stool and the corner of the bar, causing a huge hematoma on my right elbow. It scared him so badly that he called Alma to come stay with the children because he needed to take me to the ER. He explained that I'd fallen off a chair getting something from the top cabinet. I don't know why I allowed that to be the story.

It had been four weeks and my elbow had almost healed. It was Good Friday and I had shopped for Easter outfits for Laura Beth and Beau. Laura Beth's dress was a red, white, and blue organdy handkerchief tail and sleeves, and Beau's was a navy-and-white sailor suit trimmed in gold. I bought all the contents for filling the Easter baskets and dye for the egg coloring. They were excited as they ran around the family room in their new outfits, looking forward to coloring the eggs and finding their hidden Easter baskets on Easter morning before church.

The phone rang, and I answered. On the other end, I heard Mother's voice in a low quiver. "Laurel, you need to come home. Our house has been taken off the foundation by a terrible flash flood. Everything on our street is gone, and in just a few hours, God has moved us out."

Chapter 5
Maggie Coming into Grace

Beareth all things, believeth all things, hopeth all things, endureth all things. Charity never faileth; but whether there be prophecies, they shall fail; whether there be tongues, they shall cease; whether there be knowledge, it shall vanish away.
—1 Corinthians 13:7–8

I was leaving Luther even before I found out about his affair with Marge, my only friend in Tennessee. I just didn't know when. It was after the flood that it became clear. Mother and Benjamin qualified for temporary housing in a HUD mobile home, and Gee, Scarlet, and I got them moved in and situated even though they were still in shock.

I knew I was going back to Tennessee to make a plan to leave. I was both strong and weak with a strange calmness. I had the strength to know that leaving for the sake of our future was my only option to save my family. I could not bring my children up in a house of crumbling walls with Luther's secrets being harder and harder to keep. I was weak because of my naïveté and the past ten years of loving two men who did what they wanted to do, relying on my submission, as I was slowly beaten with actions and words.

As soon as I arrived, Luther sprang the news on me that we were moving back to the Cove. I knew I must make the first move.

At the same time, Marge's friend Lisa came to me with tears in her eyes. She began speaking in a halting voice, slowly informing me of the affair that had been going on between

Luther and Marge. She said, “I could not stand it any longer, and everyone knew except you.”

This news blindsided me. It was a different kind of betrayal of husband and best friend that gave me a kick to the stomach and a knot in my throat. I could not eat because swallowing was so difficult.

Cheating was a part of Mother’s life, Scarlet’s life, and my life. It seemed normal. But when it hit home again and because it was my only friend, I slumped deep into depression. I did not confront Luther but played “You Don’t Bring Me Flowers Anymore” by Barbra Streisand and Neil Diamond over and over. And then the oddest thing happened. Luther sent me flowers that said “Happy Anniversary,” but it was my birthday. I did not care what his meaning was and felt numb. I transported myself into my own world, making my plan to leave.

Finally, I went to an attorney and gave him the details of the financial irresponsibility and the affair. I asked if I could leave the state and take the children. He said he would file the court documents, and I would be able to leave as long as the children were in the jurisdiction of the court for all hearings.

Luther left for school the next morning, just like any other morning, and I told him I would drop off Laura Beth after her dental appointment. The minute he was out the door I packed our bags. I hurriedly got the money I had been saving. It was tightly wrapped in tinfoil and hidden in the freezer. In that moment, I was glad for my cold-cash idea many months earlier when I knew I would be in need of money. I then took off my wedding band and left it on his dresser with no note.

With that, I announced to the children: “We are heading toward smiling Virginia skies.”

Luther's protégé had grown up. Without realizing it, I had become a think-for-yourself woman. I was wounded deep in my soul but had a burning desire to make it on my own with my children.

I would pull myself up by the bootstraps, get a job, and find a place to live. I would no longer live waiting for the next shoe to fall—no police at my door, no subpoena in the mail, no bounced checks, and no looking for the porch light to be on. The porch light had been my way of knowing if the electricity would still be on when we returned from going out to dinner.

I glanced in the rearview mirror. My long hair was a security blanket that hid my face and my feelings. The eyes that looked back at me were haunting and empty. I took a deep breath, held my head high, and, through my tears, crossed the Tennessee-Virginia line. I was home.

The mountains were beautiful and gave me strength and hope. I had not lived that way for a long time. My faith took on a new meaning. It was in knowing the load Grandma Tori had carried on her back working from dawn to dusk, planting the fields, harvesting, and then loading her horse and taking her wares to town to barter for sugar, flour, shoes, fabric, and ribbon. It was in knowing the stoic way she bore twelve children from age fifteen to forty-four, a trait I had not thought of until now. She became important at that moment as I thought of the strong physical features in her angular face, her aqua-blue eyes, colored like the first time I saw the ocean, and her silent presence holding us up the years after Daddy died. I would draw on her mountain-woman spirit and strength to change my lot in life and that of my children.

Thinking of her strong spirit, I had to wonder if she were alive and I asked her again about Daddy and how he had gotten himself murdered, would she be as secretive as she was when we were growing up? I was determined to find out how they managed to keep us in the dark for so many years. I had to find a way to get to the truth. It was liberating as I drove the last miles to Mother's, thinking of the future and making my own way for the first time in my life.

Once I was home, Mother and I decided to move to Abingdon, Virginia, and made an appointment with Century 21 Real Estate. Her name was Vivienne Fowler, and she took a special interest in two women with three children. We looked at many houses, but the last one was God's answer to Mother in the prophecy of moving her out to a house on a hill.

The white house with blue shutters was on a hill and nestled in the woods. It had three bedrooms and a mountain stone fireplace with a sliding glass door off the fireplace room.

Mother said, "This is it, my prophecy from God coming into fruition."

Vivienne quickly got to work. Mother qualified for a 1 percent loan for ten thousand dollars due to all flood victims, and Matt cosigned. This was her start-up money to move and furnish her house.

In order to buy the house, I had to have a job to enable us to buy it together because of her age and not being employed. We lucked out because the house was through Farm Bureau. To qualify, we had to have a down payment, we needed property for sale anywhere, and I had to have a job. It was an unlikely financial statement combining the assets of mother and daughter to begin a new life together.

It turned out that the Monteagle property was for still for sale, and my name was on the deed, so that was one component that met Farm Bureau's criteria. My job would be the last qualification on the list. As a teacher, I had only made eight thousand dollars. I needed a better-paying job. I answered an ad in the *Bristol Herald Courier* for an insurance agent in southwest Virginia territory. I would have to go to insurance school, but lucky for me, it was paid for by the company. I interviewed and was one of two women and one man signed to go to school in Richmond, Virginia.

The day we went for closing, I was under a lot of pressure. Mother told me to listen to everything the lawyer said so we did not miss anything important. Right in the middle of closing, I had to go to the ladies' room and give myself a shot, knowing I was having another attack.

The lawyer said no one had ever brought cash to a closing, but that was not unusual for Mother. She'd had Scarlet and me put fifteen thousand dollars' cash in a safe-deposit box, hoping to get more child support for Benjamin by not showing cash in her bank account. We didn't bat an eye because we never questioned her. We simply took the cash out of town to a bank in Wise, Virginia, and opened a safe-deposit box. Mother was unpredictable and secretive as always, and she kept all her thoughts between herself and God. We moved into the house, and I packed to go to Richmond for insurance school.

Scarlet came over to help me pack for the trip to Richmond. She was sexy, sophisticated, and worldly, going on shopping sprees to San Francisco and Miami. I was not in her league but aspired to be. She sensed I would need advice and support and gave me my first bottle of wine, congratulated me on my new job, and handed me a book titled *Sex and the Single Girl* by Helen Gurley Brown. I was armed with an important book. She knew I always referred to books for practical guidance, and along with a new reference, my confidence soared. Never mind the book was written in 1962 when I was thirteen, the topics were just as relative in 1977, and my new status was soon to be twenty-eight-year-old single woman. The advice encouraged single women to be financially independent and experience sexual relationships with or without marriage.

I didn't care about sex for me as a single woman, but I wanted to be armed with all the modern techniques so I could navigate as a career woman and make my own choices. In my own way, I wanted to be a heroine, mastering all challenges and showing no need to be rescued. I wanted to be in charge and independent and look feminine but not use it to get ahead. I wanted to be equal to a man and not depend on one as I had done before. I didn't want sex; I wouldn't say I didn't but would present the front of "maybe."

Scarlet's plan to leave her husband continued even though she would be shocked by the events that were coming up. He came home from the service and took a job as an electrician in the coal mines at Splashdam just before they married. He was in an explosion and suffered burns to his face and hands. His face healed nicely, leaving no scars, but his hands took some time.

Scarlet took care of him with loving care and postponed her plans to leave him. It was during his recovery that she found out about his girlfriend from Colorado, whom he had met while in the service. He always called her just after leaving home and before beginning his shift. When he didn't call several nights in a row, she called the house, and Scarlet took the call. She filled Scarlet in on the love affair that had started when Bobby Joe came on leave with her brother from Fort Bragg. She said they had planned to marry, and Bobby Joe had asked her to wait for him. That was all Scarlet needed to give her the courage for her plan to leave him. Because of the accident, she stuck with him as he changed jobs.

Bobby Joe's sister was an insurance agent, and she helped him open his own agency. Both he and Scarlet went to insurance school, and she saw him through his first five-year contract. They became successful after only one year and were the up-and-coming couple everyone wanted to have at their parties. Scarlet went to North Carolina shopping on weekends for crystal, china, and new clothes for the family. All the while, she was planning to leave when she turned twenty-five. She always loved deadlines.

Scarlet waved good-bye as I was picked up by my new insurance school colleagues, Glen and Darlene, and we headed off to Richmond for insurance school. They were fun and free-spirited, and I made sure they didn't know what a wallflower I was. Once we were checked in to the hotel and had our agenda for class, we met in the hotel bar. That was my first experience with alcohol other than my once-a-month Tom Collins at Red Lobster in Chattanooga with Luther. (Of course, he chose my drink.) The Tom Collins didn't give the feeling of the Southern Comfort I was sipping while having lighthearted conversation with the classmates from all over Virginia.

This trip was also my first experience trying to play strip poker. Glen and Darlene wanted to play, and I felt daring after the Southern Comfort and said yes. But in the middle of the game, I couldn't take my blouse off, so I had to bow out. They played, and I watched as they took off their clothes. I smiled and hid my fear, getting an education of being on my own. I was trying very hard to show no shock; after all, it was harmless.

I met a well-dressed businessman at the hotel bar who showed me a lot of attention. He asked me to meet him there after closing, telling me he had paid to keep the bar open. He called the bartender over, and he acknowledged that Mr. Gregory Benson was a great customer and a gentleman. I wanted to go and was flattered, also knowing I wouldn't be leaving with him.

I wanted to look modern so I wore a pair of cargo pants with Etienne Aigner antic red, open-toed high heels with the horseshoe *A* on the strap across the arch, and a white Poor Boy T-shirt. My long red frosted hair was curly and a little wild, and it gave me a look of being hard to tame. I lined my eyes animal-like and mysterious, just the way Scarlet showed me. Next I added light, shimmering-pink lips, and my long fingernails were wine red. A splash of bronze on my cheekbones gave me a healthy tanned look.

He stood up when I walked in and seated me. I smiled and tossed back my hair, but I was extremely nervous. He broke the ice when he asked me if I knew that Adam's first wife, Lilith, had red hair. I had never heard of Lilith, only Eve, so I didn't miss a beat and said, "I would like to have your take on the first redhead." He said Lilith insisted on being equal to Adam and smiled saying, "Eve's hair turned red also after she convinced Adam to sin in the Garden of Eden."

He ordered champagne, and I excused myself to go to the ladies' room. I realized I was way over my head and was glad he didn't know my last name or room number. I headed for the elevator and didn't go back, but I liked it.

After a lot of studying and passing time with my new friends, I passed my boards and came back home a licensed insurance agent. Laura Beth and Beau had been very unhappy while I was gone, especially Laura Beth. She could not understand why we left our beautiful home and her friends. She had been sheltered from any problems and thought it was all my fault we were living with Mother. Mother was not going to allow her to say it was my fault and told her all about Luther and the irresponsible way he had put his family in jeopardy, caused my physical illness, and carried on an affair with Marge. She was too young to hear all of that, but the damage had been done. She began to have a rash on her arms, and I felt guilty about all the changes in her life. She would have to grow up fast.

Mother was immersed in her meetings and spiritual gifts of speaking in tongues, praying for a word of wisdom and hoping for a prophecy that would come into fruition. Most important, she said that the fruit of the spirit or Christlike character controlled her gifts so they wouldn't become worthless according to Paul in 1 Corinthians, chapter 13 because her character and Christlike character did not seem to have any kinship, and it was confusing. She was so different after becoming slain in the Spirit.

She would ask us, "Why don't you girls want what God has given to me?"

I was determined to take the children to church, so we chose Sinking Springs Presbyterian where our real estate agent, Vivienne, was a deacon. We had been raised Presbyterian, and I relied on tradition as a stable part of my life. Mother said Presbyterians were lukewarm Christians, so I kept a clear separation between the two. I fell in the lukewarm Christian category and wanted my children to be taught there. I soon learned being a divorced woman did not have a category at Sinking Springs. My Sunday school class talked about divorce like it was a disease. This bothered me and added to my insecurity. It was like walking around with a D on my clothes for *Divorce*. I was walking through the motions but refused to give in to my feelings and quit. I did it for my children.

I talked to Rev. Samuel Logan about how I felt ostracized in my Sunday school class. He did not give me any biblical reference on divorce. He invited me to come by his office and talk. I began to feel more comfortable with my divorce status.

One day I rushed to his office before going to work, my long hair still wet, and out of the blue he said, "You are your mother twenty years younger."

"I don't want to look like her or be like her with her religious fever and fanaticism," I said.

He asked me what I meant, and I told him about all the meetings she attended, her gifts of the spirit, and speaking in tongues. He said that what I had told him disturbed him, and he wanted to go to one of the meetings.

I told him, "I feel conflicted about her and this new religious worship taking her further and further into a world I don't understand. Gee and Scarlet want nothing to do with it either." We felt betrayal as she slipped further away from us.

Reverend Logan quickly changed the subject, saying, "You should never marry again." He put his feet on his desk and leaned back in his chair, smoking in a very cool, impressive manner. He went on to say, "I could be everything you need. I would buy you nice gifts and take you places and be there for you."

"Are you trying to teach me something? Is this a hypothetical situation?" I asked.

He replied, "When you need a plumber, you call a plumber."

I began feeling that my newfound trust in my minister was heading in a direction that I did not what to go. I said, "What would God say? And Mother? And Martha, your wife?"

He said, "Who are you more afraid of, God or your mother?"

I said, "They are one and the same, and what about Martha?"

"What about Martha?" he questioned.

I did not get up and run as I wanted to. A thought quickly flashed through my mind. If I were suicidal, this would take me over the edge. I said, "I need to get to work." I then grabbed my bag and walked to the door, hiding my feelings.

He called out after me. "Laurel, think about it."

That was the last time I visited Reverend Logan in his office at church. In fact, I avoided him whenever possible. He would leave his card at my office with a note saying, "Stop in and see me. It's been a while."

It dawned on me that he was in love with Mother but wanted the younger version. My life was a continuation of betrayal. I had no one to turn to. Once I ran into him at the Highlands Festival beside the Martha Washington Inn, and he said, "Have you lowered your standards to come slumming with us?"

What nerve! I thought as I turned in the opposite direction.

My work took me from county to county selling and servicing insurance clients. I excelled in selling insurance and renewing policies and was able to pay our bills and have some money left over. The children would ask me every evening, "Mommy, how many policies did you sell today?"

I had to stay out of town about one week a month, and Laura Beth was becoming increasingly unhappy. She was having a conflict with Mother, who was very frugal and ruled by "conquering children," just like she was taught. She believed the Bible verse, "Spare the rod and spoil the child." She tried to use the switch on Laura Beth and got the switch taken out of her hands. Laura Beth used her own money and went to the local store and bought shampoo and toiletries so she did not have to listen to Gran.

I realized we would need our own place to live. It was not working out putting the two families together. Mother said I could pay monthly for the HUD mobile home, and I could move it into a nice mobile home park near Abingdon Elementary.

I decided to go back to Tennessee and get my furniture. The first person I ran into was Marge in the driveway. She did not speak and hurried to her car, avoiding me entirely. I had the moving van loaded with no trouble from Luther. I guess it was because I had Mother with me who was praying the whole time: "God, you know of Luther's moral deficiency and the narrow passage he is walking toward Satan."

I saw our wedding bands on the dresser and picked them up. I knew Luther wore a size twelve (a lot of gold), and I put them in my purse. Gold was bringing a good price, and I sold the set together, laughing instead of crying and saying, "That will buy milk for my babies." This reminded me of "Rose of Sharon and her milk," in the ending of *The Grapes of Wrath*: despite her own need she sustains life, giving her milk to a man dying of starvation.

Laura Beth was twelve years old, and she and Beau would get off the bus at our new place. They were latchkey kids, and she became my right arm. When she entered seventh grade, she wanted to have a boy-girl party. Scarlet and I made sure she had all the things for a party, but it was hard trying to supervise preteens and I knew I was in for an awakening. I took everything to heart and felt solely responsible for how my children would grow up and turn out.

I became way too serious and was sure little Beau would be a juvenile delinquent. At age three, he had stolen a small red Bible from Sinking Springs Church. He put it up the sleeve of his camel coat, and when I patted him on the arm to tell him how good he'd been in church, I felt the Bible. I cried all the way back to the church and made him apologize to the church secretary. I was taking to heart all the newspaper and magazine articles that were saying that juvenile delinquents came from broken homes.

Scarlet was coming over more often and wanted to go out. I would come home from work on a Friday, totally exhausted, and she would be at Mother's. Her long, straight hair was curled, hanging down past the middle of her back, and she would be dressed in the latest fashion, wearing her clothes in a sexy manner. She called her shiny black pants "second skins" and was witty and in-the-know sexually. She wanted to take me to the Martha Washington Inn to Preston's Pub, which was hidden downstairs. She said almost no one knew about it unless you were part of the *in* crowd.

What I didn't understand was that Mother was all up for me to go and that she wanted me to look after Scarlet. Mother loved it when Luther would call, and she could tell him I was out in town at the Martha Washington. Mother was more than happy to keep Laura Beth and Beau, so I could watch out for Scarlet. But Scarlet was teaching me. Before we would go out, Scarlet would help me with my hair and clothes.

"Soon you will be the high school queen you once were," she said. "You are just in a shell and have forgotten who you are.

I will never let a man do to me what has been done to you all in the name of love, honor, and cherish."

We polished our long fingernails wine red, and out the door we went.

The Martha Washington Inn, originally built in 1832, was stately and beautiful. It made you feel special just to be there. Tucked away to the side downstairs, Preston's Pub was small but cozy with a fireplace. We always sat at the table for two beside the fireplace. Scarlet would coach me on sitting up straight and keeping my hair out of my face. She made me realize I was hiding behind my hair, shy and reserved. I was more tailored for business, and she was more glamorous. We were deciding what I would drink, having such limited experience. We tasted bourbon, gin, vodka, and scotch. I settled on scotch because it was not sweet, and the bartender said it was seventy calories. We had a rule to stick together—sit at a table for two or sit at the bar. That way it looked like we did not expect anyone to join us, just admire us. She was glamor, and I was sophistication.

One snowy night after two scotches we wrote a poem on a napkin about me:

"The Classy Lady"

In a bar not far enough to forget
The classy lady, in a gray tweed suit and long
string pearls
She was straight
But curved in all the right places
She was wild but only in a few men's dreams
In a bar not far enough to forget
The classy lady

We acted preoccupied, not wanting to be picked up. We fancied ourselves as poets and always discussed poetry like Marge Piercy, "The Moon Is Always Female," and all of the books by the Irish poet, Merrit Malloy: *My Song for Him Who Never Sang to Me*, *We Hardly See Each Other Any More*, *The People Who Didn't Say Good-bye*, *Beware of Older Men*, and *Things I Meant to Say to You When We Were Old.*

We were particularly fascinated with the Irish former priest James Kavanaugh's poetry about God, passion, haunting love, and loneliness, reading aloud *Laughing Down Lonely Canyons.* I began to look forward to Scarlet coming over to go to the pub.

Besides working all week and being a mother, I had created a new identity, just for me, for the first time in my life. Most important was to appear strong and in charge. I realized I did not miss sex at all. I think I was Tommy Lee's first, and he was mine, and Luther had no sex appeal once his true self was revealed because he was never handsome. This left me feeling there was something more. I asked Mother, and she said, "Women just have to bear up with a smile." But she quickly added, "I always pleased my man and never had any issues with sex." That feedback sure made me feel better.

Scarlet called and asked if I would like to go with her and her sister-in-law, Melissa, to Johnson City to see Dave and Sugar and Charlie Pride. I asked Mother, and she was all for it. We were going to stay at the Holiday Inn, and on the way, they stopped at a liquor store. I had never been in a liquor store and thought they were so brave in their tight jeans and cute tops and high heels going in and buying scotch. I sat in the car but felt alive and excited.

We went to the concert, and in the middle of "Does Your Ring Hurt Your Finger When You Go Out at Night," Melissa said, "Let's go outside and smoke. I can't stand this song."

Once we got outside they lit up Virginia Slim menthols and looked at me as if to say, "You've come a long way, baby."

"I wish I could smoke," I said.

Scarlet and Melissa gave me one and laughed. "That will never work. You look like a hooker trying to smoke." We went back in, and Dave and Sugar were singing "Queen of the Silver Dollar." We all agreed he was hot and wished he would lose Sugar.

When we got back to the Holiday Inn, the clerk asked us if we would like to go to Charlie Pride's room. We said no and then asked if Sugar was with Dave. The clerk gave us no answer about Sugar, the two female singers of the trio, and we laughed.

We drank scotch, wondering if it really was a sin like Mother believed. Melissa said, "I'm not good enough to go to church."

I told her about David and Bathsheba and their story. She was fascinated because no one ever told her David was king and a favorite of God. He saw the beautiful, married Bathsheba bathing on her roof and sent for her. She slept with him as a willing partner, although he had power over her because he was king. Her husband was off to war, and David sent him to the front lines, ensuring he would be killed, after learning she was with child. After a short period of mourning, Bathsheba became the wife of King David.

Melissa said, "That sheds a new light on God and forgiveness." She said she was going to buy a Bible and might go to church after all. Not too long after that, she was saved at a revival and was baptized.

We awakened the next morning to about six inches of snow on the ground. We had an hour drive to Abingdon, and Scarlet and Melissa had another hour to get home. When we got to the parking lot, we ran into David and Sugar standing outside their bus. He was dark and handsome and friendly.

Scarlet asked him, "Did you have to lie down on the bed to zip your pants? They fit so well."

He smiled because they were tight and then asked us if we wanted to ride the bus with them. I was scared but happy when my companions declined, saying they didn't want to risk being stranded in a snowstorm.

Mother was getting worried about Scarlet's marriage even though she had been saying she was leaving for several years. She had all the women in her Women's Aglow meetings praying, followed by speaking in tongues and asking God for an intervention.

Mother was also going to Ridgecrest, North Carolina, to conferences with people from all church denominations who couldn't be spiritually fed in their own churches. She would ask one of us to go with her for a weekend, and all three of us resisted but could not tell her no as always.

One time I went with her when Derek Prince and other prophets were there on the stage. She may have believed he was a prophet because he was from India. It seemed all prophets were from another country.

She explained to me that he was well-known worldwide for his teaching about deliverance from demonic oppression. He had an encounter of supernatural experience with Jesus. He had prayed for two people to be raised from the dead, and his prayers were answered.

The auditorium was filled to capacity. There were nuns in their habits, people were kneeling in prayer, and the big screens displayed the words for the praise music. Everyone would stand and raise their hands while singing and dancing in the aisles. Mother wanted me to go forward and get slain in the Spirit, but I did not want to go. She pushed me up, and when I got on stage, I was suddenly surrounded by six prophets who had been visited by the Holy Spirit and sent to serve their fellow man. They asked me why I had come on stage.

"Mother pushed me here to be prayed for," I admitted.

They began praying as they laid their hands on me, and I waited to be slain in the Spirit and fall back into a trance of God's grace, but it didn't happen.

I didn't receive any visions or hear God speak. I didn't feel the ecstasy or excitement that I noticed in others on the floor. I felt like something was wrong with me. Before I left the stage, one of the lady prophets told me that "God revealed to her that a curse had come to the women of our family from past generations." I had heard of the sins of the fathers before but not the mothers. I left the stage more confused.

Many times I had watched Kathryn Kuhlman on one of Mother's favorite TV shows, *I Believe in Miracles.* In one of her shows, she stated, "Jesus walked this earth as much a man and a God, subjected to temptation, which he resisted, and staked everything on the Holy Ghost."

Mother told me to stake everything on the Holy Ghost, and I still did not receive this anointing like she had. I didn't know why and could only think that I wasn't to be one of the chosen ones.

I was glad to get back from Ridgecrest, but all hell broke loose when Scarlet informed us that she was leaving Bobby Joe the day after Rachel's eighth birthday, on August 5. We had listened to her for five years as she planned this move.

"If I am not happy by the time I am twenty-five, I will be leaving," she'd said.

I suppose we thought she would never follow through with it.

Mother knew she would be staying with her until she could get a job and find her own place, just as I had. One big difference between Scarlet and me was Scarlet gave in to melancholy and would cry for hours on end. Everything centered on her unhappiness, which helped me create her nickname: Melancholy Baby.

Scarlet packed her white Chrysler New Yorker Fifth Avenue with all her precious things and planned to take a moving van back later for furniture and other belongings. She stopped on the way and bought five pairs of high heels. One pair was a clear, see-through Cinderella-looking high heel with ankle straps and big white patent bows on the open toes. She had also checked out three thousand dollars from the joint checking account. She pulled in at Mother's and got out of the car. She walked up the steps in her short shorts with her golden tan legs, ran into the house, fell into the pillows on the sofa, and broke into sobs. She took to her bed for two weeks, and everyone did everything to make her happy as we would for years to come. She just was one of those that people wanted to help.

I finally got her to get out of the bed and get dressed up in her Cinderella shoes. We were going to Preston's Pub at the Martha Washington. She got up, and when she came out in her sexy sundress and shoes, she had painted her lips ruby red and had on her fake smile that I had seen so many times before.

Mother said, "Watch out for her because she's a Powers, and that worries me."

We walked into Preston's Pub, and at the bar sat a tall, slim man with wavy auburn hair and blue eyes, just like Miss Lang saw when she read Scarlet's coffee grounds at the last reading. Scarlet looked at me, smiled her real smile, and said, "That's my next husband." At that moment, he turned around and looked her up and down with an intense stare. It was as if there were only two people in the room.

As she smiled, my heart sank, and I got that punched-in-the-stomach feeling. She had no way of knowing the man sitting before her was the son of the woman who brought Mother home the day Daddy died. She had been pregnant with him that day, and his daddy was a rounder just like ours.